Shattered Sea

THE TATTERED & TORN SERIES

CATHERINE COWLES

Editor: Susan Barnes
Copy Editor: Chelle Olson
Proofreading: Julie Deaton, Jaime Ryter, Kara Hildebrand
Paperback Formatting: Stacey Blake, Champagne Book Design
Cover Design: TRC Designs

Dedication

For everyone whose pain isn't visible to the rest of the world.
You're a warrior. Never give up the fight.

Shattered Sea

Prologue

Laiken

PAST

"**N**EXT DARE. BACKFLIP INTO A DIVE." MITCH PUFFED up his chest with each word like he was an overgrown gorilla.

I rolled my eyes and snuggled back against Jase's chest, letting the crackling bonfire warm my bare legs. I did my best to tune out Mitch and the rest of our friends and tipped my face up to the sky. It was crystal-clear, letting the stars shine like sparklers in the inky black—as if the heavens were putting on their own little show in honor of our graduation.

"You could at least pull a double," Isaac muttered, cutting into my peace. "Don't be a chicken shit."

Mitch's eyes narrowed. "I'd like to see you try."

I sighed. This endless quest to one-up each other was getting old. And I could only imagine it worsening when we left for college in a few months. The mixture of freedom and access to booze taking hold.

Jase pulled me tighter against him and nuzzled the side of my neck. "You warm enough?"

"I'm perfect."

Isaac gave Mitch a shove, and he let out a string of curses as he tripped over a rock.

"Or I would be," I said, raising my voice, "if these two idiots would quit messing with my bliss zone."

Lisbeth laughed, holding her hands out to the fire. The flames made her strawberry-blond hair look more of a true red under its glow. "Good luck with that."

Isaac's focus swung to me, a devilish grin in place. "Come on, Laik. Let loose for once. You got salutatorian and your fancy gymnastics scholarship. You can breathe."

I stiffened. Structure had been my friend since finding my love of tumbling at age four. Or maybe it really took hold when my dad bailed at six. I relished the reliability of it. The knowledge that it kept things safe and predictable. Only I was tired of feeling like the dud of the group.

I pushed out of Jase's hold and stretched. "I think we can do better than a double, don't you think, guys? How about a two and a half?"

Mitch whistled. "Shit, girl. Now we're talking."

I slapped his hand in a high-five and started for the rope swing.

Jase stood, jogging to catch up with me. He grabbed hold of my elbow. "Laik, it's dark. There could be debris in the water you don't see."

I turned to face Jase, taking in the lines of concern creasing his face. I stretched up on my tiptoes, brushing my lips against his. The touch brought with it a flush of warmth and comfort. Sometimes, I thought I knew Jase's body better than my own. From childhood best friends to middle-school crush to first everything.

"Someone has to put these idiots in their place," I whispered in his ear.

Jase's fingers tangled in my hair. "It doesn't need to be you."

"I've done flips off that rope swing a million times. Are you forgetting who the state champ on the uneven bars was?"

He shouldn't. Jase came to every meet, usually dragging the rest of our friends, too. He made ridiculous posters and sometimes t-shirts. My favorite one had read: *Number One Fan & Water Boy*.

A smile stretched across his face, but the edges were strained. "I'm not doubting your bendy, twisty prowess. It's the hard objects you could land on that make me nervous."

I scanned the water and saw more than enough to make the jump safely. "Full moon, babe. I got this. Channeling my inner gymnastics nerd."

He chuckled, wrapping his arms around me and pulling me close. "Those leotards have always been my favorite."

"Perv."

Jase nipped at my bottom lip. "You like me pervy."

Isaac made a gagging noise. "I think I'm gonna vomit."

I twisted out of Jase's hold and strode towards the rope swing. "When I do this, you have to stop giving me shit for the rest of the night."

"Aw, come on, that's no fun." He ran a hand through his blond hair, the strands long on top and shaved on the sides. A look he thought was the epitome of *cool*.

"You being silent sounds like plenty of fun to me," I called back.

I heard a grunt and curse that I was pretty sure meant someone had gotten punched in the gut.

"That's what you get for being a jackass," Jase muttered.

I tugged off my t-shirt and tossed it onto my bag near the fire, leaving me in only my bikini. Lisbeth let out a loud whistle. "Get it, Laik."

I shot her a grin. "Take a picture of Mitch and Isaac's faces when I put them to shame."

She held up her phone. "I'm going full video on this one."

"Smart. We can post it everywhere."

"You girls are brutal," Mitch muttered.

"And it would do you well to remember that," I called.

Before I could let myself have second thoughts, I grabbed hold of a wooden plank nailed to the tree. I hoisted myself up, rung after rung. My friends' voices lifted on the early summer air, but I tuned them out, focusing only on my next steps.

I reached the platform in a matter of seconds. Who knew how long it had been up here? At this point, there were layers of boards reinforced by every generation who had frequented the spot.

I grabbed hold of the rope, the rough surface biting into my palms. Any blisters would be worth it for this minor moment of glory and bragging rights for the rest of the summer. I adjusted my grip and stared down at the water. It took a few moments to discern where the shore ended, and the water began.

My heart picked up speed as I stretched up onto my tiptoes, preparing to jump. I didn't give myself a chance to reconsider; I let myself fly.

The wind whipped against my face as I swung through the night air. My palms burned, but I held tight to the rope, waiting for the moment when I knew I was fully over the lake. The rope gave a jerk, and I released my hold.

I arched into a backflip, the stars blurring overhead. Instead of releasing my tuck for a dive, I stayed in a tight ball for a second rotation, then opened into that extension. My hands and head hit the surface with a sharp sting.

The lake was colder than expected, stealing the breath right out of my lungs. I kicked towards the surface as my chest burned. Panic started to set in as my muscles seized. My face met air just in time, and I took a sharp breath.

I heard splashing by the shore as Jase waded into the water, his bare chest on display. I swam towards him. "I'm fine. Told you."

Jase hauled me into his arms. "I think that's enough daredeviling for tonight."

I wrapped my arms around his waist. "Think Mitch and Isaac will keep their traps shut?"

Jase shook his head and nuzzled my neck. "If they don't, I'll shut them for them."

I ran my fingers through his longish, dark hair. "What does it say about me that I support that move?"

He chuckled and kissed me as he strode towards the shore. "That you're my girl."

"I am, aren't I?"

"Forever and a day."

My stomach gave a healthy flip as if I'd taken another tumble from the rope swing. "Forever and two days."

"Deal."

Isaac chuckled. "Does she wear his balls on that necklace of hers?"

Jase smirked at him. "I know you're jealous that you don't have a girl as hot as mine, but you don't have to be so obvious about it."

"Whatever," he muttered, but I swore I saw a red stain rise to his cheeks.

Mitch studied me as if I were a bug. "How the hell did you do that?"

"You should've taken gymnastics with me in elementary school like your mom wanted."

Jase snorted but pulled me in closer to his side.

"Oh my God, Laik. Did you just flip off that rope swing?" Marisa's voice cut through the night as she stepped out of the trees, readjusting her clothes.

Scott wrapped an arm around his girlfriend and shot me a grin. "Of course, she did. She's a badass."

"And I have video proof, so that fact will live on in infamy," Lisbeth said, holding up her cell.

Scott mirrored the move with his phone. "Jax just texted. There's a party at the farmhouse. We should go."

Jase frowned at Scott. "My brother's throwing a party?"

"Said your aunt was looking the other way for the evening."

Jase's aunt, Gillian, was always left to look in on Jase and Jax when their parents went out of town for their sister Serena's cheer competitions. Even though Jax was twenty, and Jase was eighteen, their parents didn't trust them not to wreck the place. They could've trusted Jase, but Jax was a whole other story.

"He's such an idiot," Jase grumbled. "I'm not covering for him this time. Can I stay at your place tonight? Your mom won't mind if I crash on the couch."

She wouldn't. She was so wrapped up in her world; she probably wouldn't notice if I didn't come home for days. The Grangers weren't like that. Jase's parents, Kay and Chip, cared. Even if their family wasn't perfect, their love for each other was clear as day.

Only lately, that love seemed to be fraying around the edges in a way that gave me a stomachache. There were more raised voices and storming out of rooms. And it almost always revolved around something Jax had done. I nibbled on the corner of my lip. "Maybe we should go. We can make sure nothing gets too out of control."

A muscle in Jase's cheek fluttered. "There's no way it won't get out of hand. I should just call the cops now and get it over with."

Scott flipped Jase off. "Don't cockblock. Some of us want to have fun tonight."

I glared at him.

Isaac smirked. "I'm pretty sure your cock has gotten all it's up to tonight."

"Hey!" Marisa screeched at him, her pale complexion pinking around her cheeks.

"Enough," Jase clipped. "The last thing I want to do is try to corral my brother and his friends."

The hint of true anger in Jase's expression had my stomach cramping. I had always played referee between the brothers, but it was getting out of hand lately, and I worried there would be a break they couldn't get past. There had been tension between them ever since Jase had taken the fall for a party Jax threw over spring break. But this was more. The idea of the family I'd been lucky enough to be all but adopted into falling apart like mine had anxiety pulsing through me.

I wrapped my arms around Jase's waist and kissed the underside of his chin. "The last thing I want to do is play hall monitor tonight. But maybe we can wrap it up early and go back to our plans. A drive into the mountains in the Jeep. Some alone time." I waggled my eyebrows.

Jase's lips twitched. "I like the second part of that plan."

"I'll be your backup and play bad cop. Promise. I'm not afraid to use buckets of ice water if necessary."

Mitch's brows rose. "Harsh."

I shrugged. "Jax has earned a little bad cop."

"That's the freaking truth," Jase said.

I turned into him and pressed my lips to his. "I'm sorry things are so hard right now."

His jaw worked back and forth. "We used to be on the same team. Now, it feels like I don't even know him anymore."

Hearing him utter those words aloud broke my heart. "Maybe you two need some time. Just the two of you. Go on one of your camping trips."

"Maybe." Jase shook his head. "I can't believe Gilly left him alone. She knows he'll throw a party."

"She probably wanted to be the cool aunt. Or she got distracted by her latest art project."

Gillian was flighty and moved to the beat of her own drum, but she loved her nephews and niece. And she was always a safe place to land for me, too. She never cared if I came over to her art studio to work on homework because I didn't want to go home to an empty house. And she always asked my opinion on what she was working on as if she really cared. To me, that outweighed all the flighty.

Jase ran his fingers through my hair. "Sometimes when my parents are gone, it feels like I'm the babysitter."

"A couple more months, and we'll be out of here. You'll only have to be responsible for yourself."

He tapped the end of my nose. "And you."

"I never get into any trouble."

"Suuuuure."

Scott lifted a bucket of water and doused the fire. "Can we go or what?"

"Yeah, we can go." Jase pinned him with a stare. "But no getting wasted and puking in my mom's planter."

I scrunched up my nose as I turned to Marisa, who I saw was doing the same. "That was so gross," she said with a shiver.

I wanted to gag just thinking about it.

Scott grinned. "My tolerance is a million times better than it was at the last party."

Lisbeth turned to Isaac. "Will you and Mitch be my ride? I don't want to get stuck in a car with puke-face."

I couldn't hold in my laughter as Isaac wrapped his arm around her. "I got you, gorgeous."

Jase wrapped a towel around me and then picked up our bags. "Let's go." He tugged me towards the parking lot. "You can shower and change in my bathroom when we get there."

I just hoped no one was screwing in Jase's bed when we arrived because that had happened before.

We piled into three different vehicles. Jase turned the key in his older-model Jeep. As soon as the engine started, I hit the stereo dial and turned it to my favorite country station. He grimaced. "Are you seriously going to make me listen to that when I already know I'm going to be tortured tonight?"

"Hey, I'm partial to Tim McGraw. You know, I lost my virginity to a song by him."

The light in Jase's dark eyes danced. "You don't say."

"I do." I leaned over, my lips grazing the shell of his ear. "If you're lucky, I'll let you reenact it later."

"I'm pretty sure you don't want that. I think I lasted all of three minutes."

"It was sweet."

Jase pulled out of the lot and onto the gravel road. "It was mortifying."

"You know what they say…practice makes perfect."

"Now that's a plan I can get behind."

Jase turned onto the two-lane highway that led into Wolf Gap. The headlights from Scott's truck and Isaac's sedan swung across our back window as they followed. I bent down, pulling my cell phone out of my bag. I typed out a quick text.

Me: *I'm going to spend the night at Marisa's. I'll see you in the morning.*

My mom didn't respond—not that I had expected her to. She was all about being busy. Because if she was busy, then she never had to deal with the fact that my dad had cheated and bailed. She numbed herself with activities and a full social calendar.

My older brother was the same. He'd looked out for me at first after Dad bailed, but then he simply had better things to do. Once he left for college, he only returned for the holidays and was home for forty-eight hours tops.

Lights flashed across the windshield, and I squinted at the road. "Geez."

"Someone needs to learn how to turn off their brights."

The headlights wove back and forth in front of us.

I leaned forward, trying to see better. It looked as if the driver wasn't following the line of the road. "Are they drunk?"

Jase flipped the visor on his Jeep down. "I hope not."

The truck veered off the side of the road and then back on. My stomach dropped. "I'm calling the sheriff's department."

"Don't do that, Laik. They might just be tired."

I hit the non-emergency number stored in my phone. "They could hurt someone."

"I guess you're right." Jase flashed his lights at the oncoming vehicle.

Instead of slowing down and pulling over, the truck picked up speed, its engine revving.

"Carson County Sheriff's Department, how can I help you?"

"This is Laiken Montgomery. We're heading into town on twenty-two. I think the driver of a red pickup is intoxicated."

"Are you safe?"

Jase pulled to the side of the road as the truck weaved again.

"My boyfriend just pulled over. I think we're fine."

"Okay, I've got deputies heading that way now."

"Thank you." I hung up as Jase idled.

The truck slowed and then stopped. A guy got out from behind the wheel and wavered as he strode towards us. I vaguely recognized him but didn't know his name. He started shouting and cursing about us flashing our lights.

I gripped Jase's hand. "I think you should go now. He doesn't look like he's in his right mind."

Jase put the Jeep in drive and pulled off as our friends followed behind. The man shook his fist at us as we passed and screamed something I couldn't make out.

I didn't let out the breath I'd been holding until his taillights disappeared. "That was crazy."

"Hopefully, the sheriff arrests him."

"No kidding."

I switched the radio off; the upbeat music not a match for that close call.

Jase linked his fingers with mine. "They'll get 'em."

"I know."

The faint sound of a souped-up engine cut through the night. I turned in my seat to see headlights swerving out from behind our three vehicles to pass. The red truck had to be going about ninety miles an hour. "Is he insane?"

Before Jase could answer, the truck slammed into the side of our SUV. I screamed as we spun. There was a sickening crunch as we hit one vehicle and then another. I lost track of how many times we collided with things. And then, we were airborne.

My seat belt jerked me against the seat as the Jeep flew into a roll. Flipping over and over, the sounds were deafening until everything blinked out. No sound, no sight, no feeling. There was simply nothingness.

I didn't know how long the nothingness lasted before I blinked against it. I heard shouts from somewhere. That infiltrated my brain before the pain. But once the pain appeared, there was nothing else.

A white-hot agony ripped through my body, tearing at muscle and sinew. I let out a whimper as I tried to move. As if that would help me escape the pain. But I couldn't shift my position. The Jeep no longer resembled a vehicle. It had been crunched into something altogether different.

Panic lit through me at that thought. "Jase?"

My voice came out hoarse as if I hadn't used it in years. There was no answer. Blood rushed to my head, and for the first time, I realized we were upside down.

"Jase." His name was a plea. I tried to twist myself, but pain ripped through me. My seat was folded into the dashboard, my head and neck resting on its surface.

A low groan sounded from next to me. "Laik?"

"I'm here. Are you hurt?"

What a dumb question. Of course, he was hurt. There was no way he couldn't be.

"I don't know." Jase's voice sounded funny. As if he were on heavy-duty painkillers or something.

"Over here," a voice shouted. "I'm going down."

I tried just moving my arm. It hurt like hell, but I could weave it around the torn and bent metal. After a few tries, I felt a body. An arm. Jase's arm. I patted it until I found his hand. I linked my fingers with his. But Jase's hand was slick with blood.

My heart ricocheted around in my chest. "Jase, what do you feel?"

"Hmm?"

"Stay awake," I ordered. I didn't know much, but I knew that it was important to stay conscious.

"I'm awake."

"Tell me about the house we're gonna have one day."

It was quiet for a moment, nothing but the sounds of creaking metal.

I squeezed Jase's hand, and he started to speak. "Huge

wraparound porch. I'm gonna build you one of those porch swings that looks more like a bed. We'll make a baby on that porch swing."

My throat burned. "You'll be the best dad."

Footsteps sounded, and then a voice. "Jase? Laiken?"

"We're here," I croaked.

Out of the corner of my eye, I could just make out a face. A piece of a sheriff's department uniform. Hayes Easton sank to his knees, trying to get a visual on the inside of the SUV. "We've got more help on the way. Just sit tight."

"They have to hurry. I think Jase is hurt bad."

"Jase, can you tell me where you're feeling pain?"

There was nothing. I squeezed his hand, and his fingers fluttered. "I don't know. I feel weird."

"That's okay. We're gonna get you out. You just hold on. Stay with us." Hayes slid his hand into the tiny opening near my head. His fingers landed on my neck, checking my pulse. "What about you, Laiken?"

It took a second to think about it. The pain that had dominated my mind just minutes before had faded to the background as my worry about Jase took over. "M-my back. My side." The panic picked up again, and tears gathered in my eyes. "You gotta get us out."

Hayes' hand found mine and held on tight. "We've got people coming. They're bringing equipment to get you out. I know it's scary, but I'm with you. We'll get through this together."

I held tighter to Hayes with one hand and Jase with the other— as if Hayes could save us both if I just held on. "You hear that, Jase? Help is coming."

Jase made a sound of agreement.

I gripped his hand harder. "Tell me about our wedding."

He grunted, almost as if he were trying to laugh. "Told you I'd marry you tomorrow."

My nose stung. "We get out of this, and I'll go to the courthouse with you as soon as it opens."

"You heard her, Hayes."

Hayes let out a chuckle, but it was forced. "I'll be your witness. How about that?"

"Brand-new, fancy deputy at our wedding," Jase muttered.

"Hell, I'll see if I can get ordained," Hayes said.

"Laik, you gotta wear that white sundress and flowers in your hair. What are those ones you love?"

"Ranunculus," I said as tears spilled from my eyes.

"Those in your hair."

"Don't forget my necklace."

"You never take that thing off. I didn't have to tell you." I heard the smile in Jase's voice as he spoke.

"I don't take it off because you gave it to me."

Jase's hand loosened around mine. "Love you, Laik." His words were drawn out as if each was a struggle.

I squeezed his hand harder. "Forever and a day."

There was no response.

My fingernails dug into Jase's skin. "Forever and a day, Jase."

Nothing. His hand went limp.

My tears came harder as I shook Jase's hand. "Forever and a day."

My voice broke, and the sobs came. No matter how hard I squeezed Jase's hand, no matter how many times I said our words, he never said anything back.

"Laiken, hold on," Hayes said as he kept a grip on my other hand.

I held them both. One so full of life and strength. The other growing cold in my grasp.

"Jase…"

"I know. But you gotta hang on for me. Breathe. You're gonna hyperventilate."

I didn't want to hang on. I didn't want to breathe. I wanted to follow Jase wherever he had gone. Forever and a day.

Chapter One

Laiken

PRESENT

THE WIND PICKED UP, SENDING LEAVES SWIRLING AROUND the sidewalk. Winter had us in her grips and didn't show any signs of letting go. But I didn't mind. I loved the cold. That bite in the air that reminded you that you were alive. Even if it made your lungs ache.

Gizmo let out a little yip as he attempted to chase one of the leaves circling our feet. A woman walking towards us came to a stop, taking him in and smiling. "Does he have wheels?"

"His back legs don't work all that great, so these help him along."

She bent and gave his head a rub. "What a love."

"And a troublemaker." He was a mix of long-haired Chihuahua and who knew what else. My best guess was that he was part gremlin.

Gizmo twisted his head back towards me, and I swore he glared.

The woman chuckled as she stood. "Chihuahuas always seem to make up for their size with their personality."

I couldn't hold in my laugh. "That they do."

"Have a good day."

"You, too," I said, giving her a wave. I started forward, then waited for Gizmo to follow. "Come on. Don't sulk. You know you're my favorite."

Gizmo lifted his chin in the air and moved down the sidewalk towards The Gallery. I shook my head and took a sip of my coffee. Wolf Gap's streets were mostly quiet at eight in the morning. The cold meant fewer tourists, and most locals stayed warm at home until it was time for them to make their way to work.

I looped the leash over my wrist and pulled my keys out of my pocket. I was just about to slide them into the lock when Gillian pulled the door open.

"Get in here before you freeze to death. Every year, I swear I'm leaving these mountains and moving to Costa Rica."

"And every year when spring comes, you change your mind," I finished for her as I stepped inside.

She shut the door and crouched to greet Gizmo, who pushed his head into her hand. She looked up at me. "It's not nice to be a know-it-all."

I laughed. "I definitely don't know it all, but I do know you."

Gilly stood and pulled me into a hug. "And aren't I thankful for that?"

I tried not to wince as my back twisted in a way it didn't want to go. But Gilly must've felt the stiffening of my muscles. She released me instantly. "Is it bad today?"

I shook my head, forcing a smile. "Just stiff this morning."

She rolled her eyes. "Like you would tell me if it was."

I probably wouldn't. Not unless it was so bad that I couldn't get out of bed. But those days weren't frequent. I knew how to mitigate the pain. Every day was a series of calculations. How much one activity would take from my reserves. If I would have enough left over to do whatever else needed to be done.

I bent, unlatching Gizmo's leash. He raced towards the kitchen, and I followed in his wake. "What are you doing here so early?" I didn't usually see Gilly until noon at the earliest. She always said her muse was nocturnal.

"I was dropping off a painting and wanted to see how the next show was coming together."

Even though Gilly owned The Gallery, she mostly left me to run it. Somewhere along the way, the space had become my haven. The little apartment upstairs my home, and the exhibitions below my creative domain.

I gestured to several pieces lining the walls of the storage space next to the kitchen and the de facto break room. "Have a look. I think it's a nice variety."

I lifted the lid on a tin of treats and tossed one to Gizmo, who caught it in mid-air. Then I pulled a plate down from the cabinet. "Want half my muffin?"

Gilly waved me off, now fully engrossed in the art. "I ate around three."

"You haven't slept, have you?"

"Who needs sleep when the muse is speaking?"

I grinned as I plated my muffin and set it and my coffee on the table.

Gilly stopped in front of a photograph. It was black and white. A man whose age and grief was carved into his face, line after line. But it was his eyes that spoke volumes. They released all his pain for the world to see. "This is incredible."

She whirled to face me. "Has your artist agreed to meet me yet?"

I pressed my lips into a firm line. "They prefer to remain anonymous. They say that it helps the work stay honest."

Gilly rolled her eyes. "Dramatic artists. This mysterious photographer revealed themselves to you."

"Because I agreed to sit for them."

Gilly crossed the room, her layered necklaces jingling with the movement. "You're persuasive when you want to be. I've seen you close a deal faster than art brokers in New York." She gave me her best puppy-dog face, which was comical on a woman in her mid-sixties. "Tell them what a hoot I am. That I'm charming, and oh, so good-looking."

I couldn't hold in my laugh. "You are all those things."

She sighed, looking back at the photo. "I'd love to do a show of just their work."

"I can ask, but I doubt they'll go for that. Attention isn't really what they're after." Attention was the last thing I wanted. I'd had enough of it to last a lifetime. Funerals. Trials. Anniversary press coverage. The only thing I wanted to do was make art that showed the truth of the human experience. To be brave enough to look it in the eye and not blink. I never wanted a soul to know it was me behind the lens.

Gilly threw her hands up. "Oh, fine. I'll leave you and your mysterious artist be." Her eyes twinkled. "But you have to tell me if he's handsome."

I let out a bark of laughter. "If I told you he was handsome, you'd never drop it."

She flounced into a chair at the table. "What can I say? I'm a hopeless romantic."

I lowered myself into the chair opposite her. "I love that about you."

She reached over and squeezed my hand. "What about you? Any strapping young men ruffling your feathers?"

My lips twitched. "I can't say that's been on the agenda."

"It never is."

"I'm happy with my life the way it is. I've got good friends, Gizmo, work that makes me happy, and a boss who only annoys me every third Tuesday when she hasn't taken off to parts unknown."

Gilly laughed, one of those bawdy, uninhibited ones I loved. "She's nosy, though, and wants you to be happy."

"Good thing I already am."

"All right, all right. I'll leave the topic be. How are things with your mom?"

I broke off a piece of my muffin and popped it into my mouth. "Fine."

"You know what I think about the word *fine*. It really stands for fucked up, insecure, neurotic, and emotional."

I choked on my muffin and took a sip of coffee. "Apologies for using the f-word."

"You should apologize. You know I only want the truth. I don't ask if I don't want to know."

That much was true. Gilly never played by the rules of polite society, and I loved her for it. My phone buzzed in my pocket, and I pulled it out. "Speak of the devil."

Mom: *Change of plans. I'm heading to Chicago with some friends this afternoon so I can't come visit. Next month?*

I held my phone out to Gilly, who scanned the screen.

"How many girls' trips can one woman take? You know I like my travel, but this is getting ridiculous."

I bit my lip to keep from laughing. "She likes her busy."

I didn't begrudge my mother that. It made her happy. Never a moment to sit still and think about the realities of life. Whereas I was all about exploring whatever I felt in the moment. And right now, that was hurt. As much as I tried to lower my expectations when it came to my mother, it still stung that I was the plan that always seemed to get canceled.

Gilly patted my hand. "Want me to go to Massachusetts with you?"

"The fact that you would endure a week with my mother for me really does tell me you love me."

Travel was tough for me on a good day, and I usually needed a buddy to help me navigate it all. Gilly and Kay had both done that for me on more than one occasion, but I hated asking them.

Gilly snorted. "That's the freaking truth. I really will go if you feel like you need to see her."

I shook my head. "I'm good. I'll go once the weather's better and she's putting the pressure on to see her vegetable garden."

"Or you could tell her to fuck off. Like I've been telling you to do for years."

"I can't." When you lost someone you loved, it made it hard to let go of anyone else—even if they didn't have your best interests at heart.

"Okay, I'll drop it. I actually have a couple of other things to run by you."

I set my coffee down. "Hit me with it."

"Serena's moving back to Wolf Gap."

I stilled. "When?" Jase's sister had avoided our town much like my mother and brother did. But for her, I think it was simply too painful. Too many memories to contend with. The problem was, she hadn't been able to find her place anywhere. She'd transferred colleges four times before dropping out altogether and heading to New York to take a stab at modeling. Last I'd heard, she had followed a boyfriend to Majorca and was working in a bar there.

Gilly eyed me carefully. "Don't hate me, but I told her I could find a place for her here."

I was quiet for a beat. "I'd never hate you for that. I'm just surprised she wants to work with me." Serena and I had been close once, but all of that changed after Jase's death. She'd started acting out and getting into trouble. We'd gone more than a few rounds before the friendship dropped away altogether.

"I'm sorry, Cherub. I know it's another loss for you, but maybe this will be a chance for you two to reconnect."

"Maybe." I missed Serena. Our friendship. I couldn't deny that. But I didn't have a lot of hope for the repairs required to close that chasm.

"She's living in the apartment over the garage at her parents', and this will give her a chance to get on her feet again."

"I already have Addie helping, too. I'm not sure how many hours I'll really need someone else."

Gilly rolled the beads on one of her necklaces between her

fingers. "And I love Addie. But she's going to have a baby before too long, and you usually have two employees helping."

"That's during the summer." What I wanted to add was that Serena would likely be more work than she was help.

"You'll find something for her to do, I'm sure."

I didn't agree or disagree, I changed the subject. "What's the second thing you wanted to ask me about?"

Gilly arched a brow. "Don't think I don't see your game."

I pressed my lips together to keep from laughing. "If I ignore it, then it doesn't exist in my world."

"If only that were the truth."

"When it comes to Serena, I'm going to live in ignorance-is-bliss land."

Gilly shook her head, but her mouth curved into a smile. "Fair enough." She paused for a moment, seeming to assess me. "Kay wants to do Jase's birthday celebration Saturday afternoon. Does that work for you?"

A burning fire lit along my sternum, but I swallowed it down. "Okay."

I'd marked each of the nine years since that night with the Grangers. Every birthday. Every anniversary of Jase's death. Even though it killed a piece of me to do it. To feel their pain like a branding iron on my skin. Yet they were the only ones who truly understood mine.

But this year would be harder. Anniversaries always were. And it would be ten years this summer. Kay had thrown herself into honoring her son in every way she could think of. Benches. Statues. Scholarships. She'd even managed to fund a new wing of the local library we were christening tonight.

I forced my focus back to this weekend. "Will Jax be there?"

With Jax, I didn't feel pain. It was rage—an anger strong enough to swallow us all whole.

Gilly's mouth thinned. "He got the day off work."

"That should be fun," I mumbled.

Gilly sighed, leaning back in her chair. I saw her age then. The way the years of stress and grief had carved their way into her face. How her shoulders curved in on themselves more than they had years ago. I framed the shot in my mind. Captured the story her body told without uttering a word.

"He'll never get over it," she said quietly.

"I know he won't. I'm not saying he should."

Gilly waved me off. "I know you're not." She looked me dead in the eyes. "You're not the only one he blames. It's all of us."

The burn was back. I heard Jax's hysterical voice, echoing off the hospital walls. "Why did you make him go?" It still hurt so much that it stole my breath. Guilt eating away at my insides. If I'd never insisted that we check up on Jax. If we'd just gone back to my house, instead of heading to that stupid party. If we'd only waited another five minutes before leaving.

I drowned in what-ifs. We all did in one way or another. Our once tightly bound group of friends had shattered. Scott had lost himself in a bottle and then more, the drugs finally taking him from us. Another coffin in a line of too many.

Marisa had stuck by Scott until she found him getting high in a motel room last year, half-naked with a woman that neither of them knew. Now, she was trying to rebuild her life piece by piece while ignoring the rest of us.

Lisbeth had lost herself in work. Taking legal case after legal case and barely coming up for air. Whenever I ran into her in town, it was as if we were strangers.

Isaac had retreated from everyone. Even though I knew he still lived in Wolf Gap, I rarely saw him. But I had never pushed to, either. I knew the temptation to hide away from it all and didn't want to hurt him by forcing him to remember.

Mitch had almost instantly replaced us all with new friends. A slightly rougher crowd. He went from his construction sites to the bar in a rhythm that I knew was an attempt to numb his pain.

And I'd all but lost the family I'd built for myself. I desperately held on to Kay and Chip, even though I felt them slipping through my fingers, too. I missed Serena like a limb. I would've even settled for her screaming at me for being an interfering bitch, rather than the silence. I even missed cleaning up Jax's messes.

But most of all, I missed the warmth of how things used to be. Jax as an annoying big brother with his teasing. Serena asking me for advice about her latest crush. Kay and Chip's care.

Guilt had slowly eaten away at every last relationship. The friends. The brother and sister I'd gained through Jase. The second parents—ones who actually gave a damn. I held on as tightly as I could, but I felt the ties fading.

It was none of our faults. It was the responsibility of a man who'd gotten high on meth and lost himself to rage. He had ended all of our lives in one way or another. None of us could fully figure out how to put the pieces back together after that night—even if we had survived.

"Laiken?"

Gilly's voice pulled me from my spiral. "Sorry," I croaked. "Just thinking about everyone. How much we all carry."

"Loss has a way of carving itself into your bones. It shouldn't be any other way."

She was right in so many ways. I could still feel Jase, but his memory was blurry now. I couldn't grasp onto the love that had once felt so real. Maybe because I was a different person now. I wasn't the girl who had promised him forever. I'd been made into something new through fire and ash.

"I miss him." The thing I missed most of all was my best friend. The one who knew all my secrets and scars. The person I was most comfortable with in the world.

"Me, too, Cherub. Me, too."

"We'll celebrate all he was to us. We'll have cake and tell stories. It'll be good."

She reached over and squeezed my hand. "That's my girl."

Chapter Two

Boden

I EASED MY FOOT OFF THE ACCELERATOR AS THE SPEED LIMIT dropped to twenty miles per hour on the edge of town. "Here's home for the next bit."

I glanced over at Peaches, who had her snout pressed to the window. "All right, but no jumping out of my truck," I told her with a stern look.

I lowered the window, and Peaches instantly stuck her head out, nose in the air. I did my own survey of the town. One thing was for sure—it was tiny. I'd learned that could be a good or bad thing. If the town was on your side, you could find refuge. If they posted selfies and stealth shots on their social media accounts, the paparazzi would be here in no time.

I struggled to unclench my jaw, working it back and forth to loosen the muscles as I scanned the street. Even though it was barely forty degrees, people were out and about, ducking into shops and restaurants. The buildings had an Old West vibe to them, and that carried to the street itself. Antique lampposts lined the way, still adorned with lights from Christmas in the shape of snowflakes.

"What do you think?"

Peaches let out a happy bark that only made her look goofier. No one, not even my vet, had any idea what different breeds were in this dog. She was her own unique creation with dark fur around her nose and eyes and lighter on her body. She should've been a big dog, except her legs were comically short and stubby.

But she'd stolen my heart when I was filming in Mexico. She'd found my trailer, and once I'd given her a piece of turkey from my sandwich, that was it—she'd claimed me as hers.

Getting her back to the States had been a nightmare, but I couldn't leave her behind. I'd never forget the flight back. Peaches had climbed into my lap, all sixty-five pounds of her, shaking like a leaf. If it had been possible for her to crawl inside me, she likely would've done it.

I gave her a scratch behind the ears. "I like it, too."

Maybe this was just what we needed after being cooped up in my Malibu house for months on end. I'd had to get my assistant to take Peaches out because the paps had resorted to flying drones over my private street.

But slowly, attention waned. Some pro-baseball player had been caught having an affair while his popstar wife was pregnant at home. I was sorry for her but grateful for the diversion.

For the first time in six months, I might be able to breathe. I pulled the fresh air into my lungs, rolling my shoulders back. Pine laced the breeze, even in the dead of winter, and I could only imagine how amazing it smelled once the weather warmed. Maybe this was just the place I needed.

My phone rang through the speakers in my truck. I checked the readout and hit a button on my steering wheel. "Hey, Dad."

"Where are you? You make it there yet?"

I couldn't help but grin. "Thirty-three, and he still worries I'm gonna get kidnapped."

My dad grunted. "There are crazies on the roads these days."

"I'm just driving through Wolf Gap now. It's gorgeous here. You can see the mountains and the lake from downtown. You'd love it."

"Maybe I'll have to come for a visit."

I paused for a moment. There was nothing I'd love more than some time with my dad, but executing it was complicated when I was trying to keep a low profile.

"Towards the end of your stay," he hurried to say.

"That'd be perfect."

He was quiet for a moment. "I hate the idea of you up there all alone. You sure you don't want to hole up at the compound? Your mom and I would love to have you. You and Peaches can take the pool house so you have your own space."

"I don't think that's a good idea. Eli could show up—"

"I don't think he will. We've still got paparazzi on the street out front."

A flush of anger swept through my system at my parents having to deal with the press hounding them. My father was used to the media to some degree. He'd been a child actor before moving on to directing. But even with blockbusters and Oscar wins, he'd somehow managed to keep a low profile and be boring enough for the gossip rags to leave him mostly alone.

At least until my brother stirred up trouble. He'd always had a gift for it. But this time, it hadn't been trouble. It had been so much more. He'd torn my life apart with casual disregard. And Carissa had paid the ultimate price for it all.

"Bo?"

I blinked a few times, coming to a stop at an intersection. "Sorry. What'd you say?"

Dad was quiet again. "Say the word, and I'm on a plane."

My throat burned. He was such a good man. The best. "I'm fine, really."

"You're not, but you will be. Each day, you're working yourself towards that."

I swallowed hard. I hoped he was right. But the truth was, I'd fallen out of love with Carissa years ago. I'd stayed because we'd always been a package deal. Because she knew what it was like to grow up in the limelight. Because I'd thought staying by her side would save her.

How wrong I'd been. Being with Carissa had meant her destruction. Made Eli fixate. Because he always had to destroy what he thought made me happy.

"Thanks, Dad. I should go. I need to pay attention to these directions."

"Sure. Text me when you get there. Send your mom a picture of the house."

The corners of my mouth lifted. "I think it's just a cabin. Probably a little rough. Gaines warned me that this guy wasn't exactly making his property a welcome place for visitors."

"Are you sure this is a good idea?"

"I want to get this movie right. He's the one to give me the authenticity."

My dad made a sound in the back of his throat that wasn't exactly agreement. "He went to prison."

"His conviction was overturned."

"That kind of experience changes a man."

I turned off the main road onto a smaller one that led away from town. "I'm sure it does. But that's part of what I need to see firsthand. That and his way with the horses. Gaines said it's like nothing he's ever seen before."

"I hope it's worth it," Dad muttered.

"It will be." It had to be. For the first time, I was trying to step into Dad's shoes. I'd be in front of the camera and behind it. I'd found projects before, taking on a producer role, but as soon as I'd read this script, I'd known I wanted to be the one to bring it to life at every stage of the process. The story had worked its way into my soul, and I needed to do it justice.

"Love you, Pop."

"Love you, too. I'm here if you need me."

"I know you are. Talk later."

"Text me."

I chuckled. "I'll let you know the highway bandits didn't get me."

"Tell me where I went wrong in raising such a smartass."

"I get it from you."

"Don't tell your mom that."

I eased my truck around a turn. "Your secret's safe with me. Later."

"Later."

My dad hung up, and I refocused on the road. We seemed to be curving around the mountain. The farther we went, the fewer and fewer gates I saw for homes and properties until they ceased altogether.

"You better not make a run for it out here. You'd get lost in a second."

Peaches gave a good sniff of the air, her tongue lolling out of her mouth.

"Your destination is on your right. One mile," my navigation system informed me.

"He's certainly got the isolated thing going for him."

I knew Ramsey Bishop didn't want me here. Gaines, my key grip, who handled the camera team on as many movies as I could get him on, had met Ramsey in prison, doing a stint for jacking a car when he was seventeen. They'd become tight, and Gaines had called in a favor when I told him about this movie. But even if Ramsey were prickly, I could be charming when I needed to be. Schmoozing was required when you wanted films to get made.

I slowed my truck as I spotted a large sign that read *Private Property Keep Out*. A duplicate hung about one hundred yards down the road on the opposite side. A third read: *This is your last warning. Turn around now.*

Hell. I hoped I wasn't about to get my ass shot. I came to a stop at a large wrought-iron gate. Rustic beams framed it, the earlier message punctuated by several cameras.

I rolled down my window and pressed the intercom button.

"What?" A rough voice cut across the line.

"Hey, it's Boden Cavanaugh. I'm looking for Ramsey Bishop."

"Let me see some ID. Hold it up to the camera."

I started to laugh and then realized that he was serious. I didn't mean to be an asshole, but I'd been in dozens of movies, and my face had been splashed across magazine covers at regular intervals for the past six months.

"Sure." I leaned to the side, pulling out my wallet. I slid out my ID and held it up to a small camera beside the intercom.

"Fine. I'm gonna open the gate. Follow the road around. Stop at the guest cabin. Don't come to the main house. I'll meet you there."

Ramsey didn't wait for me to answer, simply clicked off the line. The gate buzzed and began swinging open.

"Some welcome," I muttered to Peaches.

She simply panted happily in response.

I eased my truck forward. Tall pines flanked the road, hiding any true glimpses of the property from view. All at once, the forest fell away, and I was met by sweeping pastures dotted with horses and a series of structures that could've been out of an *Architectural Digest* article on the Old West. Rustic in a way that melded with the landscape around it, a massive barn stood near a large main house that looked like a mountain lodge, and a smaller cabin set a ways apart from the rest.

I guided my vehicle towards the cabin. I pulled into a makeshift spot at the front of the building and shut off my engine. Sliding out, I rounded my truck and opened the passenger door. Peaches jumped out and began to sniff. Her whole body quivered as her eyes moved to the trees behind the cabin.

A man stepped out from the woods. He was younger than I expected. Probably not that much older than me. And he had what I could only describe as a massive beast by his side.

"Stay," I ordered Peaches.

Her whole body wagged back and forth.

"Gaines didn't say anything about a dog," the man who had to be Ramsey said.

"Should I be worried that yours will eat her?"

Ramsey scowled. "Kai likes animals just fine. It's people he's wary of."

"What is he?" I couldn't help but ask. The canine's coat was thick with various shades of grays woven through it. But the ice-blue eyes took my breath.

"He's a wolf-hybrid."

"A wolf?"

"You have a problem with that you can stay somewhere else."

I held up a hand. "No problem. Just never seen one before."

Ramsey simply grunted and then tossed me a set of keys. "That's to the cabin, and a key fob for the gate. You don't bring any visitors here. You do, and you're out."

He turned and started to walk away.

"Wait. When do you work with the horses?"

Ramsey turned back, a muscle in his cheek ticking. "A little after sunrise. Better get your beauty sleep, movie star."

I bit back the retort I wanted to let loose and simply nodded. "See you then."

Ramsey disappeared between the trees.

"Think it might take me a minute to win him over."

Peaches made a keening noise as if she wanted to follow them.

"Sorry, buddy. You're stuck with me."

I walked up the front steps to the small porch and turned to survey my new surroundings. They were a sucker punch. Fields flowed into forests, which bled into craggy mountains covered in snow. The peaks looked so huge, they reminded me of how small I was in the grand scheme of things. How miniscule my problems were compared to their backdrop.

I could lose myself here for a few months. And just maybe I'd find a piece of myself again, too.

Chapter Three

Laiken

"**L**AIKEN, YOU LOOK BEAUTIFUL." KAY PULLED ME INTO a tight hug.

I let her warmth and familiar lavender scent wash over me. "So do you."

She released me. Her hand trembled as she brushed invisible wrinkles out of her dress. "It's rare I have an excuse to get dressed up these days." Kay scanned the space, her gaze skipping over the people filling it to the bones of the room. "It turned out well, don't you think?"

I followed her line of sight, tracking over the rows of bookshelves, large tables for studying, comfortable chairs and couches, and even a few computer terminals. "He would love this. I can see him curling up on one of those couches with one of those alien battle books."

"One of his happy places, as long as you were with him."

Kay's eyes misted over, and panic gripped me. It was a delicate dance with Kay, walking down memory lane but not lingering for too long. Because she could get lost there and not want to return to the rest of us.

I squeezed Kay's arms, bringing her attention back to me. "You're doing a wonderful thing here. So many kids will get such amazing use out of this place."

She took a shaky breath. "They will, won't they?"

I smiled and knew it reached my eyes. "You're giving them a warm and welcoming place to study. To work on projects. The library and the town will be so much better for it."

"You're giving it to them, too. This wing was your brainchild."

I waved Kay off. When she asked me to sit on the board of The Jase Granger Foundation, I'd immediately agreed. Still, I usually took a backseat. "All I said was that we should do something with books and reading. You took that and ran with it."

She grinned. "You know making plans is my love language."

A smile stretched across my face as a million different memories played in my mind. Elaborate birthday parties, end-of-school scavenger hunts, backyard campouts. "You put a military strategist to shame."

"Dang straight." Her head lifted as someone called her name. "That's Cary. I really should thank him for his donation to this project."

I made a shooing motion. "Go. I'll catch up with you later."

She pulled me in for one more hug. "Love you, Laiken."

My throat burned. "Love you, too."

I watched her chat with Cary, making sure she seemed good. Stable. Kay's emotional state could go from tough as nails to fragile as an eggshell in a split second. But tonight, she seemed good. I let out the breath I'd been holding.

In seconds, I was swept into polite conversation with one casual acquaintance after another. It was one of my least favorite things. That surface-level chitchat that didn't give you even a glimpse into who you were talking with.

I liked people. Found them endlessly fascinating. But not like this. I craved raw authenticity. The kind that could terrify or comfort. Make you feel exposed, but at the same time, seen.

I excused myself from one such encounter and turned for the

bar, knocking into another partygoer. "Sorry, I didn't—" My words cut off as Lisbeth's face filled my vision. Her strawberry-blond hair had turned to more of a true red since I'd last seen her.

"Laiken." Her smile looked strained. Fake.

"How are you?" My question came out as more of a croak.

"Good. Busy. Things with the practice are crazy."

"It was nice of you to come."

Ten years. It was a lifetime and yet a split second all at the same time. She and Marisa had been my best friends, and now they were simply acquaintances at best. Lisbeth might be an acquaintance anyway. Marisa? She might consider me much worse than that.

"It was the right thing to do. For Kay and Chip," Lisbeth said, her voice growing thick.

I swallowed as if that would clear the emotion from my throat. "Have you talked to Marisa?"

"Only once since Scott's funeral."

I shifted from foot to foot, trying to alleviate the growing tension low in my back. Little ice picks stabbing into my spine. I forced myself to focus on Lisbeth. "How was she?"

"How do you think? She's a mess."

Guilt pricked at me. The last words she'd hurled at me hadn't been kind ones, but I should've tried harder to heal that divide. We were all struggling, doing the best we could, given all we'd been through. "I'll call her."

"I don't know if that's a good idea." Lisbeth's phone buzzed, and she pulled it from her purse. "I need to go. See you around, Laiken."

She took off without another word. The woman who used to be one of my closest friends. Maybe we weren't even acquaintances now, either. Maybe we truly were strangers.

The walls seemed to close in around me, my temperature ticking up a few degrees. I wove through the crowd of people. It wasn't a massive group. They were all faces I recognized to one degree or another. Yet the room felt stifling.

I moved to the bar. "Ice water, please."

The bartender sent me a wink. "You sure I can't get you something stronger?"

"Just the water."

His smile slipped a fraction, but he filled a glass with ice and then water. "Here you go."

"Thank you."

I scanned the room quickly and moved towards a somewhat-empty corner. My back throbbed as I eased myself into a chair. Too much standing for one day. I rubbed at the muscles as I took a sip.

I closed my eyes for a moment, letting the cold liquid soothe my throat. I imagined it traveling down to the worst of the agony that wrapped around my spinal column. Three surgeries, and they still hadn't found a way to lessen the pain. The last one had made it worse, and I'd made a promise to myself never to let someone slice me open again.

"Laiken."

My eyes flew open at the sound of the deep voice. It cut like a knife. So similar to the one I'd lost, yet with a hardness Jase's had never had.

"Jax. What are you doing here?"

As much as Jax had cleaned up his act after his brother's death, a library opening wasn't exactly his scene, even if the building held Jase's name.

He inclined his head in his mother's direction. "I promised Mom I'd come."

I nodded, taking another sip of my water.

"Are you coming on Saturday?"

"Of course." Pain pulsed in my back as though just thinking about the gathering for Jase's birthday had intensified it.

Jax's jaw worked back and forth. "I don't know if 'of course' really fits the bill. Haven't seen you around much lately."

I lifted my gaze to his. There was pain there, but Jax had transformed that pain into anger. I got it. Anger was sometimes easier to live with than grief. "I come when you're at work."

It was easier that way. I'd given up on trying to reach Jax, attempting to explain to the person who had once been a brother that I'd give anything, even my life, for things to be different. Nothing would ever be enough for him. Because after Robert Aaron had gone to prison, Jax had lost his punching bag. He'd needed someone to blame, and I was a handy target.

A muscle ticked in his cheek. "Never could handle confrontation."

"I don't see a point in it when it doesn't help a damn thing," I gritted out.

"Maybe you should stop showing up altogether. It might be better if the birthday celebrations were just family."

I reared back as if Jax had slapped me. He might as well have; it would've been less painful. Since kindergarten, the Grangers *had* been my family. Jax had been more of a big brother to me than mine. But now, only derision bled from his gaze.

"We all lost someone we loved," I whispered.

"No. You lost a fuck buddy. I lost my goddamned brother!"

My hand trembled, and I lowered the glass to rest on my knee. "I loved him, too."

Jax's dark eyes flashed. "Did you?"

I pushed to my feet. "You know I did. You saw it every damned day. Don't you dare question that." My hand began shaking again.

"It was your damn grand idea to come play fun police and break up my party. If you hadn't been such a tight-assed bitch, my brother would still be here."

I lost my grip on the glass. It dropped to the floor, smashing into a million tiny pieces—shards so small there was no way to put them back together. Not in a way that would make a working glass again. Sometimes, like now, I felt just like that glass. Shattered beyond recognition.

Kay hurried over, a worried look on her face as her gaze bounced back and forth between Jax and me. "Accident?" She waved over a waiter. "Can you please find a dustpan and broom so we can clean this up?"

"Of course, ma'am."

Jax's hot gaze hadn't left my face. It bored into me as if he could strike me down with it. I'd wanted authenticity, anything but polite conversation. But it was like they said: *Be careful what you wish for*.

"I'm sorry, Kay. I'm not feeling well. I need to head home."

Worry lined her expression. "Do you need me to drive you?"

Gilly hurried over, patting Kay's shoulder. "No, you stay. I can give Laiken a ride."

"No." The single word came out more harshly than intended. I softened it with a shaky smile. "I just need to rest for a little bit."

Gilly's gaze narrowed on me, but she nodded. "You promise to text if you need anything?"

"I promise."

Jax scoffed. "Yeah, bend over backwards for *Laik*. Not like she hasn't already fucked everything up."

I whirled on him, white-hot pain lancing up my spine. "You don't get to call me that. You lost that right a long time ago. Maybe you never should've had it."

Jax stumbled back a step, and I caught a hint of booze on his breath. He held up both hands, a smirk playing on his lips. "Why don't you get out of here before you cause more of a scene?"

My gaze darted around the room. So many sets of eyes focused directly on us. The attention grated against my skin, leaving it raw and exposed.

I turned and headed for the door, but I didn't take a full breath until I sank into the driver's seat of my car. My hands tightened around the wheel as the burning behind my eyes intensified. It was all a mess. Everything twisted and shattered like the vehicle they'd pulled my and Jase's bodies from. And it was only getting worse.

Chapter Four

Laiken

I WAS SWIMMING IN A DARK SEA, THE WAVES BATTERING ME. *I heard Jase's voice calling out for me. "Love you, Laik. Forever and a day."*

I tried to get my answer out. To tell him, "Forever and two days." But the water choked me, and the sea darkened even more.

Jax's voice replaced Jase's. "You killed him."

I shot up in bed, my heart hammering against my ribs. My pajamas clung to my damp skin. Gizmo let out a little whimper as he dragged himself closer to me and licked my arm.

I brushed a hand over his head. "It's okay. We're okay."

Gizmo pressed into my hand. I lifted him, cuddling his little body against my chest. "What would I do without you?"

My muscles still trembled. The dreams always felt so real. Sometimes, I woke up and swore I'd swum a mile in them.

I glanced at the clock on my nightstand. A little after five. It wasn't worth trying to find sleep again, especially in damp sheets.

I swung my legs over the side of the bed and stood. I bent, setting Gizmo down and hooking him up to his wheels. "There you go. Let me get cleaned up and then I'll take you out and get you some breakfast."

He danced and spun at the word *out*.

"Give me ten minutes."

I moved into the tiny bathroom off my bedroom area. The apartment was really just a single large space with a closet and a bathroom, but I'd done my best to make it mine. It was cozy. Decorated with pieces of art I'd collected over my years working at The Gallery. My attempts at watercolor and oils before finally finding my love of photography. It was me, a one-of-a-kind mess. And I loved it just like that.

I stripped off my PJs and tossed them into my hamper. I turned on the shower spray, waiting for it to get warm. I swore I still heard the echo of voices in my head from the dream. I stepped into the clawfoot tub and shower combo, pulling the curtain, and held my face up to the spray.

I didn't move as the water coursed over me. I tried to picture Jase's face. To grab hold of one of our beautiful memories. My favorites were always the times we were in a friendship more than anything else. It made me wonder if we would've lasted to forever like we'd always promised.

I knew one thing for sure. I would have loved him always. For being the boy who made me feel safe and cherished. As the best friend I'd ever had. Even if that love had transformed into something else, it still would've been one of the best gifts I'd ever received.

I turned under the stream of water, soaking my hair, even though it would take forever for the thick, dark strands to dry. I soaped up my scalp, taking breaks when I needed to if the pain got to be too much. I conditioned, then washed my face and body. I bent to shave my legs. The sharp, stabbing sensations ricocheted up my spine, but I was determined to finish the task, even if my tears mixed with the shower spray.

When I finished, I stepped out and wrapped a thick towel around myself. I put my hair in another. Gizmo sat, waiting politely, but he stared me down in a way that told me to hurry up.

I made quick work of brushing my teeth and dressing. I kept my hair in the towel as I took Gizmo downstairs and out the back door. There was a small patch of grass back there where he could do his business before we took our longer walk later.

Footsteps sounded near the other end of the pseudo-alley. My eyes strained against the darkness, trying to see as my heart rate picked up to keep time with the footsteps. I tugged on Gizmo's leash. "Let's get inside."

As soon as we were in, I slammed and locked the door. There were no windows along the back wall of the shop, no peephole to peer through. I listened and swore I heard the footsteps slow at The Gallery's back door. Then they picked up again, walking away.

A chill skated over my skin as Gizmo let out a low growl. I bent and gave him a good rub. "It's okay. I guess early mornings make me jumpy."

But I knew that wasn't the truth. It was the perfect storm that had me on edge. My run-in with Jax the night before. The lack of sleep. The nightmare. And it didn't help that I knew I'd have to face the onslaught of memories again this weekend.

I held the bag of bagels in one hand and Gizmo's leash in the other as I headed up the stairs to Addie and Beckett's house. Well, it was actually Beckett's brother's home, but Hayes had given them use of it until the couple's new house was built.

I looked up at the sound of the front door opening and closing.

"Hey, Laik," Beckett greeted. Nothing about the man read *doctor*, from his slightly shaggy hair to his leather jacket. But he was one of the best.

"Morning."

He bent to give Gizmo a scratch. "The crew's inside. And I'm gonna be honest, I'm pissed this is a girls-only breakfast because it smells amazing."

I chuckled. "Are you honestly telling me that Addie is letting you starve?"

His lips twitched. "She might've snuck me a little something."

"That's what I thought."

"Head on in, the door's unlocked."

The statement was a simple one, but after everything Addie and Beckett had been through in the past few months, the knowledge that they felt safe enough to leave their front door open warmed something inside me. "Thanks. Save lots of lives today."

"Let's hope I don't need to save any. I'm going for scraped knees and colds."

"That works, too." I gave him a wave and headed through the front door.

Voices sounded from the kitchen, and I bent to unhook Gizmo's leash. As soon as the latch released, he took off like a racehorse towards the sounds and smells of the gathering.

Addie's laughter sifted through the air. "Gizmo. Did you bring your mom, or did you make the walk on your own?"

"He probably would if I'd let him," I said as I rounded the corner.

Gizmo was already in Addie's arms, licking her face. She nuzzled his face as she balanced him against her small baby bump. "That's because we're best pals."

Addie's cousin, Everly, smiled. "She's a born mama."

"She's definitely got the gentle touch down, but you're also going to have to learn to be a referee if you have more than one," Hadley said.

Addie grinned. "I'll leave bad cop to Beckett."

Hadley snorted. "Good luck with that. My brother is a total pushover."

A look of such tenderness passed over Addie's face, it had me looking away.

"I love that about him."

Hadley laughed. "She's definitely a goner."

Addie set Gizmo down, moving to the container of treats she

kept just for him. "Yup. And I'm fine with that." She tossed a treat down to my dog, who gobbled it up.

I set the bag on the counter and moved to wash my hands, Addie following behind me to do the same. "I brought bagels. I hope that goes with whatever smells so good."

"It's a savory breakfast casserole, so bagels are perfect." Addie's cheeks heated. "I was going to make biscuits to go with it, but I lost track of time this morning."

I waggled my eyebrows. "Lost track of time? Or Beckett distracted you?"

Addie buried her face in the hand towel. "I don't know what you're talking about."

"Don't be embarrassed. Beck is hot," Everly said.

"Ev," Addie scolded. "He's your brother-in-law."

"So? I can still objectively say he's hot."

Hadley made a gagging noise. "Subject change. For the love of God, subject change."

Everly sent Hadley an evil grin. "What? You don't want to hear about your brother's hotness?"

"Gross. How about we talk about your other hotness sighting?"

Everly shook her head. "Hayes said there was no way it was him."

"Who?" Addie asked as she pulled the casserole out of the oven.

"Ev thinks she saw Boden Cavanaugh driving through town yesterday," Hadley explained.

"I swear it was him. He had the window of his truck down, and his dog stuck its head out."

I slid onto one of the stools at the counter. "The actor?"

"You mean the heartthrob?" Hadley asked.

Ev broke off a piece of bagel. "He definitely makes my heart go pitter-patter."

"Which one is he again?" Addie asked as she moved the casserole to the island.

Ev reached for the cream cheese. "Remember that movie we watched two weekends ago?"

"The one that sent me into a heaving mess?"

Everly's lips twitched. "I thought Beckett was going to throttle me."

Addie laughed. "He doesn't handle my tears well."

"Understatement. Anyway, Boden Cavanaugh played the lead in that one."

Addie's eyes widened. "And he's in Wolf Gap?"

"I swear it was him."

I moved the stack of plates closer to Addie so she could dish up her casserole. "Seems like an odd destination in the middle of winter."

Hadley took a sip of her orange juice and then set it down. "I wonder if he's trying to lay low after everything that happened."

Ev turned to her. "I completely forgot about that."

"What?" I asked.

"His longtime girlfriend died about six months ago. The family didn't share how, and that only made the press more bloodthirsty," Hadley said. "They hounded him for months."

Ev took the plate Addie handed her. "Maybe he's moving to Wolf Gap. I wouldn't blame him after going through that."

Hadley shook her head. "It was awful. There were even some disgusting tabloids that suggested he had something to do with it, even though there was zero proof."

My rib cage tightened around my lungs as I struggled to breathe normally. I knew what that was like, but I didn't have the eyes of the world on me, just a tiny town. "If he is in town, I hope people leave him alone here."

Addie reached over and squeezed my arm. "I do, too. No one should have to deal with ugliness like that, especially when they're mourning."

No, they shouldn't. But life was rarely what it should be. You simply had to do your best to make something beautiful out of the shattered pieces.

Chapter Five

Boden

I LEANED BACK IN THE ROCKER, THE RAILS MAKING A SOOTHING sound as they traveled back and forth over the planks of the front porch. Only Peaches' soft snores punctuated the song. She'd never been one for early mornings. I took a sip of my coffee and watched the sun crest the horizon.

I could get used to this. For the first time in what felt like forever, I'd slept through the night without any dreams taunting me. I'd kept the window in my bedroom cracked, and I wondered if the cool, crisp air had kept me comatose. I hadn't needed my alarm because I'd woken up just fine on my own.

I caught sight of a figure moving from the main house towards the barn. I stayed put. Somehow, I didn't think Ramsey would appreciate me showing up first thing. I'd wait until I saw him move a horse from the barn.

One minute bled into the next, and before long, half an hour had passed. I rose from my rocker to make my way towards the structure when I saw them. It was the sound of thundering hooves that caught my attention first, bringing my gaze to the back of the barn. One horse, then another, took off across the field—a herd of about a dozen, charging over the land.

I had no choice but to stop dead. They were a sight to behold. As if given a silent command, they turned, heading across the horizon.

The crunch of gravel had me pulling my focus away from the majestic sight towards a pickup truck and trailer heading down the lane.

"I thought you'd still be sleeping."

I turned to see Ramsey heading in my direction. "I'm not sure what you know about making movies, but when we're on days, my call times are usually around four in the morning."

He gave a slight chin lift, an acknowledgment that he'd heard me but nothing else.

So, we weren't going to find our way to friendship anytime soon. Peaches danced at my side as she caught sight of the large wolf-dog next to Ramsey. I rubbed her head. "You need to play it cool. I don't want us kicked out of here."

I gave her the command to stay, and she lay down on the porch. I moved down the steps as the truck backed its trailer up to the round pen. "New horse?"

Ramsey nodded. "You'll need to stay clear of the pen."

"No problem."

When the trailer was in place, a woman who looked to be in her sixties jumped down from the cab of the truck. She crossed to us, her eyes widening slightly at the sight of me, but she immediately turned her focus back to Ramsey. "She's feeling a lot of feelings."

Ramsey's eyes shifted to the trailer. A whinny sounded, followed by a swift kick to the trailer wall. "You get any additional information?"

The woman's lips pursed. "When she wasn't doing what they wanted, the owners tried force."

The set of Ramsey's jaw hardened to stone. "Idiots."

"They are that. You'll get her where she needs to go." The

woman turned back to me. "Since Ramsey here isn't one for polite introductions, I'll have to start. I'm Loren, but everyone calls me Lor."

"Boden Cavanaugh."

Her eyes twinkled in the early morning light. "Oh, I know who you are, cutie. What brings you to Wolf Gap?"

"I'm prepping a movie and am here doing research."

"He's making a movie on one of the prison wild horse programs," Ramsey said.

Lor's eyes snapped to me, wariness there now. "Are you?"

"I'm here because it's important for me to get it right." And not just to make the movie successful. The script was fictional, but its bones were rooted in reality. A program where inmates near the end of their sentences were eligible to work with wild horses to prepare them for their future homes. I'd visited a couple of different programs to get a feel for how they worked, but I needed a closer look. To understand from someone who'd been through it.

Lor turned to Ramsey. "And you agreed to this?"

His mouth thinned. "Gaines roped me into it."

A smile spread across Lor's face, and she turned to me. "Of course, he did. How is that big lug?"

"He's good. Great. Got a little girl who just turned two and an amazing wife. How do you know him?" I asked.

"I started one of the first prison programs."

My jaw went slack. "I'd love to pick your brain."

Her expression hardened again. "We'll see."

The horse in the trailer gave another swift kick, rattling the wall.

"If you two are done with your tea party, I'd like to help her out of that tin can," Ramsey gritted out.

Lor moved towards the trailer. "Let's set her free. I couldn't get close enough to harness her. Could only get her loaded up using a training flag, so she's gonna come straight out."

Ramsey gave another of those slight chin lifts to acknowledge that he'd heard Lor. She moved to one side of the trailer and unbolted the latch. Ramsey grabbed the door and pulled it open until it was flush with the pen wall.

The mare exploded out of the trailer, bucking and kicking out her hind legs. As soon as she was free, Ramsey closed the door, and Lor latched it. He then closed the opening to the pen, checking to make sure it was secure. "Move the trailer. I don't want her thinking she's going back in there."

Lor nodded and climbed behind the wheel. When the engine turned over, the horse gave another series of bucks. Ramsey simply watched her, not reacting at all. Once the truck and trailer were out of sight, he ducked between the fence rails and moved into the round pen, only a rope in hand.

The horse gave a good kick and began racing along the fence line, showing her displeasure at having someone in her space. I bit back the urge to ask him if this was really a good idea.

Ramsey gave her a minute and then began walking in circles, raising and lowering his looped rope. The horse would charge in bursts, throwing in a buck here and there, but Ramsey never reacted. Nerves of steel. One of those hooves could cave in a man's skull.

I watched from a couple of feet away as something in the mare slowly quieted. Her bursts of speed weren't quite as intense, and the bucks stopped altogether.

Ramsey slowed then, too. He faced the mare. She studied him, taking his measure.

"She's wondering if he'll hurt her the way her other owners did. But he's already proven that he won't."

I hadn't even heard Lor come up alongside me. I glanced at her and then focused back on the horse and man. "It's pretty incredible."

"You haven't seen anything yet. Ramsey's a walking miracle." Her eyes narrowed on me. "If you try to use what he's been through as fodder for your movie, I'll come for you. And it won't be pleasant."

I watched as the mare sidled up to Ramsey. She pressed her muzzle into his arm.

"Holy hell," I muttered to myself. Lor had left an hour or so ago, but I'd stayed glued to the spot, riveted, watching the dance play out.

Ramsey rubbed her face, not saying a word. Then he bent, reaching for something on the other side of the fence. As soon as he set the bucket of grain on the ground, the mare pounced on it. As she did, Ramsey ducked out of the pen.

"That was unbelievable. What will you work on next with her?"

He snapped his fingers, and Kai instantly came to his side, eyeing me suspiciously. "You talk a lot."

I swallowed a strangled laugh. "I think that's the only thing I've said in the past two hours."

Ramsey ignored my defense. "I'm breaking for lunch. You can come back this afternoon or tomorrow at sunrise. Your choice."

I'd been dismissed. But I hadn't been kicked out. I was already playing over a million different things in my mind, building the character from the ground up. Taking pieces from how Ramsey held himself or the way he moved and then creating embellishments of my own rooted in the hero's backstory. There was enough for me to chew on for days.

Hell, I probably had most of what I needed for the entire movie in the span of the past few hours. But I wasn't anxious to leave this place anytime soon. There was a magic in the air that I'd been missing for a long time.

"I'll see you later…" My words trailed off because Ramsey was already halfway to his house.

Peaches whined from the porch.

"Sorry, girl." I gave her the signal for release, and she lumbered over to me, jumping up and down in a slow prance. "What do you say we go for a ride?" She let out a happy bark. "Thought you might like that."

I pulled my keys from my pocket and beeped the locks. Opening the passenger door, Peaches charged, her stubby legs propelling her into the air. Jumps like these sometimes ended with her missing the mark and doing some sort of flip, but this time she landed soundly in the passenger seat.

I climbed behind the wheel and started the engine. As soon as the windows were down, Peaches was in heaven. Panting, she let her tongue loll. I took a roundabout way into town. I didn't know exactly where I was going, but I knew the rough direction I was headed in. I looped around the mountains and drove by the lake. Eventually, I had to put the heat on, even though Peaches' window was down because temperatures in the twenties were too much for my Los Angeles blood.

By the time I pulled into a parking spot in front of a small grocery store on the main drag, Peaches had curled into a ball on the seat and was snoring away again. I gave her head a rub. "You gotta stay here while I get groceries."

Her eyes opened a fraction and then closed again. I chuckled. Two things you didn't come between with Peaches: her food and her naps.

My phone buzzed in the cupholder, and I pulled it out.

Unknown Number: *I'm trying to keep a low profile like Dad asked but I'm running low on funds. Can you spot me?*

My back teeth ground together as I stared at the screen. How had we gotten here? This place where Eli's phone number changed every other week because people were looking for him. The one where he despised me yet was willing to hit me up for money. A world where Carissa no longer existed.

It was the last thought that had me blocking the number. I'd tried time and time again to be there for Eli. The only thing it had gotten me was a lifetime of heartache and cleaning up his messes. I was done.

I shoved my phone into my pocket and pulled on my ballcap. Sliding out of my truck, I slammed the door with a little more force than necessary, and Peaches' ears twitched. I'd get her a treat to make up for it. But as I headed for the grocery store, I couldn't make myself go inside. I was too keyed up. Twitchy.

Instead, I headed down the sidewalk, tugging my hat down low. I shouldn't have worried about it. Only a handful of people were on the street, and none of them expected to see me in this tiny town.

I welcomed the bite of cold air, not caring that I'd left my jacket back at the cabin. Something about the way the temperature attacked my skin mirrored how I felt at the moment. There was a feral edge to us both.

I lost myself in the sights of the town and that feeling. They didn't match up. Wolf Gap was what my mom would call *quaint*. It had a charming, welcoming quality to it that didn't fit with the air or my mood. Hand-painted signs proclaimed coffee shops and pizza parlors. Tourist shops and cafes.

My steps faltered as a building with large windows came into view. It wasn't the building itself that had my feet slowing. It was an image—a photograph. A woman bent over in a field, her body contorted and hair hanging in front of her face.

Something about it pulled me in. Before I could think about the wisdom of the action, I was opening the door and stepping into the gallery space. But I didn't have eyes for any other pieces of art. Only the one that had drawn me in.

I felt a tugging sensation in the center of my chest as if an invisible tether pulled me closer. I stopped just two feet shy of the piece. Now I could see the woman's face. A tear tracked down her cheek. Even though her dark hair hid some of her gorgeous features, her eyes shot straight to me.

No, they shot *through* me. It was as though those amber orbs saw everything I'd gotten so good at hiding from the world. Those eyes were unflinchingly honest. Let you see all the pain below. And for the first time in forever, I didn't feel quite so alone.

Chapter Six

Laiken

I MOVED FROM THE BACK ROOM INTO THE GALLERY, LEAVING Gizmo on his bed, happily chewing on a bully stick. My steps faltered as I took in the man in front of my photograph, his back to me. He wore dark jeans that hugged his hips, a flannel shirt, and a baseball cap. It was too cold for only a flannel shirt, yet I couldn't find it in me to be sad that it was what he wore.

The shirt ghosted over defined muscles and showed just how broad his shoulders were. What was it about good shoulders? I was woman enough to admit they were my weakness.

But it was the energy that flowed off him that had me stepping forward. He paid rapt attention to the photograph in front of him. I couldn't help the question that tumbled out of my mouth. "What do you think?"

The man didn't turn around. "It's one of the most visceral pieces of art I've ever seen."

Visceral. This man didn't know he'd just paid me one of the highest compliments possible. "Most people think it's depressing." I'd seen more than one patron scrunch up their nose at it and turn away in favor of a pretty watercolor landscape.

"It's real. A piece of the human experience. Isn't that what art should be?"

My heart hammered in my chest. "I think so. That and to make us feel seen. Less alone in one way or another." That was what it had done for me time and time again. It was why I had been brave enough to shoot this self-portrait. Because I hoped to give that gift to someone else.

"Less alone," he muttered as he stared at the image. After a few beats, he turned around.

I sucked in a sharp breath as I took in his angled features that I'd seen gracing the covers of magazines at the grocery store checkout so many times. But those photos didn't come anywhere close to doing his eyes justice. The swirling green and gold could hold a person in a trance. "Oh, crap."

Boden Cavanaugh chuckled. "That isn't usually the reaction I get, but I like the honesty." He held out his hand. "I'm Boden."

I shook on autopilot. I expected his palm to be soft, pampered, but rough calluses dotted his skin. "Laiken."

"The woman in the photo."

I cleared my throat and tugged my hand from his. "I am. And gallery manager. Nice to meet you."

His gaze tracked over my face as if he were committing every detail to memory. "Is the photograph for sale?"

"It is—"

"I'll take it."

I arched a brow. "You didn't even ask how much it is."

He grinned, and the effect was devastating. "Rookie mistake. You know how much I want it now and can highball me."

My lips twitched. "Lucky for you, there's a price point on the exhibit label. I won't be able to con you out of millions."

"I guess luck is on my side." He turned back to the photo and the plaque to check the price. "This photographer should be charging triple."

"I'll be sure to tell them."

Boden turned back to me. "I don't see a name. I'd love to look for more of their work."

"They prefer to remain anonymous, but I can give you a link to their website. And we have a couple more pieces that will be in the next showing in a few weeks."

His eyes narrowed a fraction. "Why the anonymity?"

I shrugged. "They say it allows the art to be more free."

Boden glanced at the photograph again. "It's the hardest to be vulnerable in front of prying eyes."

"Yet you manage to do it." Countless awards told me as much.

He smiled. "I try."

That curve of the lips was charming. Beautiful, even. But I studied smiles, and I knew a fake one when I saw it. In the midst of such a real conversation, I hated the falsity slipping in. I headed to the reception desk. "I can take payment now if you'd like, but you won't be able to pick up the photograph until the end of the exhibit in a few weeks. If you won't be here, then I can have it shipped wherever you'd like."

Boden followed behind me. "I can pay now."

He moved to pull his wallet out when a bark sounded, and Gizmo charged out of the back room, wheels bouncing as he ran.

"I'll be damned," Boden said as he crouched. Gizmo launched himself at Boden the best he could with wheels still attached. "Don't flip yourself over." He lifted his eyes to me as he gave my dog a good rub. "Who's this?"

The bite of earlier frustration melted away at his tenderness with my pup. "Gizmo, troublemaker and gallery mascot."

Boden scratched behind Gizmo's ears. "All the best dogs are at least a little troublemaker."

"I'd say he has more than a little in him." Gizmo licked Boden's cheek. "He's clearly fond of you."

"He can probably smell my dog on me. She's waiting in my truck."

"Oh—"

The door opening cut me off, the bell overhead tinkling.

"Laiken, good, you're still here. I wanted to run something by—oh, I'm so sorry. Here I am, yammering on, and we have a patron." Gilly's eyes widened a fraction as she placed his face. "Quite the patron, I see. She held out a hand. I'm Gillian, owner of The Gallery."

She sent me a sheepish smile. "Though owner in name only, really. Laiken runs this ship."

His gaze tracked back to me, staying a moment longer than necessary. "She clearly knows what she's doing. It's a wonderful collection of pieces."

"She has the best eye out there. Are you looking for anything in particular?"

"I found it. That photograph by your anonymous artist."

I fought the urge to squirm, instead keeping my face an impassive mask.

"Ah, one of my favorites." Gilly turned to the photo, her gaze sweeping over it like a caress.

Even though no one knew I was the artist, I still felt Gilly's support. Every time she pushed to meet the photographer. Every time she lingered at one of my pieces or gasped when I revealed a new work. She was my champion without even knowing it.

"So, do you know the mysterious artist?" Boden asked.

Gilly chuckled. "I wish. I've been pushing Laiken for an introduction for years now. She never gives in."

Boden glanced back at me. "A good keeper of secrets, then."

"The best." I was a master at keeping my grief and pain hidden from those around me. But I was also tired. Sometimes, it felt as if I were constantly bracing myself for a blow. I needed to set that down. To give my muscles a chance to relax.

"Laiken?"

Gilly's voice cut through my spiral of thoughts. "Sorry. What?"

Concern lined the planes of Boden's face. "I was asking if anyone tried bribing you."

I laughed but knew it came across as forced. "I'm above bribing."

Boden winked. "We'll just have to see about that."

Gilly's lips pressed into a firm line as she seemed to struggle to keep from laughing.

I rolled my eyes and stepped behind the desk, waking up my computer. "How about you just pay for your photo instead?"

Boden handed over his credit card. "I can do that. For now."

A pleasant shiver skated down my spine. I focused back on the screen, typing in the amount and the buyer details. "Is there a phone number or email you'd like me to contact when the photo is ready to be taken home?"

"If you want my phone number, you can just ask. I'll give it to you."

I couldn't hold in my snort. "I'll be sure to block my number when I call you. Wouldn't want to gain a stalker."

Boden let out a bark of laughter. "Laiken, I think you're my new favorite person." He pulled a card out of his wallet as I handed him back his credit card. "Here's all my information. Call anytime."

"I'll call when the photograph is ready." And not a second before. Not even when the man in front of me was more than intriguing. I wished for an afternoon in the mountains, just me, him, and my camera. I wanted to strip away the layers of charm and flirt and expose the real man underneath.

The corner of Boden's mouth kicked up. "We'll see." He gave Gilly a nod. "Lovely to meet you."

She blinked a few times as if coming out of a daze, then cleared her throat. "You, too. Stop by anytime."

"Thank you, I will." And then he was gone.

I grinned at Gilly. "How are you going to make sure you're here when he comes back?"

She bent, lifting Gizmo into her arms. "I'm going to rely on my bestest employee and dear friend to text me. Should we come up with a code word?"

A snort escaped me. "How about '*the hottie has landed*?'"

Gilly's mouth curved. "I like it." She paused for a moment, surveying my face. "And he likes you."

"He doesn't know me."

"He could if you gave him a chance."

I lowered myself into the desk chair. My back protested the movement. "Not interested."

Gilly stared at me as she pulled out one of the chairs opposite the desk and eased into it.

"My life is full. So many wonderful people, a job I love, a pup who adores me and makes me laugh."

"You still miss him."

"Of course, I do."

But not in the way Gilly thought. I missed Jase like a security blanket. When he died, I'd realized that life didn't always work out the way you wanted it to. Sometimes, it twisted into something altogether different. Sometimes, *you* twisted into something different. I wasn't the same girl who'd loved that boy. But through the pain and grief, I'd realized just how strong I was. How much I could carry on my shoulders. I'd realized what was truly important to me and what I could let go.

I lifted my gaze to Gilly. "He'll always be a part of me. In so many ways, he's made me who I am today."

Her expression softened. "I'm glad you carry him with you."

But I carried so much along with it. Grief. Guilt. The weight of Kay's struggles and Jax's anger. Serena's disappearance and Chip's distance.

Gilly studied me. "Everything okay?"

"I'm fine. Last night was just a lot."

Her lips pressed together. "Jax was out of line. He'd been drinking and—"

"Jax and I will never see eye to eye. It breaks something in Kay every time he and I get into it. I don't want to put her through that."

"She loves you like you were her own. And she's used to her children squabbling."

But this was so much more than squabbling.

Gilly was quiet for a bit as she continued to stroke Gizmo. "Losing Jase shaped us all."

"I know that. And I'd never want to tell someone what to feel. But I can't be the receptacle for his pain. It's not fair to me, and it hurts too damn much."

She reached across the table and squeezed my hand. "I know, Cherub. It kills me that he puts you through that. I've tried talking to him, but it might be time for another conversation—"

I held up a hand, cutting her off. "Don't do that. I don't want you to put yourself in the middle."

"You know I'd do anything for you."

"Let me try to sort it out on my own. After Saturday, I won't have to see him for a while. That should help."

Gilly's gaze roamed over my face. "You're happy here, aren't you?"

I really thought about it for a moment. My life was full of so many good things. Infinite gratitude. "There's so much I love. So much that makes me happy. This gallery. My home. Addie, Ev, and Hadley. You. These mountains. Sometimes, I think the feel of this place is what fuels me."

"The muse is a powerful thing. Don't ignore that."

I chuckled. "The muse is your number one, always."

Her lips twitched. "What can I say? I'm an artist through and through."

I looked around the space I had poured so much of myself into. I didn't want to lose that. And as hard as my relationship was with Jax, I couldn't imagine not seeing Kay and Gilly on a weekly basis. It was all a jumble of emotions. But I'd just have to find a way to live with that mess.

Chapter Seven

Boden

I LEANED AGAINST THE SIDE OF THE ROUND PEN, PEACHES sitting next to me as we watched Ramsey work. The bay mare followed him around the ring. He'd head in one direction for a while and then switch the opposite way. She behaved more like a dog than a horse, and it was night and day from yesterday.

Ramsey stopped, and the mare did the same. He moved to the fence and removed a halter from one of the posts. The horse quivered, no longer following. He halted, not moving forward or back.

I would've given anything to read minds at that moment. To know how Ramsey decided when to push forward, when to pull back, when to stop. The mare eyed him, the contraption in his hands, and pawed at the ground.

Ramsey stood his ground. Then he held out his hand free of the halter. The horse lifted her head, straining her neck but not yet moving her hooves.

Ramsey kept his hand extended in an open invitation. She took one step, her eyes going back and forth between the halter and his hand. Then another step. She waited there for a while. He still didn't move.

Finally, the horse closed the distance. Ramsey stroked her face. He whispered things to her I couldn't make out. As he petted her, he lifted the halter with his other hand. The movement was slow and steady, in clear view of the mare.

She quivered, and he halted again. They repeated the dance over and over until she finally allowed contact with the device. But Ramsey didn't try to slip it onto her. He first gave her a good rub with it, moving it over her neck and back. Showing the horse what the nylon and metal buckles would feel like against her coat. That they wouldn't cause her pain. Then, so slowly it was almost painful, Ramsey slipped the halter over her head.

After he buckled it in place, he gave her a good rubdown. Whispered more sweet nothings that I couldn't make out. Just as I was about to ask him one of the millions of questions swirling in my mind, movement caught my attention.

Kai lifted his head, sniffing the air before taking off at a dead run towards a figure on the hill behind the round pen. The woman was close enough that I could just make out her features, her hair billowing behind her in the breeze as she sat, a horse grazing at her side.

"Uh, Ramsey?"

He looked at me in question.

I pointed to the rise. "Is your wolf-dog gonna eat her?"

Ramsey's head snapped in the direction I'd indicated. His shoulders relaxed a fraction as he took the woman in. "No."

The massive dog closed the distance to the woman.

"I thought you said he didn't like people."

"He doesn't."

The dog launched, and my heart jerked in my chest. I barely heard faint laughter caught on the breeze as the woman rolled with the creature. Ruffling his fur.

Ramsey lifted his gaze to me. "She's the exception."

Interesting. "Who is she?"

"No one you need to worry about." His eyes hardened. "You don't approach her."

I held up both hands. "I wasn't planning on it."

He nodded, ducking between the fence rails. "That's enough for today."

"Okay, but could I ask you a few questions?"

Ramsey sighed.

"Look, the sooner I understand how you work, the sooner I'll be out of here." Except that wasn't exactly true. Something about these mountains called to me. I'd slept like a rock again last night, even with my brother's text message playing in my head before I dropped off. I might need to look into finding a second home here.

"Ask," Ramsey said through gritted teeth.

Peaches trotted over to him and looked up with adoring eyes. Something in his demeanor softened a fraction, and he bent to scratch behind her ears.

"How do you know when it's time to move on to the next step of training?"

Ramsey lowered himself to a bench that ran along one section of the fence. "There aren't steps."

"Okay…"

"It's all a journey. The horse wants to go one way, you want to go the other, you have to find the path that belongs to both of you."

I leaned against the fence. "That sounds more like poetry."

Ramsey shrugged. "Maybe it is. It's something we create together. To find it, you have to listen. You can't listen if you're making too much noise or looking in the wrong direction."

Ramsey had stillness down to an art. How many times had I needed to move around the corral because I'd started to feel twitchy? I couldn't count. That stillness would be at the center of the character I was creating. I knew that much.

I always looked for the hook with the person I was playing. The one thing I could root everything else in. This was it. "How do you keep so still for so long?"

His eyes flared a fraction. "It's just something that's been ingrained in me. Not something you can teach." His lips twitched.

"I guess you could do some of that meditation and yoga stuff they preach about in LA. Maybe that would help."

"Don't knock yoga."

Ramsey shook his head as he stood. "Whatever gets your rocks off. I gotta get back to work."

I'd noticed that he didn't seem to have any help with tending to the horses, other than Lor stopping by occasionally. This phantom woman on the rise was the only other person I'd seen on the property at all.

"Wait, one other question."

He stopped, turning back to me. "No, I won't do sunrise yoga with you."

I choked on a laugh. "Did you just make a joke?"

Ramsey scowled at me.

"Sorry. No jokes. I was wondering if you knew anything about the woman who manages the gallery in town. Her name is Laiken."

I couldn't help the pull to know more about her. Any little piece of information would be like gold. She was utterly fascinating. The conversation we'd had before I turned around had been one of my most honest in recent memory. The way she'd shifted from one moment to the next throughout our talk had me riveted. Open and transparent one moment. Locked up tight the next.

Ramsey's scowl only deepened. "Do I look like the town gossip?"

"No, but I'm assuming you know the people who live here. I thought you might know her."

"I don't. If you want to run around chasing locals, fine. Just remember you can't bring them back here."

"I'm not chasing locals—"

Ramsey started towards the barn, waving me off. "I don't have time for this."

I snapped my mouth closed and glanced down at Peaches. "That went well."

Chapter Eight

Laiken

THE BELL OVER THE DOOR JINGLED, AND I LOOKED UP FROM the papers Addie and I were huddled over at my desk. My breath caught in my throat. Serena. She looked different yet undeniably familiar. My chest constricted as memories danced in the back of my mind. So many, it was a wonder I could hold them all.

"Laiken," she greeted.

There wasn't warmth in her tone, but there wasn't anger, either.

"Welcome home, Serena." I pushed to my feet and crossed to her. Nothing about her demeanor said she would've welcomed a hug, but I found myself wanting to try anyway. I resisted the urge. "How are you?"

"I'm back in the middle of nowhere. How do you think I am?"

Okay, so coming home wasn't her choice. I ignored the dig and gestured to Addie. "This is my friend and the other gallery employee, Addie. Addie, this is Gilly's niece, Serena."

Addie gave her a warm smile. "Nice to meet you."

"You, too," she said, looking around the space.

"Want me to give you the tour?"

Serena's head snapped in my direction. "I think I remember Gilly's gallery well enough. There are two rooms. I'm not going to get lost."

"Fair enough. Why don't you refamiliarize yourself with the place, and then we can go over your duties?"

She scoffed. "Whatever."

It was going to be a long day.

Heels clacked on the polished cement of the gallery floor. "I really don't get why someone would want this in their house."

Addie sent me a sidelong look from the chair she'd pulled up to the desk.

I squeezed the bridge of my nose. "Tastes in art are subjective, Serena."

She snorted. "Clearly, since this depressing thing sold."

Serena had only been working here a matter of hours, and I was already fighting the urge to throw her through the plate glass window. One morning, and I might have to tell Gilly that I quit, no matter how much I loved my job.

Addie cleared her throat. "I went over the guest list for the past three openings and combined them into one master list. Take a look and see if there's anyone you think we should add or cut."

Serena's heels picked up their clacking again as she hurried over. "I want to see. I'm the perfect person to handle the guest list."

I moved the paper out of her reach. "Have you finished organizing the crating supplies in the back room?"

She frowned at me. "I'm not wearing the right kind of clothes for that. Gilly didn't inform me that there would be manual labor involved in this job."

"There's a little bit of everything involved, but that includes cleaning, building crates, and other less glamorous tasks."

Serena's mouth curved into a smile that I was sure typically got her what she wanted. With her blond hair highlighted and curled to perfection and her expertly applied makeup, there was no denying that she was beautiful. "Don't you think it would work better to play to my strengths? I can plan a party with the best of them. I know the best caterers, and we could do live music. Maybe a string quartet—"

"Serena," I stopped her gently. "Those are lovely ideas, but we don't have that kind of budget."

"What are you spending all my aunt's money on then?"

I stiffened, but Addie hurried to answer. "A lot goes into keeping The Gallery running. Rent for the building, utilities, salaries for everyone who works here, the website, computer software, promotional materials, shipping."

"None of that will take you to the next level of success. You need to be talked about in the right circles," Serena pushed.

I glanced at my watch. It was after two, and I was starving. "You know what? I think that's enough for today. I can wrap things up on my own." We only stayed open until four in the winter months, and if I had to deal with Serena for two more hours, one of us would end up dead, and the other would be arrested for murder.

"Are you sure?" Addie asked.

Serena grabbed her purse from where she'd left it on one of the chairs. "As long as I get paid for the full day, I don't care."

And with that, she was gone, the bell reverberating against the door and the sound echoing in my skull. I dropped my head to my desk. "Do you think if I pay her, I can just tell her not to come in?"

Addie rubbed a hand up and down my back. "It's hard to believe she's related to Gilly and Kay."

"After Jase died, her parents spoiled her," I muttered against the desk's surface. "I understand why, but it's like she turned into a person I don't even recognize anymore." I missed the girl who had long heart-to-hearts with me, picked wildflowers in the meadow, and wanted nothing more than to tag along with her big brothers.

Addie continued her soothing strokes, and I reveled in the feeling. How long had it been since someone had consoled me like this? I honestly couldn't remember. I rarely let my guard fully down around Gilly and Kay because I didn't want my pain to weigh on them. The simple human kindness of Addie's touch made my eyes burn.

"I think she's going to need some firm boundaries. I'm just sorry you'll have to be the one to put them in place. Unless you think Gilly will step up?"

I straightened in my chair, Addie's hand slipping away. I shook my head. "She won't. After she lost Jase, it's too hard for her to be firm with Serena and Jax." Addie knew the broad strokes of what had happened but not the fine details. Not how I'd held Jase's hand as he slipped away, or just how complicated my relationships were with the other members of his family.

Her mouth thinned. "It's not fair for that pressure to fall to you, though."

It wasn't. In the same way I didn't want to be the dumpster for Jax's pain anymore. It took too much. "You're right, but it's complicated."

"It always is. You just let me know how I can help."

I reached over and squeezed her arm. "Thank you. Just having you here is helping me not lose my mind."

She chuckled. "I'll do whatever I can to keep you sane."

"A true friend."

I pushed away from the desk and stood, but as I moved, my back spasmed. I clamped my mouth shut as I braced myself on the surface in front of me.

"What is it?" Addie asked, moving instantly to my side.

I pulled air in through my nose and let it slowly out through my mouth. "I'm okay."

"No, you're not."

The cramp slowly subsided, and I was able to straighten again. "My back just wasn't happy about sitting in that chair for so long."

Addie's eyes narrowed on me. She'd seen more glimpses of my pain than anyone else in recent years. It was harder to hide when you worked with someone multiple days a week for long hours.

"Really. Just kinks in these old muscles."

"You aren't old, Laiken."

"Sometimes, I feel like I'm at least ninety."

Addie continued studying me, trying to read between every word I said. "Why don't you go lay down, and I'll pick you up something to eat?"

"No, I'm fine. You should take off. I'll probably close early today."

She moved then pulled me into a hug. "I'm here if you need me. I know it's not always easy to ask for help, but it's always worth it in the end."

My throat burned as my arms closed around her. "Thanks, Addie."

Help was a tricky thing, though. If you started to count on it, that help could make you weak when it was no longer there.

Addie gave me one last squeeze before releasing me. "I'm just a phone call away."

"Love knowing that."

She moved into the back room, grabbing her belongings from the lockers before heading out the back door. When the door snicked closed, I let out a breath. I moved from behind the desk and walked in a circle around the gallery.

I didn't need to be feeling the pain I was in now. I'd been distracted by Serena's presence today and had sat for far too long. That led to my body revolting, the muscles and sinew twisting themselves into intricate knots that could take me days to undo.

Gizmo's tags jingled as he followed along in step with me. I looked down at his happy face. "A little workout for both of us, huh?"

He panted in response.

I looped around the space a few more times, my muscles releasing a bit more with each pass. I slowed, folding over into a stretch. Scratching Gizmo's ears, I nuzzled his face. "That's the good stuff, right?"

The bell over the door tinkled, and I straightened. "Hayes." My chest tightened the same way it did every time I saw him. It wasn't bad exactly. It was probably similar to how brothers in arms felt, seeing each other after the battle was done. I'd be forever grateful to the man who had tethered me to this Earth when all I wanted to do was leave with Jase. The man who hadn't once let go of my hand, even when the machine began cutting into the car.

He dipped his head in greeting. "It's good to see you, Laiken."

"You, too. You just missed Addie, if that's who you were looking for."

His mouth curved into a smile. "Saw her on my way over. Think she was headed to give Beck a surprise visit."

I couldn't help my answering smile. "Your brother's a lucky man."

"That he is."

"So, you're here to see me?"

It wasn't that Hayes and I didn't run into each other, especially since Everly and I had become such good friends. But he didn't usually stop by The Gallery for a friendly chat.

A little of the warmth in Hayes' expression slipped away. "I have some hard news. I didn't want you to hear it from anyone else."

My heart picked up speed as names and faces flew through my mind. A million different grisly what-ifs playing on a loop.

"There was an accident this morning. Lisbeth's car went off the road on one of the mountain passes."

Nausea swept through me as my stomach cramped. "Is she?"

"She didn't make it."

My throat and eyes burned as I fought to keep the tears at bay. "I'm so sorry, Laiken."

I swallowed, trying to clear the fire in my throat. "Do they know what caused it?"

Hayes was a master at the blank mask, but I was an expert at faces. I didn't miss the slight shifting of his eyes. "What?"

"There weren't any brake marks at the scene."

My hands fisted so hard I wouldn't have been surprised if I'd broken a knuckle. "What does that mean?" I asked the question, even though I knew the answer.

"There are two possibilities. Something happened with her brakes—and we'll test for that. Or she didn't try to brake."

I closed my eyes as if that would somehow keep back the pain. Lisbeth had always been a nervous driver. She never drove over the speed limit, and I doubted she'd ever miss a service appointment for her vehicle or drive it if she felt that anything was off. I forced my eyes open again. "Do her parents know?"

"I called them earlier. They'll catch a plane later today."

"Will you—?" I couldn't finish the rest of the sentence.

"I'll tell the others," Hayes said softly.

Sometimes, I wondered if my group of high school friends was cursed. Tragedy had a firm grip on us and didn't seem to want to let go. "Thank you for telling me. You didn't have to—"

"Laiken."

Hayes' voice brought my gaze back to his.

"We share a bond. I feel Jase's loss, too. Feel how it's marked all of you. You're not alone in that."

"Thank you," I said hoarsely.

"Do you want me to call Ev? Have her come be with you?"

I shook my head. "I think I need to be alone for a little while."

"Okay. You call or text if that changes."

"I will." But I wouldn't. I'd felt weak so many times in my life. I didn't want anyone to see me that way a moment more than absolutely necessary.

Hayes hovered for another few seconds as if he weren't sure he should leave me alone.

"I'll be okay."

"I know. You always are." He gave me a tilt of his head and headed out.

I closed the door after him and flipped the sign to *Closed*. But I couldn't find it within myself to move. I simply sank to the floor where I stood.

Gizmo climbed onto my lap, wheels and all. I cuddled him to my chest and let the tears fall. For Lisbeth. For Scott. For Jase. For all of us who would never be the same.

Chapter Nine

Boden

I DUCKED OUT OF THE LITTLE CAFÉ CALLED SPOONS AND headed down the street. The waitress behind the counter had looked at me a second longer than usual but then shook her head and took my order. When people weren't expecting to see you, you could get away with a lot more.

My stomach rumbled as the scents wafted out of my takeout bag. Some sort of egg salad BLT was calling my name. I'd made an impulse decision when I saw it on the menu and had gotten two, along with a few whoopie pies from the bakery case.

It was dumb—monumentally stupid, really—to try to get to know the dark-haired beauty better. My life was a mess. Likely always would be. I didn't need to drag anyone else into that. Yet my feet took me in the gallery's direction.

My pace slowed as I took in a man in a uniform through the window. From my spot across the street, I could just make out the patches that signified the sheriff's department. My heart slammed against my ribs as my gaze moved to Laiken. Her typically tanned, golden skin was ashen now, far too pale for this to be a friendly visit.

I started across the street just as the man exited the building. His eyes paused on me, doing a double-take. "I'll be damned. Ev was right."

"Is everything okay?"

He blinked a couple of times. "Excuse me?"

"Is everything okay with Laiken?"

"I'm sorry, are you two friends?"

The thought that this guy might be more than a local law enforcement officer ate at me, but I dismissed the idea. If he was, he would still be in there with Laiken, not on the sidewalk with me. "I met her the other day." The words sounded pathetic, even to my ears.

The man extended a hand to me. "Hayes Easton."

"Boden Cavanaugh."

"I figured. My fiancée said she thought she saw you driving through town the other day, but I told her she had to be mistaken."

"I'm doing some research for a film. Staying out at Ramsey Bishop's ranch."

Hayes' eyes widened. "He let you on the property? Am I in the *Twilight Zone* or something?"

I would've laughed if I weren't so worried about Laiken. "A mutual friend pressured him into it."

"Never heard of another soul allowed out there other than Lor."

An image of the young woman on the rise flashed in my mind, but I had a feeling if I blew the whistle on that one, Ramsey would kick me right off his property. I shrugged. "I guess I'm just lucky enough to follow his grumpy ass around."

Hayes let out a bark of laughter. "He's not exactly the warm and fuzzy sort."

"Not so much." I glanced towards The Gallery. I could barely make out the top of Laiken's head. She had to be sitting on the floor. My chest constricted. "Can you tell me what happened?"

Hayes shook his head. Not declining my request, more trying to make sense of what he was about to tell me. "She lost a friend. Car accident."

"Hell," I muttered. "I was going to bring her some lunch—"

"Do it."

I looked back at Hayes in question.

"She's got walls thicker than Fort Knox, but if you can figure out a way through them, I think she could use a friend."

My brow lifted. "You a cop or a therapist?"

"I'm the sheriff, but the job usually comes with a bit of both." He pulled a card from his wallet and handed it to me. "My cell's on there. You run into any issues around town, give me a call. But the locals are pretty respectful."

"I'm trying to keep a low profile."

"This would be a good place to do it. Need anything at all, give me a shout."

I shook his hand again. "Thanks. I'll just…"

Hayes' lips twitched. "Good luck."

I watched as he jogged across the street and then walked towards The Gallery's door. The sign said it was closed, but I gave the handle a try anyway. It pulled right open, the bell jingling.

"I'm sorry, we're closed early for the day," Laiken said, not looking up.

I didn't say anything, just moved to a spot on the wall a couple of feet from her and lowered myself to the floor. "Hey."

She blinked a few times, holding her tiny dog to her chest. "We're closed."

"I know."

A hint of anger flared to life in those eyes. "Famous Hollywood star probably used to getting whatever he wants. There are no closed stores, right?"

"Definitely don't get everything I want."

"Sure," she scoffed.

I searched for something to say. Anything that might bring comfort. But there were never the right words when it came to situations like these. The only thing that helped was to know you weren't alone in it. "My girlfriend died six months ago. Overdose."

All the fight went out of Laiken in a single breath. "I'm sorry."

She stared down at her hands. "I can't imagine how hard that must've been."

"She was my best friend for my whole life. More of a friend than lover, if I'm honest. But I'd take her in my life in any way I could get her." The words tumbled out of me, ones I hadn't given to a single other human being. "It crushed me in more ways than I can count."

"I know what that's like." Her voice was rough. As if she'd smoked a pack of cigarettes and downed a fifth of whiskey. Something about that tone told me it was more than just the friend who had died today. Grief had etched itself into Laiken's very soul.

"I'm sorry about your friend."

She blinked a few times. "How did you know?"

"I ran into the sheriff outside."

"Never knew Hayes to be a gossip," she muttered.

"I don't think he is. I was pushy."

"Of course, you were."

I chuckled, but the sound died out quickly. "I was worried about you."

"You don't even know me."

"I've gotten a couple of glimpses. I'd like to know you better."

"Boden, I have no interest in sleeping with you. Don't get me wrong, you're hot. Gorgeous in a way that I'm sure has had smart women doing some very stupid things. But I don't need that kind of complication in my life right now."

I opened my takeout bag and handed Laiken a sandwich. "Fair enough. I won't lie. I think there's a spark here."

"I didn't say there wasn't."

The corner of my mouth kicked up at that. "But I respect having a complicated life. Truth is, mine is too complicated to bring anyone else into it. How would you feel about friendship?"

Laiken stared down at the parcel in her lap. "You brought me a sandwich?"

"I did."

She peeled back the paper. "An egg salad BLT from Spoons?"

I grinned. "I take it that was a good pick?"

"My favorite."

Gizmo sniffed the air.

"Uh-uh, baby. Not good for dogs."

He let out a little whine.

I unwrapped my sandwich and broke off a tiny piece of bacon. "Can I give him this?"

She shook her head. "He'll never leave you alone if you do."

"I'll risk it." I gave Gizmo the bacon, and he immediately left Laiken's side to sit by me.

"Traitor," she mumbled.

I laughed and pulled two drinks out of my bag. "Coke or iced tea?"

"Tea, please."

I handed her the bottle.

"You think of everything."

"Even dessert."

Her mouth curved into the barest smile. "If there are whoopie pies in there, I'll marry you. It'll be a loveless, sexless marriage, you understand. But I'll marry you."

I barked out a laugh. "Looks like we're getting hitched."

"Worth it." Laiken took a bite of her BLT and washed it down with iced tea. "Why did you bring me a sandwich?"

"Kept finding myself thinking about you these past few days."

"You must be bored."

I fought a grin as I took a swig of my Coke. "Plenty to think about, yet you always seem to fight your way in there. You and your photo."

"It's not mine."

"Fine, the photo of you."

She looked up at the piece. "It's one of my favorites, too."

"Made me curious about you."

Laiken grunted.

"How about a question for a question?"

"Do I get veto power?"

"Sure."

She broke off a corner of bread. "Okay."

"From Wolf Gap originally?"

"Born and raised."

That wasn't surprising. Laiken seemed to fit here. As if she and the town melded together. Maybe it was how the landscape in that photo surrounded her, but they went hand-in-hand in my mind.

"Did you like growing up in a small town?" I asked.

"Sometimes, I loved it. Other times, I hated it." She tossed the piece of bread at me. "I get two questions now."

Gizmo gobbled up the bread as it bounced off my chest.

"Fair enough."

"What are you doing in Wolf Gap?"

"Learning how to whisper to horses."

Laiken stilled. "From Ramsey? How much did you have to pay him to get him to do that?"

"Not a penny." He'd been insulted when I offered. "That's two. My turn. Tell me something about your friend."

A shadow passed over her eyes, and I wanted to kick myself. "Never mind. Dumb question."

"No. It's okay. It might be nice to talk about her. We weren't friends anymore. Not really. But we were close at one of those fundamental times in your life. Those relationships stamp themselves into your bones."

"They do."

"She had a mischievous streak. Loved a practical joke. But she'd also do anything for her friends. Anything to make sure they knew she loved them. You'd think with that kind of care, nothing bad could've happened to any of us."

Something in Laiken's voice told me that something bad *had* happened to them. And it had marked her.

Chapter Ten

Laiken

THE BELL OVER THE DOOR JINGLED JUST AS I HIT THE bottom step from my apartment into the gallery. It was almost ten, but I'd slept as late as I could after tossing and turning last night. Thoughts of Lisbeth and a million different memories played in my head on repeat. Once I finally slipped off, the hazel eyes of a man who'd brought me lunch circled in my subconscious.

I moved into the space. "Morning, Addie. Thanks for manning the ship today."

"Of course."

As she stepped into the shop, Hadley moved in behind her. Hadley strode across the floor and pulled me into a hug. "I'm so sorry about Lisbeth."

I awkwardly returned the embrace. "Thanks." I didn't know what else to say. Didn't want to go there when I already had to face the realities of grief today.

Pulling back, I shuffled my feet. "Not on duty this morning?"

Hadley's eyes narrowed a fraction. "Don't want to talk about it?"

"Not at the moment."

Addie bumped my shoulder with hers. "We all deal with things the best way we can in the moment."

I leaned into her. "Thanks."

"Well, if you don't want to go there, how about you tell us what happened when a certain movie star came to The Gallery?"

Addie whirled on me. "What? You never said anything."

My cheeks heated, and I glared at Hadley. "Prepare for payback."

She laughed. "Worth it."

"Tell us what happened," Addie urged.

I shrugged. "He bought a photograph."

"And then he came back," Hadley said, waggling her eyebrows.

I let out a little growl. "Do you have cameras in here or something?"

"I had dinner with Hayes and Everly last night."

"Boden's wrong. Hayes *is* a gossip."

"Boden?" Addie squeaked. "You say his name like you're best friends."

"What else should I call him?"

"I don't know, Mr. Cavanaugh?"

"He's just a normal human. I'll call him by his normal name. Just like I do with you."

Hadley shook her head. "I don't know that winning Oscars and Golden Globes is all that *normal*."

"Or being the third highest-paid actor in Hollywood." Addie gave a sheepish shrug. "I Googled him."

I sighed. "He's trying to keep a low profile. Maybe don't share with people that he's in town?" I rubbed a spot on my chest. I couldn't imagine grieving when the whole world was trying to take your picture.

Hadley made a motion of locking her lips and throwing away the key. "I told Shiloh, but you know she doesn't talk to anyone."

Hadley's sister had never really been the same after she was kidnapped as a child. We'd been in the same grade growing up, and our classmates had treated her more like a fascinating science experiment than anything else. "I know she won't say anything."

Addie pressed her lips together. "You should invite him to dinner at my and Beckett's place."

"What?" Shock bled into my tone. Both at the fact that Addie would welcome a stranger into our fold and that she was pushing me to basically make a move on him.

Her eyes misted over. "I know what it's like to feel alone. He must be feeling some of that, losing someone he loves, being in a strange place. You guys were so wonderful to me. Boden should have some of that, too."

I took Addie's hand and squeezed. "You have the best heart."

"You'll ask him?"

I was a sucker when it came to requests from Addie. She'd battled through so much to find her freedom, and I couldn't tell her no. "I'll ask."

She beamed. "I can't wait to meet him."

Hell. What had I gotten myself into?

A breeze lifted the hair around my face as I moved towards the picnic table in the center of a grove of Aspen trees. It had always been one of Jase's favorite spots, but it had lost some of its magic over the years.

For the first couple of years, the group that gathered for Jase's birthday had been a large one. Friends, teachers, coaches. It had dwindled to just family and me. Kay and Chip. Jax. Gilly. Serena.

Now, we all stood somewhat awkwardly. It was so different than what birthday parties had been like all those years ago—full of laughter and good-natured teasing. Games and fighting over who had given the best present.

No bond in our group was as tight as it had been back then, and my heart ached with the knowledge. My gaze caught on Chip as he stared off into the distance, not completely here with us. I remembered when he had stepped into all the roles my father had so carelessly given away. Now, he was in danger of becoming a stranger, too.

He caught me looking his way and gave me a forced smile and a pat on the shoulder. "How are things with The Gallery?"

"Good." I toyed with the zipper on my jacket. "I'm putting the finishing touches on an exhibit that opens in a couple of weeks. You should come."

Serena let out a little scoff. "I thought the guest list was limited."

I worked my jaw back and forth, swallowing down the retort I wanted to send her way. "It is, but there's always space for family."

"This isn't your family," Jax bit out.

"Jackson Granger," Gilly scolded. "Laiken is a member of this family in every way that counts."

But I wasn't. At one point, I had been. They had been my refuge when my mom got too intense. The happy chaos of their ranch was always a balm to my soul. All of that had changed when we lost Jase—slowly and in a split second.

"She's not. I'm only stating the truth. If she can't handle that, then maybe she should leave."

Serena looked on, her brow furrowing while Chip shifted uncomfortably.

"Jax," he said in a low tone, one that carried so much fatigue. "Now isn't the time for this."

"When is, then?" he barked. "You act like it's normal that she's here."

"I invited her," Kay said softly. The flatness of it had my stomach cramping. The same way it always did when her voice was absent of emotion. It was a sign that things were taking a turn. "Jase would want her at his birthday." Her eyes were glassy as she stared at the cake, the candles flickering in the wind. She let them burn until the wax melted onto the frosting.

Her knuckles bleached white as she focused on the dessert. It was as if she believed if she held on long enough, her son would show up to blow out the candles. That determined hope carved a hole in my chest.

"Mom, you're gonna burn yourself." Jax stepped up and bent to blow out the candles.

"No!" she shrieked. "No, no, no. Those are your brother's candles. You can't blow them out. You can't. They're his candles!"

Chip wrapped an arm around her as Kay dissolved into sobs, her entire body shaking. "He'll come. Jase will come. He always comes."

Jax's face paled as he took a step back. "I'm sorry. I just didn't want her to get hurt."

Chip's jaw flexed as he held his wife close. "I think I need to get her inside."

"We need presents. There has to be presents. That was his favorite part."

"Come on, Kay. We'll do presents later. After dinner. You need to rest now," Chip said as he guided her away from the table.

Gilly patted his shoulder as they passed. "Her medication is in the drawer in her nightstand."

We all watched in silence as he led her towards the house. It wasn't until they slipped inside that someone spoke.

"Well, that was fun," Serena mumbled.

"Shut up," Jax snapped.

"Hey, don't take it out on me because you sent Mom into a freak-out."

He stalked towards her, his face reddening. "You have no idea what we've been through these past few years. Because you took off, gallivanting all over who knows where and spending all their money. You're pathetic."

She blanched. "Jax…"

He threw up his hands. "I'm done with you. Jase would be ashamed of the way you bailed on your family."

Serena promptly burst into tears and took off running for her apartment over the garage.

"Jackson," Gilly said softly, shaking her head.

"You know I'm right. She's selfish and immature. And she needs a reality check."

"The truth isn't always a kindness. It would be good for you to remember that."

"Whatever," he muttered and started towards his truck.

I slowly let out the breath I'd been holding since Kay's outburst. Releasing it hurt. As if it scratched at my lungs and throat on the way out.

So much pain. It seemed impossible that one moment had caused all of this. One man's reckless decision to get high. Drugs that had fueled his rage and taken away his normal thought processes.

But he wasn't here for the Grangers to take their anger out on. He'd spent years in prison and then moved as far away from Wolf Gap as he could get. So, the anger and pain the Grangers were feeling was eating them alive instead. And I had no idea how to help.

"I'm sorry, Laiken."

I looked up at Gilly's voice. "You don't have anything to apologize for. I thought she was doing better."

She lowered herself to the picnic table. "Me, too."

I sat down next to her. "What about the psychiatrist she's been seeing?"

Gilly glanced towards the house. "I don't know anymore. He doesn't seem to be helping all that much."

"Maybe it's time to try someone new."

"Maybe." She toyed with a bead on her bracelet. "Chip doesn't want to do anything to upset her. And on days like this one, the only thing Kay wants is to be numb."

I knew that feeling. Weeks in the hospital where every time I got too upset, they pumped something into my IV. Then the months afterwards where I had a ready supply of painkillers that made me feel nothing at all.

I could still remember lining them up on my desk in neat rows one afternoon. Counting each one and wondering how many it would take for me to cease to exist altogether. That had been the wake-up call. I'd flushed them down the toilet and told my doctor I didn't want any more.

It hadn't been an easy road, but at the end of the day—painkillers or not—I hurt. Now, I only used them when I had to be on my feet for an event, which was only a handful of times a year. I used them to live instead of using them to check out. That was the difference.

But I remembered that deep pull towards nothingness. I knew that devil was more tempting than anything when you were hurting. And the last thing I wanted was for Kay to lose that battle.

"Do you think there's anything I can do?" I asked.

Gilly patted my hand. "You're doing it. I'm sure another visit here and there would help." She lifted her gaze to the horizon. "She always used to talk about you and Jase getting married on this land. Maybe building a house here one day. Giving her grandbabies."

My chest tightened, making it hard to breathe normally. "It would've been a beautiful life."

"Maybe you can talk to her about the good memories from the past. She needs people to remember Jase with."

"I can do that." No matter how hard those conversations were to navigate, I could do that for Kay. For the endless support she'd always shown me. And for her incredible son, who had loved me so well.

Gilly pushed to her feet and picked up the cake. "I'm going to take this inside and see if Kay needs anything."

"Call me if *you* need anything."

She gave me a half-smile. "You know I'm damn good at taking care of myself."

Gilly was that. A force of nature. Could do anything she put her mind to. But that didn't mean she didn't need support every now and then. "Why don't I just offer friendship then?"

"That, I will always take, Cherub." She bent and kissed my cheek. "Drive safe. I think we'll be getting snow soon."

I looked to the gray sky and inhaled deeply. It smelled like snow. I was ready for it. We'd only had a couple of inches so far this year, and each time they fell, they melted within a week. "Safety is my middle name."

Gilly snorted and waved me off.

I headed to my SUV, but movement caught my attention over the garage, a flutter of the curtains. My gaze locked with Serena's, her mouth set in a hard line. A beat later, she let the curtain fall closed again.

Hell. I wondered how she would spin this to be my fault. Serena wouldn't stay mad at her brother for long. Somehow, this would all fall back on my shoulders.

I pulled open the door to my SUV and slid inside. Gizmo's head popped up from where he'd been happily chewing on a bully stick while wrapped in a blanket. I turned, scratching behind his ears. "How would you feel about a little adventure?"

He licked my hand in response.

"I was hoping you'd say that."

I pulled out my keys and started the engine. That familiar crawling-out-of-my-skin sensation was back. I needed to release some of the pent-up emotion that was swirling inside. When I was younger, I probably would've gone for a run, but my body couldn't handle that anymore. I needed my new outlet. The only thing that truly made me feel seen anymore.

I guided my SUV away from the Grangers' ranch and towards the mountains. They looked a purplish-gray in the overcast light. Their stark, snow-capped peaks the backdrop I needed today.

I turned off the main road and wound around the southern mountain. After a few turns, I finally found the trailhead I was looking for. I pulled into a spot. There was only one other vehicle in the lot, a pickup truck I'd seen countless times before.

As I climbed out of my SUV, the owner appeared. I waved. "Hey, Brett."

He grinned. "Hey, Laiken. Afternoon hike?"

I nodded. "Guess you were doing the same."

"Needed to get in a little workout before my shift."

"Oh, yeah, I heard it's Deputy Williams now."

A hint of pink hit his cheeks. "I guess so."

"Congrats. That's great."

He shuffled his feet, glancing down at his hiking boots. "I'm real sorry about Lisbeth. She was good people."

My throat burned. "She was." And I never should've let our friendship fall apart the way it had. I thought about seeking Marisa out to see how she was, but our last conversation, one where we'd both said some harsh things, still played in my mind.

"Her parents are going to do a memorial here in a few days. See you there?"

The last thing I wanted was to sit in a church, dressed in black. Not again. I didn't want to hear the soft sniffles and the louder cries. "I'll see you there."

Brett nodded and headed for his truck.

I zipped my coat up higher, the cold of the altitude setting in, and then grabbed my gear from the trunk. I ignored the protest my back made as I hoisted the backpack. Then I strapped Gizmo's carrier on. By the time I opened the back passenger door, he was dancing.

I lifted him out and placed him in the contraption probably made for babies. "You know I'd never leave you behind on an adventure."

He licked my chin.

I let out a laugh. It felt damn good. Gizmo was always a balm to my soul.

I started up the trail, thankful that I wouldn't have to worry about running into anyone else. At three in the afternoon in the dead of winter, I'd have the place to myself. I lost myself in the rhythm of my feet on packed dirt and the sounds of nature.

It all soothed away some of the worst of the day. But it wasn't quite enough. That would come, though. As the trail bent, I veered off, finding the exact place I wanted. The meadow had gone golden after going through the summer and fall months without much rain.

The sea of dried-up color was perfect against the craggy mountain. I slid off my backpack first. Opening it, I pulled out a blanket for Gizmo, then my camera gear. Once he was positioned back with his bully stick, I got to work setting up the tripod.

I tried a few different positions before landing on one. I brought the tripod low to give myself a unique angle on all the elements I wanted. Shrugging off my jacket, I stepped in front of the lens.

The only thing I did was breathe. Inhale and let the emotions come. Exhale and set them free.

I thought of Kay's broken grief. Jax's rage. Serena's version of numbing. The way Chip was barely hanging on.

I thought of how badly I wanted to fix it all for them. My hands fisted in the grass at my impotence in all of it. I clicked the remote to the shutter.

I sank deeper into the grass, turning my head into the breeze as it picked up. Tears tracked down my cheeks as I let it all go. The pain, the grief, the brokenness.

I let every emotion fly and tried to capture them all.

Chapter Eleven

Boden

MY PHONE BUZZED IN MY CUPHOLDER AS I TURNED off the main road and onto a smaller one that curved around the mountain. I pressed a button on my steering wheel, and an animatronic voice read out the message. "From unknown number. You think you're so much better than me. You're not. Carissa didn't think you were better. She picked me in the end. Me—"

I fumbled to hit the button again. Even with that disembodied voice reading the words, I could still hear my brother's tone bleeding through. Nausea swept through me, and I pulled into a trailhead, rolling down my window. I needed air.

I swiped up my phone, staring at the screen. Another text message popped up.

Unknown Number: *You're a coward. Running and hiding. What do you think would happen if the media found out where you were?*

I locked the phone, throwing it onto the passenger seat. My rib cage tightened, making it hard to breathe. I'd never escape Eli. Never be free. My hands flexed around the wheel, the desire to move strong. To run like my brother had accused me of. But it was only to try to get away from *him.*

I rolled up the window and climbed out of my truck, beeping the locks. I had to get out some of the energy thrumming through me. I hadn't planned for a hike, but at least I had on boots and a jacket. I'd just go for a little while. Long enough to slow the thrumming at my pulse points and still the twitch in my muscles.

I started up the trail with only my keys. I should've brought my phone to send it hurtling over a cliff. So much betrayal. And with Eli, it had become an obsession. Any way he could find to knock me down a peg, he took.

Beyond the grief of losing Carissa, that was where most of my pain lingered. The fact that Eli would do anything to hurt me. His own brother. And for what? Because I'd had more success in the business? That I shared that love with Mom and Dad?

Eli had tried his hand at a few different things in entertainment. Acting? You had to show up to set too early. Producing? Too detail-oriented. He'd even played in a band for a while. He'd been damn good at that, but it had ultimately only led to more partying. Nothing lasted more than a few months tops, and after a while, people stopped giving him shots.

Somehow, that was my fault, too. I could hear his voice echoing in my head. "*They all want me to be you.*"

We used to be similar. Had the same interests, which usually revolved around us chasing Carissa around our Brentwood property. Epic games of hide-and-seek. Those had evolved into some sort of water gun tag in the summer.

Dad would put up a big tent in the backyard, and we'd camp out. He'd tell stories, and we'd make s'mores. Even with the media attention, and the kind of pressure that growing up in the spotlight put on us, we'd had a good childhood.

But somewhere along the line, that had changed. Middle school, maybe? Carissa and I had started dating, and Eli had fallen in with a rougher crowd. Kids whose parents gave them so much free rein, they had no consequences.

My hands fisted and flexed at my sides as I ran through things in my mind. All the times Carissa and I had broken up, only for her to end up in tears on my doorstep weeks or months later. What if I would've let her go? Told her the truth? That I'd always love her, but we weren't good for each other. Maybe then Eli wouldn't have fixated.

But he had. And I had to carry the weight of that now.

I shook out my hands as I pushed up the path. My steps faltered as I took in the figure in the field ahead. Dark brown hair lifting on the breeze, eyes cast up to the sky.

I was walking towards her before I even knew what was happening. She had that pull. Something in her mirrored something in me.

As I got closer, I saw the tears on her face. It wasn't until I was just feet away that I took in the camera—the camera with no one behind it.

Gizmo's head popped up, and he let out a happy bark.

Laiken's head snapped in my direction, her eyes widening as she quickly wiped away the tears. I saw the layers of her mask weaving back into place. She carefully packed away whatever she'd come here to let loose.

I crouched, scratching behind Gizmo's ears, my gaze not straying from the gorgeous woman in front of me. "Does Gillian know you're the photographer?"

Laiken opened her mouth to say something and then snapped it closed again. Her shoulders curved in on themselves, drooping. Everything in her posture spoke of defeat. I hated everything about the emotion being carved into Laiken. I moved without thinking, coming in close. My hand found her cheek, lifting her head. "Hey. I'm not going to say anything."

Her amber eyes glowed in the late afternoon light. "No one's supposed to know."

"Why?"

"It's the only way I can be free in making it."

I studied her for a moment, trying to come up with the right words. "You want to expose the truth in people but not let anyone know it's you exposing it."

Laiken turned away from my gaze, facing the mountains. "I guess that makes me a coward."

When she moved, my hand fell away from her cheek. But even with the absence of the touch, my palm tingled. I flexed my fingers at my side. "I didn't say that."

"It's what you were thinking, though."

"*Coward* is a pretty strong word. I was thinking more that you've got a strong self-protective instinct."

She laughed, but it had a scoffing edge to it. "I guess that much is true."

Laiken moved towards her gear, pulling on her jacket. "Look, I'd appreciate it if you didn't tell anyone. I want to keep this mine."

"I already told you I wouldn't."

As she crouched to remove her camera from the tripod, her knees buckled. I moved on instinct, catching her just before she hit the ground. "Shit, are you okay?"

Laiken struggled out of my grip, righting herself. But her legs were unsteady. "I'm fine. Just lost my balance."

But it hadn't been that. Her legs had given out on her and were still trembling even now. "Laiken."

"I'm fine."

She was an expert at those masks of hers, but I could make out the lines of strain around her eyes and mouth. "You're hurting."

"We're all hurting, aren't we?"

"I'm not talking about philosophical pain here. Something's hurting you."

Her mouth pressed into a firm line, and her eyes flashed. God, I admired that stubborn streak. That strength. But I wanted nothing more than for her to let me in a little. Maybe even let me help.

"Something's always hurting."

She said the words so softly, I wouldn't have heard her at all if the wind hadn't carried them to me.

"Are you sick?" A million worst-case scenarios flew through my mind. Cancer. Some sort of autoimmune disease.

"I'm not sick." She turned back to the mountains she always seemed to look to for reassurance.

"What is it then?" I was pushing my luck, and I knew it, but I had to try.

"I was in a car accident in high school. It was pretty bad. My body's never been quite the same since."

"I'm sorry." The words were incredibly lame, but it was all I seemed to be able to come up with. "Doctors can't do anything else to help?"

Laiken shrugged, focusing back on me. "I'm sure they'd love to cut me open again, but every time they do, it makes something worse. I've learned to live with it."

My jaw tightened, my back teeth grinding together. "You still come up to the mountains by yourself." Even though her body could give out on her. What would've happened if I hadn't been here today? What if she fell on a trail and broke an ankle? There wasn't exactly cell service up here.

"I do it because it's important."

"I get that. But what if you get hurt?"

"Then I get back to my car however I can and call for help."

A muscle in my jaw ticked. "Is Gizmo going to carry you?"

Laiken laughed, the sound warming that place in the cavern of my chest that had been so damn cold for so long. "If I had a cart, he probably could."

I looked down at the tiny Chihuahua currently chewing on a bully stick half the size of his head. "He does seem determined."

"We can all learn a little something from Gizmo."

"I don't doubt it." I scanned all the gear on the ground plus Gizmo. "Did you carry all of this up here?"

"I'm not an invalid."

"I know that. But it has to weigh a fair amount."

Laiken's jaw worked back and forth. "I make it work."

"What if you could make it work better?"

Her eyes narrowed on me. "How?"

I gave Laiken my most charming smile. "How would you feel about an assistant?"

Chapter Twelve

Laiken

"AN ASSISTANT?" I PARROTED.

"You know, someone to boss around and make carry all your stuff. I have to think you'd get more accomplished with someone helping."

I'd lost count of how many times I'd wished for just that. Times when I'd been in tears after a long day, just trying to get my body to cooperate in the ways I wanted it to. "I don't think that's a good idea."

Boden's smile fell. "Why not?"

A million different answers flew through my brain, but the one that stuck was: *I don't want to rely on you.* If you always leaned on someone, you became dependent. When they weren't there anymore, figuring out how to walk on your own again was the hardest thing you'd ever have to do.

"I'm taking that silence as you not having a reason. I'm an excellent partner in crime. I can send you references if you'd like. You're welcome to run a background check to make sure I'm not a serial killer."

I couldn't help the smile that pulled at my lips. "Maybe you're a good serial killer. One who's never been caught."

"What if I promise to only use my murder-y tendencies for good, taking out bad guys and the like?"

I arched a brow. "Wasn't that a storyline in one of your movies?"

A grin stretched across Boden's face. I'd seen him smile before, but this was such an honest one, and the authenticity stole my breath.

"I knew you were a fan."

I barked out a laugh. "I'm pretty sure everyone and their brother saw that movie. I don't know that my viewing qualifies me as a fan."

"I still have the damn spandex suit somewhere. I could get it shipped up here, and we could role-play."

My laughter came harder. "If you think I'm wearing what the heroine did in that movie, you're delirious." It had been some skintight, barely-there creation that I had to think made fighting a challenge. At least, without flashing your lady bits to everyone.

"I'm a fan of that outfit…"

I rolled my eyes, but my smile was still in place. "I'm sure you are."

He shook his head. "Ella bitched and moaned about it every day, but at least it was quick to put on. Mine took hours. And don't get me started about what happened if I had to pee."

The mental image of a ruggedly handsome Boden crossing his legs on set filled my mind, and I couldn't help but laugh again. I'd laughed more in the past ten minutes than I had in weeks. Maybe months. Even as I stood with my back aching and a fiery nerve pain engulfing my legs, Boden made me laugh. That was worth something. "You can be my assistant."

This time, Boden didn't grin. He full-out *beamed*. It engulfed his face, making him look altogether different. I'd never seen a photo of him where he'd looked like this. Something told me it was because he didn't show it to many other people.

"I'm at your service, my lady."

"If you show up to our first session in armor, you're fired."

He chuckled. "How about hiking boots instead?"

My lips twitched. "Clothes, too? Or just the hiking boots?"

"I'd be down for some naked hiking. But only if you're playing, too."

"You do realize it's about thirty degrees this week, right? You could lose a ball."

Boden cupped himself. "Don't say something like that. It makes them hurt."

I shook my head. "Come on, we should get back to the trailhead. We're losing light." Even in the gray, overcast sky, I saw that the sun was now hanging low. I moved towards my backpack, but Boden took my elbow.

"Let me. You can show me how to load everything up so I don't break something."

"Okay." I pointed out how the camera fit into the specially made backpack, then the tripod, and the rest of my odds and ends.

Boden studied the other contraption on the ground. "Is that a baby carrier?"

I pressed my lips together to keep from laughing. "I have to get Gizmo up here somehow. He doesn't like being left behind, and his wheels don't work well on these kinds of trails."

Boden shook his head and looked balefully at Gizmo. "You're really gonna make me wear that, aren't you?"

Gizmo just panted up at him, a smile on his doggy face.

"If you're not man enough…"

Boden's hazel eyes shot to mine. "Oh, I'm gonna rock this baby carrier."

I bent to pick up Gizmo as Boden strapped the thing on. My back cried out as I moved, but I bit the inside of my cheek to keep from making a sound. I lifted Gizmo into the carrier and secured him in place.

Stepping back, I couldn't help but smile. I slid my phone out from my back pocket and toggled over to the camera. "This is too good a picture to pass up." I clicked the shot. "How much do you think *US Weekly* would pay for something like this?"

Boden gave me a wan smile. "I'd be worried, except I'm the only one who knows your true identity. I think my baby carrier ways are safe."

I huffed. "Why did you have to go and ruin it? I was already mentally spending my millions."

"I hate to break it to you, but I don't think that photo is worth millions."

"Ruining it again. Let me live in my dream world."

"Fair enough." Boden started down the path, and I fell into step beside him. "So, what would you spend your millions on?"

"Hmm. A massive soaking tub."

"I support that choice."

"A dog castle for Gizmo."

Boden's brow lifted. "A dog castle?"

"There's this company that makes castles for dogs. They're really just fancy forms of crates with dog beds inside, but I've always wanted to get him one. He is a prince, after all."

Boden chuckled and rubbed Gizmo's head. "He is that. What else?"

"A private plane so I could go anywhere I wanted without having to deal with the hassle of regular airport stuff." I paused, looking over at him. "You have a private plane, don't you?"

He gave me a sheepish smile. "It's not mine. It's my family's. But it does come in handy now and again."

I shook my head. "You're living in a whole different world." Something about that made me sad. The fact that Boden and I didn't belong in the same universe. It was just some weird hiccup in the space-time continuum that had brought us together, and it wouldn't last.

"Only the accessories are different. Don't get me wrong, I know I'm beyond fortunate. I don't take that for granted for a second. But money doesn't miraculously fix all your problems. Sometimes, it makes more of them."

"It made more for your girlfriend?" I struggled to get the word out.

"In a lot of ways. There's pressure growing up in that world. To always have more. Money, power, prestige. It can taunt people."

"I would have a hard time with that."

"Carissa did, too. And her spirit was so gentle. Easily broken." A muscle along Boden's jaw fluttered. "Maybe I fixed too many things for her for too long. She never really learned how to stand on her own two feet."

I never wanted to live through something like the accident again. Losing Jase, my friendships fracturing, all the pain of that recovery. But in so many ways, it had made me more determined than ever before. I fought for what I wanted and never gave up, even if it took me ten times as long to get there as everyone else.

"When we love someone, it's easy to want to fix everything for them."

"It's rarely the right move, though. At some point, you have to start carrying some of your own weight."

"Says the man carrying all of my belongings."

The corner of Boden's mouth kicked up. "That's different."

"Maybe. Maybe not. I still have to carry it when you're gone. I can't lose the muscle tone it requires to do that."

He frowned as we curved around the path. "I guess that makes sense."

"Then why do you look like someone kicked your puppy?"

"I don't like the idea of you having to do something that causes you pain."

My steps slowed. "Doing the things that cause us pain sometimes brings the greatest reward in the end. You know you were strong enough to make it through, and the view from where you've gotten to is always that much sweeter."

"You've got a better attitude than I do. I'm always the one crying when my trainer's taking me through my third set of burpees. He'd like you."

I grinned as I picked up my pace again. "I'd like some video proof of those tears."

"Masochist."

I chuckled.

As the parking lot came into view, a figure pushed off a sheriff's department SUV. Hayes' gaze jumped from Boden to me and back again, zeroing in on Gizmo. "Is that a baby carrier?"

"I'm never going to live this down," Boden grumbled.

Hayes shook his head, but as he focused back on me, the strains of humor in his expression fled. "Williams said you were out this way."

My stomach cramped. "Is something wrong?"

"I'm afraid so." He paused, seeming to search for words. "I'm sorry, Laiken. Mitch is dead."

Those cramps turned to waves of nausea. This wasn't happening. Not another of us. Even if Mitch had traded us in for a new set of friends, he would always be one of us. Except now, he had ceased to be at all.

"How?" I croaked.

"Looks like a hunting accident."

"Looks like?"

"It had been a day or two before someone found him."

Bile crept up my throat.

Boden wrapped an arm around me, his warmth bleeding into me.

Hayes tracked the movement, but he didn't say anything. "Laiken, that's three people involved in the accident who have died in the past few months."

"We're cursed," I said softly.

Boden's grip on me tightened. "What?"

"We're cursed. Car accident, overdose, another car accident, and now this? How else do you explain that? Maybe none of us were supposed to make it past that night. Maybe this is the Universe trying to right that."

"Or maybe someone is helping the Universe along," Hayes said.

I stiffened, my spine going ramrod straight.

"What do you mean, *helping*?" Boden growled.

Hayes scrubbed a hand over his jaw. "I'm reopening the investigation into Scott's death, and I'll be taking a much closer look at Lisbeth and Mitch."

Boden looked down at me, not letting go of my shoulders. "They were all in the car accident with you?"

I swallowed, my throat desert-dry. "We were driving from the lake to a party. Three separate cars. We passed someone on the road who was clearly intoxicated. Jase flashed his lights at him, trying to get him to slow down. He didn't like that. He forced us off the road, and the rest of the vehicles were in a pileup. But Jase was the only one who didn't make it."

"What about the guy that drove them off the road? Have you looked into him?" Boden asked Hayes.

"He got out of prison a little over a year ago. Moved back east. I'm making some calls to locate him."

I could still see Robert Aaron's face as clear as day. It was burned into my brain. How emotionless it had been as he stood trial. He didn't even blink when the judge read his sentence. One that had made the town rage for how light it was—manslaughter, when it should've been murder. The defense attorney wove a case that we had provoked Robert on the road. Kids out looking for a party.

Boden bent his head so that his lips were next to my ear. "I'm so sorry."

"Me, too."

I looked up at Hayes. "Do you really think these weren't accidents?"

He blew out a breath. "I don't know. But I don't like the odds. Not in a town of this size."

Wolf Gap had experienced its share of heartbreak. Even a murder or two—but they were far from common. "How will you know?"

"We look closely at everything. If these weren't accidents, we'll find a sign."

I shivered, and Boden pulled me closer.

"Thank you for coming to find me. For telling me in person," I said.

"Of course." Hayes looked over at my vehicle and then back at me. "How would you feel about staying with Ev and me for a while? I don't like the idea of you in that apartment alone when we don't know what's going on."

"I appreciate that, Hayes. More than you know. But I love my apartment. My routine. It's important to me to stay in it."

"I thought you'd say as much. I'll have The Gallery on our drive-by route. You triple-check locks and call me if you hear anything."

"I will. I promise."

Hayes' fingers drummed a beat against his leg. "It wouldn't hurt to get a Taser or some pepper spray."

I could just picture it, spraying myself in the face instead of an intruder. "I'll think about it. Or I could always go with a bat."

"That works, too. Call me if you need anything."

"Thanks."

He gave Boden a chin lift. "Nice to see you, Boden."

"Wish I could say the same."

"Eventually, I do get to bring good news."

"I'll be looking forward to that, then," Boden muttered.

"Me, too." Hayes climbed into his SUV and pulled out of the lot.

I pulled my keys out of my pocket and beeped my locks. "I should get going. Gizmo needs dinner—"

"Laiken."

"I'm fine. It's awful and horrible, but I've been through this before. I'll deal."

Boden's mouth pressed into a firm line, and he nodded.

I pulled open the back passenger door, and we got Gizmo

situated. Boden pulled off the backpack and set it on the seat next to the car seat. "Will you be okay to drive?"

"Of course."

"You have my number if you need anything," he pushed.

"Thanks." I quickly ducked into the driver's seat and closed the door.

Boden lingered for a moment and then headed to his truck. It wasn't until he was behind his slightly tinted windows across the lot that tears started to fall. But once they began, I couldn't do a damn thing to stop them.

Chapter Thirteen

Boden

I SAT IN MY TRUCK, STARING AT LAIKEN'S SUV. THROUGH MY tinted windows, I could just make out her shoulders shaking. Each tiny movement tore at my chest, shredding whatever was left of my heart.

She'd endured more than anyone ever should and was finally breaking. I didn't let myself think about my actions, I simply moved. Climbing out of my truck, I strode across the parking lot and pulled open Laiken's door.

She gave a small jolt but didn't try to cover her tears. They were coming too fast and too hard for her to stuff them back in. I turned her so she faced me, then wrapped my arms around her and pulled her close.

Laiken didn't fight the movements, but she didn't reciprocate, either. Her whole body shook with the force of her sobs. "It's too much," she got out between cries.

"I know."

Far too heavy a burden for anyone. Too many people lost. And now, there was the very real possibility that she was in danger on top of it.

I held her tighter against me as she continued to let her tears flow. Laiken's hands fisted in my jacket, the first contact she'd sought out. The first comfort. I wanted to give her everything I had. Anything to ease a little of her pain.

"Let it go."

Another hiccupped sob escaped her lips. "If I let it out, it could break me."

"You're way too damn strong for that." I'd only known her for a week, and I already knew that with unshakeable certainty. She was a force to be reckoned with. "But you're only going to hurt yourself if you don't let it free. If you don't tell someone how you're feeling."

Laiken pulled back a fraction, her red and swollen eyes meeting mine. "And who do you talk to?"

"My dad." I hadn't given him everything, but I'd given him the bulk of it. He'd holed up with me in my Malibu house for weeks after Carissa's death, drinking whiskey and talking it all through. Or not talking and simply staring at the ocean. But I'd known I wasn't alone. I wasn't sure Laiken had that. A person she could fully let her guard down around. I felt a swift tug in my chest, a demand to be set free. To be that person for her.

Laiken's tears turned silent. Tracking down her cheeks and leaving artful trails behind. She was a work of art, even in her worst pain. "I'm glad you have him."

"Who do you have?"

She swallowed, her throat moving with the effort of the action. "I have myself."

"The most important bond we'll ever have. But it's not the only one we need. Who do you have, Laiken?"

A flicker of temper flashed in her eyes, so much better than the grief that had been drowning them a second ago. "I have Addie, Ev, and Hadley. I had Gilly, Kay, and Chip."

"Do you let them in on this? How much it's eating you alive? Do you let them *really* know you? Or are you keeping them at arm's length?" I was being a pushy bastard, and I knew it. But this was my one shot to make sure Laiken heard me. When her defenses were a little shocked and lowered.

She opened her mouth and then snapped it closed again. "I'm a private person."

"I understand that." Better than probably anyone else in her life, I got the need to draw the curtains. When your life had been displayed and dissected, it was natural. When it had been picked apart at your worst moments, it was a vital self-protective instinct.

I trailed a hand up and down Laiken's back, my fingers doing a delicate dance over the ridges in her spine. "I'm so sorry about your friend."

More tears spilled, but no sobs came. "We weren't even friends anymore. That friendship died with Jase. I should've fought harder, I should've—"

"You did the best you could."

"Did I? I'm not sure that's true."

"There's only so much someone can handle. You were recovering from injuries. You'd just lost someone you cared about—"

"Loved. I lost the boy I thought I'd marry." Her hands fisted in my jacket. "We had our whole lives planned out. College, my fancy gymnastics scholarship, getting engaged senior year, married the summer after we graduated, moving home, having babies. It all seemed so simple."

My body went ramrod straight. Something that felt a lot like jealousy whipped through me. Laiken didn't speak of this boy with an all-consuming passion. It was more like warm comfort and simple surety. She had loved someone she'd thought she'd spend forever with. And that forever had been ripped out from under her.

"I'm so sorry. It sounds like a beautiful life." One profound in its simple wants. In that moment, I would've given anything to give it back to her. That future she'd so badly wanted.

"I don't know that we even would've made it."

I pulled back a fraction, my gaze sweeping over her face, searching. "What makes you say that?"

Laiken's fingers twisted tighter in my jacket. "We were so young. And I sometimes wonder if we were only meant to be best friends. Wonder if that was our destiny. Then I feel like a traitor for even having that thought."

It was as if she'd ripped the words from my soul. I knew that battle so well. "It's like what you had was meant to stay in that innocent part of your lives. The time before the world got complicated, and everything changed."

"Exactly. I know that Jase would've always been in my life. That I would've always loved him—"

"But it was a different kind of love."

Laiken's eyes searched mine. "Carissa?"

I nodded. "We turned our relationship into something ugly when it started out so beautiful. We twisted it, trying to force it into a mold it didn't fit in anymore. I would give anything now to have let her go."

Laiken's fingers released my jacket, and she took my hands. Her skin was petal-soft. Her bones so delicate. "Her death isn't your fault."

Not in an exact sort of way. But it was. I'd brought the darkness that was Eli into her orbit. Sometimes, I wished I would've chosen to sit by someone else that day in kindergarten when we became friends. Then, maybe Carissa's light would still be shining.

Laiken squeezed my hands hard. "It's not."

"It's complicated."

"It always is. You think I don't carry around scars of guilt? It was my bright idea to leave the lake we were at and go to the party that Jase's brother was throwing. I just had to make sure Jax was under control. So obsessed with making sure the family I'd become a part of didn't fall apart like mine."

I felt a twisting sensation deep in my chest. As if the flesh and organs were tying themselves in knots. "Deciding to drive from one place to another doesn't put the blame on your shoulders."

"No, it doesn't. The blame lies with the man who decided to smoke meth and get behind the wheel of his truck. But that doesn't mean the what-ifs don't haunt me—so many I could drown in them."

I pulled Laiken into my arms again, my face finding the crook of her neck. I knew what it was to drown in those questions. To barely be able to find the air to suck into your lungs.

Laiken let out a shuddering breath. "I really should go. It's getting dark—"

"Stay with me tonight." The words were out before I could stop them. "There's a second bedroom in my cabin." She was quiet, not moving or speaking. "I really don't feel like being alone tonight."

Too many ghosts had been stirred up. And the idea of Laiken going back to an empty apartment when someone might be looking to hurt her? It was almost more than I could take.

"Okay." Laiken said the word almost inaudibly, but I felt it form against my neck, her warm breath raising the tiny hairs there.

"I'll lead the way. Stay close."

Chapter Fourteen

Laiken

DUMB. DUMB. DUMB. THIS WAS SO MONUMENTALLY stupid, yet I kept following behind Boden's truck as we curved around the mountain roads. Because if I were honest, I didn't want to be alone tonight, either. I wanted to know that someone was close by. Not that he could save me from the demons battering at my door, but at least I didn't have to face them in solitude.

Boden came to a stop in front of a massive gate and rolled down his window, swiping something over a keypad. The gates began to open. I'd known Ramsey lived in this general area, but I certainly had never been out here. I would've given anything for a little light to see the space. I had to imagine that he had amazing views. They would make for some killer photos.

I followed Boden's truck over the gravel road until he pulled up to a cabin. I took the spot next to him and stared up at the building. It was rustic yet impeccably designed at the same time. And it fit perfectly with the landscapes of eastern Oregon.

My door opened, and I fought not to jump.

"Not having second thoughts, are you?"

I looked up at the handsome face in front of me with its jaw seemingly carved out of stone and eyes that cut you to the quick. "Of course, I am."

"Too late." Boden moved to the back passenger door, opening it and scooping Gizmo into his arms. He grabbed my belongings from back there, as well. "Let's go. I have frozen pizza inside."

"Should've known you'd be bossy. A movie star used to getting his way."

Boden chuckled, the sound skating over my skin and creating a pleasant shiver. He started up the steps, pulling out his keys. "Might be a little spoiled."

I arched a brow.

"Okay, more than a little." He unlocked the front door and pulled it open.

As we stepped inside, an adorably goofy dog sleepily raised its head, blinking a few times.

"Peaches, were you napping this whole time?" Boden asked.

The dog thumped her tail. Gizmo let out an excited series of barks, and Peaches' ears twitched. She stood, hurrying over to Boden.

He shook his head and pointed to the door. "Uh-uh, go do your business first."

She let out a series of grumbled whines that could only be taken for disagreement but headed for the open door.

Boden looked at me. "Is Gizmo good with other dogs?"

"Loves them."

Boden set him down and hooked Gizmo's wheels to his harness. Gizmo charged for the front porch just as Peaches came back up the steps. They circled each other, tails wagging until Peaches dipped her head and gave Gizmo what could only be described as a nuzzle.

"I'll be damned," Boden muttered.

Something about the movement made my chest ache. "She's so sweet."

"When she wants to be. She's also one of the most stubborn dogs on the planet."

I grinned. "That's good. You need someone who doesn't always let you have your way."

"Hell, now you're going to start ganging up on me with my dog."

A laugh bubbled out of me, and the sound felt so damn good.

Boden's expression softened before he headed into the kitchen. "You good with pepperoni?"

"It's one of my favorites."

"I knew I liked you."

As the dogs worked their way inside, I shut the door. With nothing else to do, I stood awkwardly, studying Boden's space. "How long are you here for?" It was a question I hadn't thought to ask until that very moment, but the idea of Boden leaving sent a pang along my sternum.

"Undecided." He put the frozen pizza on a tray and stuck it into the still-preheating oven. "I like it here, though. Might need to think about looking for a place."

"In middle-of-nowhere Oregon?"

He shrugged. "Finding a place that speaks to your soul isn't to be underestimated."

"Those mountains are a sucker punch."

"In the best possible way. But it's more than that. There's a sense of peace here I haven't felt in a long time. It's the same way my parents feel about Big Sur."

I settled onto a stool at the kitchen island, keeping an eye on the dogs, who were still doing their sniffing dance. "That's where they live? Not Los Angeles?"

Boden nodded. "It used to be our vacation home growing up. We spent most summers up there. But after Eli and I graduated high school, they moved up there full time."

"Is Eli your brother?"

The stiffening of his spine was so minute, I would've missed it if I weren't a student of faces and bodies and how they gave away so much more than a person would say. "Yeah, my brother."

"You two aren't close?"

"It's—"

"Complicated," I finished for him.

I knew the reality of those tender spots you didn't want others to bring into the light, but I'd just opened up to Boden more than I had with anyone in years. It stung that he wasn't ready to do the same. The urge to retreat was so strong, it battled against my skin.

A moment later, Boden's face filled my line of vision. "Sorry, I just…"

"It's okay. You don't owe me anything."

Boden frowned. "We don't get along. We used to be close, but he went down a dark path. Didn't appreciate all the attention I was getting. The comparisons between us."

The worst of the sting melted away. "That's hard."

"It's not a picnic in the park."

The way Boden's muscles tightened told me the little he'd shared was only the tip of the iceberg. That tension called to me, and I reached out, kneading the flesh along his shoulders. His head fell to my own shoulder, and he sighed. "I'll only let you do that forever."

I chuckled. "I do have the magic touch."

"You could be making millions with those hands."

"I only use them on very special recipients. They aren't for sale."

Boden straightened, but as he did, he came closer. Our faces were close. Lips just a breath away. The urge to lean forward, to know what he felt like, tasted like, was strong. Boden's hand skated up my arm to my neck to tangle in my hair. He leaned in just a little closer.

Gizmo let out a shrill bark, startling us apart. Boden's gaze jerked in the dogs' direction, and his mouth fell open. "Is he trying to hump Peaches?"

I followed his line of sight to Gizmo trying to balance on his wheels and take advantage of poor Peaches. "Gizmo," I scolded. "You just met her."

"She doesn't look like she minds," Boden said with a laugh.

Peaches cast love-filled eyes at Gizmo as he humped away.

I slid off the chair and attempted to extricate my dog from clamoring all over Boden's. "Gizmo, this is embarrassing." I looked up at Boden, cheeks heating. "He's clearly quite enamored."

The corner of his mouth kicked up. "He's not the only one."

My stomach gave a healthy flip. I wasn't sure whether the comment was directed at himself or his dog, but I knew that Boden Cavanaugh was more than dangerous. But like a moth to a flame, I kept getting closer.

"That hit the spot. Thank you." I slid off the chair, my back twinging with the movement. My legs weren't exactly thrilled, either. The fiery nerve pain licked its way across my flesh and embedded itself there.

Boden followed behind me to the sink with our cups. "I can make frozen pizza with the best of them."

"That's about as far as I make it in the kitchen."

"Damn. I was hoping you were a culinary master."

I shook my head as I rinsed our plates. "Sorry to disappoint. I make a killer sandwich, though."

"I'm a great judge of sandwiches."

I laughed. "Is that a request?"

Boden gave me puppy-dog eyes. "Take pity on me out here, living off frozen meals."

"All right. I'll make you a sandwich. And Addie wanted me to invite you to dinner."

"Who's Addie?"

"A friend of mine. Married to Hayes' brother, Beckett. She's got a heart of gold, and when she heard you were in town and didn't have friends here, she made it her mission to make you feel welcome."

I watched Boden's reaction, on the lookout for any sign that he might bristle at locals trying to worm their way into his life. Instead, a grin spread across his face. "You're talking to your friends about me?"

I rolled my eyes. "Please don't get a big head. Ev saw you drive through town. That's how the whole conversation started."

"Mm-hmm, sure."

I slapped Boden with a kitchen towel. "Someone needs to have a look at your ego, it might cause a brain bleed."

"I'd love to go to dinner with your friends. Just tell me where and when."

I fought the urge to squirm. "I'll ask Addie."

I bent to put a plate into the dishwasher, and my back spasmed. I lost my grip on the dish, and it clattered into the machine.

Boden was at my side in a flash, helping me stand. "What is it? Your back?"

I nodded, eyes watering. "Sitting on chairs with no back isn't always the best."

He glared at me. "Why didn't you say something? We could've eaten at the dining table."

"I thought it would be okay. It wasn't long."

"But you've had a long day, and your back was already hurting."

I bit the inside of my cheek so I didn't bite Boden's head off. "Sometimes, I don't want everyone around me to have to make concessions because my body can't keep up like the rest of yours."

"Sitting at a table instead of a bar is hardly a concession." He guided me towards the large couch in the living room that was practically wide enough to be a double bed. "Sit down."

"Stop bossing me."

"I will when you sit down."

I scowled at Boden as I lowered myself to the cushion but couldn't hold back my wince as I did.

He sat next to me. "Is there some medicine you can take?"

"Not really. I only take the hard stuff for special occasions when I have to be on my feet for hours."

"Like exhibit openings."

I nodded. "The rest of the time, I muddle through." It was the deal I'd made with myself long ago, and it was a promise I planned to keep.

"What does it feel like?"

My gaze shot to Boden's face. No one had ever asked that before. No one besides a doctor, anyway. People would ask if I was in pain, but they didn't try to understand it. Because they didn't want to know all the ways a body could betray you.

For the first time in years, I tried to put the sensations into words. "My back is like a mortar and pestle. Like someone's grinding into the muscle and bone there. Sometimes, I get a cramp or spasm—like now—and it can take time for my body to calm down. To realize we're not about to do battle."

"It's not just your back."

It wasn't a question, but I shook my head anyway. "I get pretty bad nerve pain in my legs. It makes them feel as if they're on fire. Usually, an ice bath helps with that if I can maneuver a bag of ice to my tub."

Boden's jaw worked back and forth. "Are you feeling that now?"

I nodded slowly. "It's not too bad."

He stood. "Stay here. I have an idea."

Boden disappeared down the hall towards what I assumed were the bedrooms. It didn't take a genius to realize he was a fixer. A person who saw someone hurting and instantly wanted to remedy it. I'd known people like that before. The thing was, they got really frustrated when they realized you weren't fixable.

Boden appeared with a massive duffel bag slung over his shoulder. My brows rose. "If you think playing a game of hockey will help my pain, I'm worried about where you get your medical advice."

He chuckled and set it down on the coffee table in front of me.

"No hockey. Promise." He pulled out what looked like thigh-high boots or black casts of some sort.

"What are they?"

"They work similarly to ice packs or an ice bath. I use them for recovery when I'm in training for something."

I watched as he set to work setting up the device. "Are you in training for something now?"

"I'm supposed to be. Don't tell my trainer I've been slacking."

"The same one who makes you cry?"

"The one and only."

Boden moved to the couch and sat. He lifted one leg into his lap. His fingers deftly untied the laces of my boot and tugged it free. He copied the move with my second foot. Grabbing one of the cast-like devices, Boden slid it up my leg. His knuckles grazed my jeans-clad flesh, and my breath hitched.

Boden's eyes locked with mine, the gold in his hazel depths burning brighter. "Does this hurt?"

I shook my head. "No." The single syllable came out as a whisper.

He tugged the second device up my other leg. The sensation of his fingers on my thigh was almost more than I could take. The urge to squirm—or worse, seek out more of that contact— was so strong.

Boden reached for a control and turned a couple of dials. "You'll start to feel the cold pretty quickly."

I already was. As the coldness seeped into my legs, the worst of the fiery pain began to ebb. There were times I spent hours in an ice bath to get the same effect. I'd be shaking like a leaf but still desperate for any bit of relief. This way, it was only my legs that were cold, not the rest of me.

I stared at the boots, my eyes burning. It was such a simple kindness. The desire to relieve some of my hurt. I forced my gaze to Boden's. "It's working."

He beamed. "I'm glad." He grabbed a remote from the coffee table. "Now, how about a movie? My only rule is no musicals."

My lips twitched. "That's all I like to watch."

Boden's head swung in my direction, panic lacing his expression.

I burst out laughing. "I can't dance worth a damn, and if I sang, I'd probably make your ears bleed."

"That wasn't nice."

"Someone has to keep you on your toes."

His gaze tracked to my lips. "Somehow, I think you could do that in your sleep."

Chapter Fifteen

Laiken

I WOKE TO HEAT. SO MUCH HEAT PRESSED AGAINST MY FRONT, I'd dreamed I was lying on the sunbaked sand of a beautiful beach. But this surface was harder. My eyes fluttered.

It took me several moments to put the pieces together. The unfamiliar cabin. The male chest. The rhythmic breath.

Crap. The soft strains of the television played in the background as the first rays of sunlight poured in through the window. Sometime between the first and second *Iron Man* movies, we must've fallen asleep. Only I'd taken it a step further, plastering myself to Boden's front. It was mortifying.

Now, I had to figure out how to extricate myself from his grasp without him knowing. I took a deep breath and rolled to my side.

Boden's arm tightened around me. "Don't move. It's cold, and you're like my own electric blanket."

"You're awake?" I squeaked.

He grinned against my hair. "Very awake."

I squirmed against him.

"You might not want to do that first thing in the morning."

I froze, a growing hardness between us making itself known. "Boden…"

"I can't help it. There's a gorgeous woman in my arms, and I just woke up."

My thighs squeezed together without my permission. I quickly rolled off Boden and off the couch altogether, struggling to my feet. That kind of proximity was far too dangerous for my own good. "I should go."

I looked around the room for Gizmo. Peaches spooned him on a dog bed, and the little guy had a look of bliss on his face.

Boden pushed himself to sitting. "Stay. I've got four kinds of cereal and plenty of fruit. Have breakfast with me."

I stared at the man in front of me, his sun-streaked brown hair mussed from sleep, those hazel eyes half-hooded. All I wanted to do was say, "*Yes.*" More, I wanted to sink onto his lap and lose the day with him. To know what it was like to disappear into the magic that was Boden Cavanaugh.

"I need to go," I said softly. The words tore at my chest—the lie scraping against muscle and bone.

His face lost a little of that adorable boyishness. "All right." He plucked up my cell phone from the table and hit a few buttons. "I have your number." His eyes lifted to mine. "I'll be calling."

It was a promise laced with a threat. Not a menacing one. A vow that he wasn't backing down. I swallowed and nodded, hurrying to gather my things. But I had a feeling that no matter how quickly I got out of Boden's space, he'd already embedded himself in my skin—and worse, my heart.

⌒

I balanced the two coffees in one hand as I pulled open the door to the sheriff's station. I didn't recognize the woman behind the front desk, but she gave me a pleasant smile. "How can I help you?"

"Is Hayes in yet?" It was a little after nine, so I hoped the answer was yes. After a very cold shower and an attempt to put myself back together, I was still rattled. I'd slept too well curled around Boden last night. No nightmares, no waking in fits of pain. Pure, dreamless sleep.

"Let me see if he's available. Your name?"

"Laiken."

The woman picked up the phone and shared a few hushed words with who I assumed was Hayes. "He'll be right out."

"Thanks." I let my gaze sweep over the entryway. It was stark efficiency laced with a rustic mountain vibe. Yet as I tried to focus on the details of the space, my mind kept filling with images of Boden's face. The way my fingers itched to run through his hair. The hint of hurt as I drove away that morning.

"Laiken."

I turned at Hayes' voice, extending one of the two cups I held in his direction. "I brought coffee."

His mouth curved as he took the cup. "How'd you know it was a multi-cup morning?"

"I figured sheriffs could never have enough."

"Tell that to Ev. She's trying to wean me down to two cups a day." Hayes motioned me to follow him.

"That's cruel and unusual punishment. You might have to arrest her."

"Think a night in lockup will have her reconsidering?"

I shook my head. "She's too tough. It'll probably only make her double down."

Hayes ushered me into his office. "You're probably right. I'll just have to swear my coworkers to secrecy and get all my caffeine here."

I laughed. "She'll find out somehow."

"Dammit, I know you're right." He lowered himself into his desk chair. "You hanging in there?"

I sat, toying with the lid of my cup. "Yeah. Have you talked to Marisa and Isaac?"

Three. That was all that was left. How was that possible? So many lives cut short.

"I got in touch with Marisa but haven't been able to find Isaac yet. I think he's out of town on a job."

Guilt pricked at me. I didn't even know what Isaac was doing these days. I rarely saw him around town, and if I did, he passed me with a polite hello that someone would give a stranger. Not like we'd once been the closest of friends. Not as if we'd mourned the loss of someone we loved together.

My stomach cramped. "I hope he's okay."

"At this point, I think out of town is a good thing."

I picked at my cup's lid. "You're pretty sure, aren't you?"

Hayes' dark blue eyes hardened a fraction. "That there's something off about these deaths?"

I nodded.

"Came in this morning to Lisbeth's tox screen on my computer. It was positive for high levels of opiates in her system. The same kind that was in Scott's system at the time of his death. It'll take a few days to get the results on Mitch."

My fingers curled around the arm of the chair, gripping it tightly. "Lisbeth didn't do drugs."

Hayes was quiet for a moment. "We don't always know what people get up to in the private moments of their lives."

"Hayes, she wouldn't. Not after what we went through. She wouldn't get behind the wheel of a car while high."

"Scott had a drug problem. It was documented. I brought him in at least a dozen times."

My back teeth ground together. "Did you ever once arrest him for driving under the influence?"

"No. He was never arrested for that."

"Because we all went through hell because someone drove high. None of us, not one, would do that."

Hayes held up both hands as if trying to calm a wild animal. "You don't have to convince me that something seems off here. I agree. I'm looking into it with the force of the whole department behind me. But this could also be something else entirely. I want you to be prepared for that."

"I just want you to find the truth."

His eyes locked with mine. "I promise you, Laiken, I won't stop until we know for sure what happened."

But the truth wasn't always such a simple thing to find. The world wasn't black and white. It was shades of gray that twirled and twisted. Sometimes, the truth hid beneath all those knots. And sometimes, it was impossible to see it at all.

Chapter Sixteen

Boden

Banging on my door had Peaches barking like mad, even though she didn't move from her bed. I sent her a wan look. "Some guard dog you are."

I crossed to the door, pulling it open. I hadn't said a word before Ramsey barged into my space. "I gave you one rule. No guests. I don't let people onto my property. I made an exception for Gaines because he's my brother in every way that counts. You betrayed that trust, and now you can get the hell out."

My jaw went slack. It was the most words I'd ever heard Ramsey say. And I could feel the rage flowing off him in hot waves. "I'm sorry. You're right. It was a breach. I should've called you." Not that I had his number.

"I don't want you to call me. I want you to respect the rules I laid out, not bring your conquests back to my property."

"Her friend died."

Ramsey stilled. "What?"

"Laiken. She's had two friends die in the last week. The sheriff is wondering if foul play is involved. They were all part of an accident in their senior year of high school. Now, they all seem to be dying, one by one."

Ramsey's eyes narrowed. "I remember that. The Granger kid."

"Her boyfriend at the time. Laiken was hurt. I'm not sure about the others."

A muscle along Ramsey's jaw ticked. "She was hurt the worst. In the hospital the longest."

A deep ache spread through my chest, thinking about Laiken in the hospital alone. Had she gotten the support she needed then? It didn't seem like her family was a huge part of her life. What about Jase's?

"Last night, she was alone and hurting. I brought her back here without thinking. She needed someone, but I should've gone to her place."

Ramsey's gaze cut to me. "The sheriff thinks someone might try to hurt her?"

"There's a chance. He doesn't know what's what right now."

"Tell her to stay here."

This time, my jaw fell fully open. "What?"

"Tell her to stay in your cabin." His eyes narrowed. "No one else. Laiken, and that's it."

"Thank you. I'm not sure she'll take me up on that offer."

The corner of his mouth kicked up. "Use some of that famous charm of yours, movie star. I'm sure you can convince her."

And with those parting words, he was gone. When it came to Ramsey, that might as well have been a friendship bracelet.

I pulled up my text messages for the hundredth time that day and stared at the screen.

Me: *How are you feeling?*

There was no response. Laiken was likely working, but how long did it take to type back a quick text? Thirty seconds?

My grip on the device tightened. I'd seen the panic in her eyes that morning. I'd seen beneath the carefully crafted mask, and she hadn't liked it. For once, she'd let her guard down, and now she was running scared.

I typed out a text to someone else instead of sending another to Laiken the way I wanted to.

Me: *It's Boden. Can I treat you to lunch?*

A few seconds later, my phone dinged in response.

Hayes: *Meet me at The Wolf Gap Bar & Grill in ten.*

Me: *See you there.*

I typed the name of the restaurant into my internet browser and pulled up the location. It was only a couple of blocks from where I was parked, and I could use the now-familiar bite of winter air.

Sliding out of my truck, I beeped the locks. I took the long way to the bar and grill, letting the brisk cold really settle into my skin. Pine still laced the air, but it was mixed with something else now: the promise of snow. I wouldn't mind a good snowstorm. Peaches had never seen the white stuff. An image of Laiken and me curled up on the couch in front of a fire filled my mind, but I shoved it down.

As I rounded the corner, Hayes lifted a hand in greeting. "This place has the best burgers and nachos you could ever hope for."

"That sounds promising."

"I'm glad you texted."

I took his hand in a shake. "I'm glad you accepted my bribe."

He chuckled. "Careful what you say to a sheriff."

"If you put me in lockup, I doubt my dog will bail me out."

"We don't accept bones as payment."

I pulled open the door and held it for Hayes. "Guess I'd better stay on the straight and narrow."

"Guess so." Hayes smiled at the woman behind the hostess station. "Hey, Cammie. Got a table for two?"

"Sure do. A booth and everything—" Her words cut off as she registered me next to Hayes. "Oh, my God. No way. You're—you're—"

"A friend of mine, who is trying to keep a low profile and away from prying eyes," Hayes finished for her.

Cammie's eyes were still wide, but her head bobbed up and down. "Got it. Top-secret status." She all but vibrated but kept her voice barely above a whisper. "That movie you did with Ava Arndt? I've probably seen it a million times. I know it by heart."

I reached out a hand to her in a shake. "It's nice to meet you, Cammie. I'm sure I can rustle up some swag from the film. Maybe a poster and sign it for you. Get Hayes to pass it along."

She let out a little squeak. "That would be amazing. Just amazing."

"Happy to. And thanks for keeping my secret. If the paparazzi show up here, I'll probably have to go back to LA."

Cammie shook her head vigorously. "I won't tell a soul." Her cheeks pinked. "Well, I'll tell everyone and their brother, but not till after you're gone. I swear."

I chuckled, but something about her words grated on me. I didn't want to leave. Wolf Gap, with its sweeping landscapes and calming air, was becoming like a drug. And it wasn't the only thing. Laiken's face filled my mind, slack with sleep. When she rolled on top of me, I'd watched her for hours. The way the hair around her face fluttered with each breath. The movement of her eyes beneath her lids. I hadn't wanted to miss a second of what it felt like to be wrapped up with her. And I wanted more.

"Thanks, Cammie."

She motioned us forward. "I've got a table for you in the corner. It's got dividers so no one will have a good view. And I'll wait on your table personally so no other waitstaff sees you."

Hayes patted her on the shoulder. "I knew we could count on you."

We settled into the booth, and Cammie jogged off to get us a couple of Cokes. Hayes let free the laughter he'd clearly been holding in. "Is it always like that for you?"

"In LA, not so much. People pay attention, but they try to play it cool. This is better. More honest. I'd prefer someone come and talk to me rather than try to sneak a picture when I'm not looking."

"That has to be exhausting, always feeling like you're being watched."

I shrugged. "It's the price I pay to do what I love."

Cammie slid the sodas across the table. "Do you know what you want, or do you need a minute with the menu?" She grinned. "I know he doesn't need a minute. Burger or nachos?"

"One day, I'm going to stump you," Hayes said. "I'll take a burger."

"If you order something else, I'll faint on the spot."

This was the kind of thing I'd missed growing up in LA. The small-town, everyone-knows-each-other feel. The simple comfort of someone knowing your restaurant order like the back of their hand. "I'll do the burger, too. Medium. With American cheese."

"Coming right up." She turned on her heel and headed for the kitchen.

"So, you just bored, or did you call this lunch with a purpose?" Hayes asked.

I guessed there was no sense in dancing around the issue. "I'm worried about Laiken."

Hayes set up straighter. "In what way?"

"If someone is out for the people involved in the accident, who's watching her back? Anyone could walk into that gallery. All day long. And what about at night? It doesn't seem like there's stellar security on the building."

"I've got it on regular drive-bys. Which is how I know her car never made it there last night. One of my guys saw her following you back to Ramsey's."

Why did I feel the sudden urge to blush? "She was rattled. We stayed up doing an *Iron Man* marathon and fell asleep on the couch."

Hayes held up both hands. "I'm not asking what your intentions are with Laiken. I'm just saying we're paying attention. I'll do whatever it takes to help keep her safe. But it wouldn't hurt if you stayed close, too."

Close was exactly where I wanted to be, and not just because Laiken might be in danger. I wanted more of her understanding and warmth. More of that strength and stubbornness. "I'm trying."

"It's not easy for her."

"I'm getting that. What I'd like to do is get her out of Wolf Gap altogether until you catch whoever's doing this."

Hayes stilled with his Coke halfway to his mouth. "That's not a bad idea."

"She's not going to take off with me. She's not a runner."

"What if you couched it as a getaway? Even just a few days would give me some time to investigate."

I scrubbed a hand over my jaw. "Hayes, I don't know what you think is happening between Laiken and me, but it's not that."

He arched a brow. "Not yet?"

I chuckled. "Hope springs eternal."

"I can tell you care about her. If you were looking for quick and easy, you would've seen that she was upset and turned away. Instead, at least twice now that I know of, you've made sure that she was okay and did what you could to help. But I've also seen how you two look at each other. There's something there."

Hayes' words should've scared the hell out of me. And I couldn't deny my rib cage tightened. But I wasn't running. I should. I should go straight back to Ramsey's, pack my stuff, and go back to LA. Or maybe to stay with my parents in Big Sur.

Instead, I wanted to chase down the woman with shadows in her eyes. Wanted to soothe them and do everything I could to protect her. "I don't know the first thing about a healthy relationship. I might not be good for her."

Hayes traced a design in the condensation on his glass. "Neither did I. But Ev and I figured it out. Had plenty of bumps in the road, but we found our way."

There was a flicker of something that felt a lot like hope deep in my gut.

"I have a friend who owns a cabin higher up the mountain. I'm sure he'd let you use it for a few days. It's off the beaten path."

My mind started whirling, putting together pieces for how I could get Laiken to agree to walk away from Wolf Gap for a few days. "I bet it has some gorgeous views."

"The best."

I glanced down at my phone. "I'd love to take Laiken up there. But it would probably help if I could get her to text me back first."

Hayes burst out laughing. "I guess movie stars don't get everything they want."

"Trust me. My life is far from perfect." Another flicker of guilt swept through me at bringing Laiken into the darkness that sometimes swamped my world.

The humor fled Hayes' expression. "We all bring baggage into relationships. But it's nice to have someone help us carry it for a while."

Chapter Seventeen

Laiken

I PULLED INTO A MAKESHIFT SPOT IN FRONT OF THE GRANGERS' house. I simply sat there for a moment, taking in the familiar view. There was comfort in how well I knew it, down to which boards creaked when you walked up the front steps. How many times had Jase pushed me in the swing out front? Or chased me with a stash of water balloons? There were so many beautiful memories here, and I didn't want to lose a single one. I didn't want the loss of Jase and the aftermath that had twisted us all to taint them.

Shutting off my SUV's engine, I pulled air into my lungs and then slowly let it out. I climbed out of the vehicle and headed for the front door. It opened before I reached the top step.

Chip smiled, but I saw strain around his eyes. "Hey, Laiken."

I lifted a bag. "I brought lunch. Have you guys eaten yet?"

He shook his head. "I was just about to scrounge something up."

"Well, now you don't have to." I pulled out a sandwich and a drink. "Why don't you take a break? I'll sit with Kay for a while."

He reached out and squeezed my shoulder. "Thank you."

The simple touch made my eyes burn. Chip used to throw affection around with casual ease. But somewhere along the line, that changed. His actions had become stilted, forced, and far less frequent. I hadn't realized how much I'd needed that point of contact to assure myself that he was still here. "I'll do anything I can to help. *Anything.*"

Chip's eyes reddened. "I know, Laiken. I wish there were a magic button you could press to fix it all. But, sometimes, the break is too great."

My heart twisted and squeezed. "I can't imagine the burden you're carrying, but if I can help shoulder the weight in any way, all you have to do is ask."

He nodded, his feet shuffling. "This is good. Right here." He pressed a kiss to the top of my head. "You're a good woman, Laiken. He would've been honored to stand by your side."

My throat burned. There were things I knew that Jase would be proud of, but there were others I knew he'd shake his head at. Things I was scared to step into. Things like the text message waiting, unanswered, on my phone.

"He's so much of who I've become."

Chip's mouth curved the barest amount. "I like to think that he had a part in that. It's like he lives on through you." His eyes misted over, and he motioned me inside. "I'm going to head out to the barn. Kay's in the living room."

I didn't try to stop him. Chip needed his privacy to let the emotions go. I could give him that.

I moved through the entryway and into the living space. Kay sat with her back to me, staring out the large windows at the back of the house and the view of the field and forest. You could even see cattle grazing and a creek weaving through the space.

Circling the couch, I lowered myself to the cushions. "Hey, Kay."

Her head swung in my direction, and she blinked a few times as if trying to bring me into focus. "Laiken."

"How are you feeling?"

Her mouth trembled. "I'm having a few bad days."

I reached out, taking her hand in mine. "It happens to all of us."

She nodded slowly, her gaze returning to the windows. "I miss him."

"Me, too."

"Sometimes, I get mad. So angry at everyone, I feel like it could burn me alive."

I squeezed her hand a little tighter, a silent acknowledgment that I was here. Listening.

Tears filled Kay's eyes. "They don't miss him as much as they should. They don't feel this pain like I do. They aren't being eaten alive from the inside out."

"Kay. No one will ever miss Jase as much as you do. You're his mother. He came from you. It's a kind of pain no one can understand unless they've been through it. But that doesn't mean everyone else isn't missing him, too. They just may have a different way of showing it."

Her head snapped in my direction, her eyes heating with anger. "They don't talk about him. They just go on with their lives like everything's fine. Even Jax and Serena barely say his name."

Likely because they were afraid of sending their mother into a state like she was in now. These episodes had gotten fewer and further apart, but I knew they must shake Jax and Serena. I swept my thumb back and forth across the back of Kay's hand. "Have you tried asking them about it? Telling them that you'd like to talk about Jase more?"

Her lips pursed. "No."

"I think we all need more communication. If you share what might help you, I bet they'll jump at the chance to do it. They love you. More than anything. Tell them what you need."

Tears filled her eyes. "You're right. I need to talk to them." She let out a shaky breath. "Will you talk about him with me now?"

I smiled. "I'd love to."

The bell signaled as I opened the door to the gallery. Raised voices greeted me.

"For the love of all that's holy, Serena. We are not painting the walls in here pink." Gilly's bracelets jangled as she gestured around the space.

Serena stiffened her spine. "I wasn't suggesting a magenta or anything. Just a soft blush. It would set us apart from the other galleries in town."

Gilly pinched the bridge of her nose. "There's a reason they don't have pink walls. It skews the way the art shows."

"I was thinking about that, too. We should go for things with a softer color palette. They'd be more aesthetically pleasing."

Addie's gaze ping-ponged from the two women to me and back, her eyes wide.

If I'd been stuck here with Serena all day, I likely would've been pulling my hair out. But now, I simply laughed. This was an element of her personality that hadn't changed. She'd always been a tornado of ideas, so sure that her plan was the best one. Seeing a hint of the girl I used to know had warmth spreading through me.

Gilly grasped Serena's shoulders. "Babycakes, you know I love you more than the sun and the moon and the stars, but after a morning with you, I need to go smoke a joint and find my Zen. Maybe a shot of tequila wouldn't hurt, either."

Addie let out a squeak of laughter.

Serena's gaze cut to her, her eyes narrowing into slits. "It's a good idea."

"You know, I think we could work with the color scheme you're talking about," I said, stepping farther into the room.

Gilly's hands dropped from Serena's shoulders. "Excuse me?" The undercurrent of those words asked if I had lost my mind.

"We are getting access to the small space next door, remember?" I asked.

Gilly nodded slowly. "For the gift shop."

"Exactly. It would be smart to have a delineation between the two—shop and gallery. I think a blush pink would make for a warm and inviting space in there."

Serena's jaw tightened. "I don't need your pity."

My hands curled, nails biting into my palms. "It's not pity. It's finding your idea useful."

"If you found it *useful,* you'd paint the walls in here pink. This is your condescending way of throwing me a bone. It's insulting, and I don't need it."

So much for seeing a glimmer of the girl I used to know. "All right, no pink. We'll go with the photos you hate so much on every available surface, and I'll call it the Serena Granger Gift Shop in your honor."

Addie choked on a laugh, but Gilly just let hers fly. She grinned at me. "I like it."

"You're all awful." Serena whirled on Gilly. "I would've thought at least you would be kind. You know what I've been through. How hard it was for me to come back."

Gilly's gaze hardened. "We've all been through hardships, Serena. It doesn't give you an excuse to be an asshole."

Serena's jaw dropped open. "You—you didn't."

Gilly shrugged. "I call 'em like I see 'em."

Tears filled Serena's eyes, and she charged towards the back room. Seconds later, the door to the bathroom slammed.

I let out a breath, looking between Addie and Gilly. "Has it been a fun morning?"

Addie smiled, shaking her head. "It hasn't been boring."

Gilly's shoulders slumped. "That girl is exhausting."

I wrapped an arm around her. "But you love her."

"I do. And I'm going to need to go back there and make sure she's all right. But, sometimes, I don't even recognize her anymore."

I knew the feeling so well. But I had to remember what I'd just told Kay an hour ago. "We all deal with grief differently. We don't like how Serena is dealing with hers, but we don't get to dictate that. She has to find her own way through it."

"It's turning my beautiful girl ugly, and I don't like seeing that."

I leaned my head against Gilly's. "I know. But she's home now. Maybe coming face-to-face with her memories and her pain will be the breakthrough she needs."

Gilly smiled, amusement filling her eyes. "Look who's trying to keep Serena around now."

I chuckled. "What can I say? I'm a sucker for the Granger clan."

She gave my waist a squeeze. "I'm going to go see if I can make some progress with her now."

"Good luck." I released her and worried my bottom lip. Gilly took too much on her shoulders, too. Trying to look after her sister, keep Jax and Serena in line, make sure Chip had the help he needed on the ranch. I needed to do some checking up on Gilly, too.

I turned to Addie. "I'm so sorry you got caught up in World War III while I was gone."

She waved me off. "I've just been sending out invoices while those two went at it. It was kind of like one of those reality tv shows. Entertaining."

I could only imagine.

The bell above the door sounded, and I looked up. My heart gave a stutter-step in my chest as I met hazel eyes across the space. I fought the urge to squirm as Boden strode into the gallery. His very presence dominated the space—taking over and sucking you in.

"Boden." My voice was a fraction more high-pitched than normal. "What are you doing here?"

"Came to see if your phone broke or if you'd been kidnapped by a roving band of bigfoot. What is the plural of that? Bigfoots? Bigfeet?"

Addie let out a sound behind me.

"It's just been a busy day." The words sounded like the lie they were. "Boden, this is my good friend, Addie. Addie, this is Boden."

That charming smile spread across his face as he crossed to the desk. "It's lovely to meet you, Addie. Did Laiken tell you I'd love to come to dinner?"

Addie sent me a sidelong glance. "No, she left that detail out."

"Can't trust anyone to deliver a message these days." Boden pulled his wallet out of his back pocket and slid out a business card. "This has my cell on it. Call or text, and we can figure out a day."

"I'll text as soon as I talk to Beckett and get his schedule at the clinic." She glanced at me, mischief in her eyes. "This will be fun, don't you think, Laiken?"

"Tons of fun," I said in a deadpan voice.

Boden let out a bark of laughter. "You'd think we were going to torture her."

Addie rolled her eyes. "A meal she doesn't have to cook with friends. So awful."

"You know, I don't think I like you two getting to be friends."

Boden grinned and leaned a little closer to Addie. "I think we should come up with a special handshake."

"I love that idea."

"I'll get brainstorming," Boden said as Addie stood from the desk.

"We can practice at dinner." She looked between the two of us. "I need to organize some inventory in the back. I'll leave you two to…talk."

I glared at her. I knew damn well she'd organized the inventory yesterday.

Boden ambled towards me as if he were in no hurry. "I like your friend."

My pulse thrummed. "Clearly."

He came to a stop just a foot away, close enough that I felt a bit of the heat rolling off him. Boden's gaze tracked over my face, searching for something. "Why didn't you text me back?"

"I told you. I was busy."

He didn't look away, his stare pinning me to the spot. "Were you really busy? Or were you avoiding me?"

So much avoidance was happening, it wasn't even funny. "I was busy. I needed to go see Jase's mom. When I got back, Serena and Gilly were making a scene. They're both worried about Kay, and neither of them handles it well."

Boden's brows pulled together. "Gilly is related to Jase?"

"His aunt. Serena's his sister."

Sympathy swept over his expression. "That's a hard loss."

Boden's kindness and understanding bled the defensiveness right out of me. "I was avoiding you."

One side of his mouth lifted in that half-smile I was growing addicted to. "I know."

"You don't have to sound so cocky."

"It's not cocky to understand someone."

"You think you understand me?"

The smile fell a fraction. "I know pieces of you. Understand them because I've lost, too. It's a club no one wants to be a part of."

"No, it's not."

Boden moved in closer. "What are you scared of?"

I stared into those swirling, hazel eyes. It was as if they bewitched me into speaking. "Getting used to having you here." It wasn't the whole truth, but it hinted at it.

"What if I want you to get used to it?"

"You don't live here. You're from a different universe. You travel the world, making movies. My whole life revolves around this tiny town."

"Those are the details, not the important things. Connection, understanding, *feeling*, that's the important stuff. We can figure out the rest."

I scoffed. "Those things are important to me. My routine, knowing what I can count on. I need that."

Hurt flashed in Boden's eyes. "You can count on me."

"You can't just say that and demand that I believe it. You have to earn it."

Boden ran a hand through his hair, his fingers leaving disheveled trails in their wake. "Then give me a damn chance to earn it. Don't push me out because I saw you in less than your full suit of armor."

I froze. "I'm not…" My words trailed off because that was precisely what I'd done. Pushed him away because it felt safe. I was brave in so many areas of my life. But this one? I was nothing but a coward.

Boden sensed an opening. "Let me cook you dinner."

"I'm not good at this…stuff." I'd had exactly one boyfriend. I'd dated some in the years in between, but nothing had felt *right* enough to let it get truly serious. Maybe because I'd always chosen guys that I didn't see a future with.

"I'm not, either. Out of practice, and probably awkward as hell. But I think we can muddle through it together."

I studied the man in front of me. The one who overflowed with such kindness. Who seemed to know just how much to push. "Okay."

Boden beamed—that uninhibited smile that was a rare treasure. "Okay, then. Is there anything you don't eat?"

"Wait, didn't you say that you had no idea how to cook? That you were existing on frozen meals alone?" The last thing we needed was to end up with an epic case of food poisoning.

He chuckled, and I swore I felt the vibrations of it on my skin.

"When I said I was going to cook, what I really meant was that I would pick up copious amounts of takeout."

"That sounds much safer."

Boden reached out, his fingers tangling in a strand of my hair as he tucked it behind my ear. "Is that a yes to copious amounts of takeout with me tonight?"

"It's a yes."

Chapter Eighteen

Laiken

"WAS THAT—?" SERENA STARTED, her expression full of awe. "There's no way."

"There is definitely a way," Addie said, a huge smile on her face. "The fancy movie star has a thing for Laiken."

A hint of worry flashed across Gilly's expression. "How long is he here for?"

My stomach twisted at the question. "I'm not sure."

She toyed with a bead on her bracelet, forcing a smile. "He's got all the handsome going for him." Her eyes took on an authentic twinkle. "Think I could convince him to sit for me? Or maybe I could have *you* convince him to sit for me."

I snorted. "I feel like you've got the convincing down better than I do."

Gilly ran a hand through her silvering hair in an exaggerated motion. "Careful, Laiken. I could give you some real competition where that man's concerned."

A grin stretched across my face. "There's zero competition. You'd trounce me."

She laughed as she wrapped an arm around my shoulders. "Oh, Cherub, you're good for my old soul."

Serena stood, gaping at us. "Is someone going to tell me what the hell is going on?"

"Boden Cavanaugh is in town for a while doing some research for a film," I explained. God, I hoped Serena wouldn't blow this wide open. "He's trying to keep a low profile, so please don't share that."

Her mouth pinched together. "If it's so secret, then why was he in here flirting with you?"

Gilly's grip on my shoulder tightened. "Serena."

"What? Now I can't ask a simple question?"

"We're friends." That seemed like so much less than we were, but it was all I could handle claiming right now. Friends was safe. Except an intimacy with Boden was far from that. He had a living, breathing flame inside him that was pulling me in.

Serena scoffed. "He's probably just looking for a piece of ass while he's on vacation."

"Stop it." Addie's words whipped out, her tone harsher than I'd ever heard it.

"Excuse me?"

"You heard me. Stop it. Your ugliness to Laiken needs to end. She's been nothing but kind to you, and you've been a brat since your first shift here."

Serena's jaw fell open. "You have no idea what you're talking about. What we've been through."

Addie's expression gentled a fraction, but there was still steel beneath it. "I know enough. I know you're hurting. But you don't take that out on her. It's not fair, and it doesn't help anything."

"Life isn't fair. It wasn't fair when my brother was stolen from me, and my family imploded. It wasn't fair when Laiken all but ditched me. When she turned from a friend to a constant lecturer. It wasn't fair when I didn't have anyone to lean on. That's not fucking fair." Tears gathered in Serena's eyes, and she furiously wiped them away. She opened her mouth to say something more but then shook her head and moved for the door. She didn't slam anything this time. There was only the bell and a soft snick in her wake. But it might as well have been a cannon.

Gilly started for the door. "I need to talk to her."

"I'm so sorry. I shouldn't have said anything—"

I waved Addie off. "No, I think that was good. It's the first time Serena has been honest about what she's feeling. She's so used to covering it with that bitchy air. That's not who she is. Not deep down." I stared at the window. "I had no idea she felt like I left her."

Addie moved closer, taking my hand. "You were grieving, trying to recover from your injuries. I'm sure everyone did the best they could."

"She was younger, though. Maybe too young to fully grasp that. I'm sure we all hurt her. It's no wonder she doesn't like coming home."

"She's here now."

She was. And I needed to find a way to heal the break between us.

I stared at the impressive gate for a moment, considering turning around and heading home—to the safety of my apartment and my routine. Gizmo barked from his car seat in the back as if to tell me to stop being such a wimp.

I pulled out my phone and hit a contact I never had before.

Boden answered on the second ring. "You here?"

I tried to speak but couldn't get the words to come easily. I cleared my throat. "I'm at the gate."

"Hold on."

I heard a buzz through my closed window, and the gates began to open.

"You know where the cabin is."

I did. Yet I didn't pull forward.

"Laiken?"

"I'm here."

"Don't bail on me now."

Something about the raw vulnerability in Boden's voice had my foot moving from the brake to the accelerator. "I'm not."

"Good. I'll reward you with food when you get here."

My mouth curved. "It's a good bribe." And with that, I hung up.

I guided my SUV around the gravel road, taking in the breathtaking sights and wondering if Ramsey knew how lucky he was to have this kind of spread. There was a different view from every direction, and each one was magical. I itched to pull over and grab my camera from the trunk, yet somehow, I didn't think the reclusive man would appreciate that.

I pulled into a makeshift spot next to Boden's truck and climbed out of my SUV. By the time I got Gizmo out of his car seat, Boden was waiting. The door bracketed him as he leaned against the frame. It would've made for a hell of a picture. I clicked the shutter in my mind, wanting to keep the image with me forever.

"Hey," he greeted with a lazy smile.

"Hey."

Peaches all but danced at his side.

I smiled at her. "Hey, pretty girl. You ready for your boyfriend?"

She let out a bark, and I set Gizmo and his wheels down. He charged for her instantly, and they circled and licked.

One side of Boden's mouth kicked up. "I'm a little jealous of that greeting."

My stomach flipped. An image of Boden's mouth on mine, his hands tangled in my hair filled my mind. I shoved it out. "I could lift Gizmo up. I'm sure he'd give you an exceedingly warm welcome."

Boden chuckled. "I think I'll pass on that one. Come inside before you freeze to death. I've got a fire going."

I hadn't felt the bitter edge of the cold. All I felt was that flame in Boden, the one that tempted me closer. "Thanks."

I stepped inside to the smells of an Italian feast. I looked towards the kitchen. "Dough Boys?" Our local pizza joint was the only place you could get decent Italian food around here.

Boden nodded. "I got a little bit of everything. It's just sitting in the oven to keep warm. You want to eat now?"

My stomach rumbled in answer.

"I'll take that as a yes. What can I get you to drink? Wine, water, soda?"

"A soda would be great."

Boden moved to the refrigerator and pulled it open. "Coke or Sprite?"

"Coke, please. What can I do to help?"

"Grab some plates from the cabinet over there." He inclined his head to the left.

We moved in a slightly awkward synchronicity. It worked but was unpracticed, my nerves making my movements jumpy.

When Boden opened the oven, my jaw dropped. "How many people are you planning on feeding?"

He shrugged a little sheepishly. "I wanted to make sure I had something you liked."

"Anything that combines cheese and carbs makes me happy."

"Then I'd say we've got you covered."

The understatement of the century. There was garlic bread, salad, eggplant parmesan, chicken parmesan, ravioli, and fettuccini Alfredo. "You'll be eating leftovers for a month."

"That's not exactly a hardship."

I eased into a chair at the dining table where Boden had set us up. "I do love a good leftover."

Boden's gaze tracked over me as I sat. "Is that chair comfortable? Do you want another one? Or a pillow?"

Warmth lit in me at his words. His thoughtfulness. "This is good. I just need the back for support."

He nodded but didn't look altogether convinced.

"So, how was your day?" My cheeks heated at the question. It screamed: *married couple.* But Boden didn't seem to think it odd.

"Good, even though I had to have cereal alone."

I squirmed in my seat as I reached for a piece of garlic bread. "I'm sure you survived."

"Barely. Spent the morning watching Ramsey with his new mare."

"I still can't get over the fact that he welcomed you into his world."

Boden dished a few different pastas onto his plate. "*Welcomed* might be too strong a word. Tolerate would be better."

"It's more than I've seen him give anyone else other than Lor."

Boden was quiet for a moment, seeming to search for the words he wanted. "He actually said you could stay here for a while if you'd like."

"Stay on his ranch?"

"In my cabin. I've got the extra bedroom, and this place is off the beaten path. Good security from what I can tell. And you wouldn't be alone."

"You want me to move in here? With you?" My voice came out more high-pitched than intended.

Boden sent me a devilish grin. "You already told me you'd marry me for whoopie pies. What's being roommates on top of it?"

Such a bad idea. The worst. Yet a piece of me would've loved to hole up in this cozy cabin with Boden and shut out the world. "I can't."

"Can't or won't?"

"A little of both, honestly. My life works well how it is now. I have things the way I need them. How I like them. We don't even know for sure if foul play was involved in these deaths." All of that was the truth. But I had my doubts that everything that had happened could be a coincidence.

"I hate the idea of you being in that apartment all alone."

"I'm not alone. I have Gizmo."

Boden glanced towards our dogs, who were cuddled up together on the dog bed. "Ferocious."

My lips twitched. "He's a good first-warning system. He has a very loud bark."

"I guess that's better than nothing."

"I've talked to Hayes. He has patrols coming by on a regular basis."

Boden took a sip of his soda. "But he hasn't made any new discoveries."

I shook my head. "I talked to him right before I drove out here. No additional test results yet. Hopefully, on Monday." I picked at the corner of my bread. "It's Lisbeth's memorial tomorrow. He said he'll have plainclothes officers there, observing. Taking photos."

"Are you going?"

I nodded. "I need to."

Boden's eyes roamed my face. "But you don't want to."

"I don't do well with funerals. It brings back a lot of hard memories of a dark time. I hate the idea of caskets."

A shadow passed over his features. "It's the sea of black and the crowd that gets to me. Makes it feel like you're suffocating, even if you're standing out in the sunshine. Carissa's had so many people. Had to be hundreds. People who didn't even know her. All just wanting a look."

"I'm sorry. That must have been incredibly hard."

Boden lifted his gaze to me. "It couldn't have been a walk in the park for you, either."

"It wasn't. They waited until I was out of the hospital, but I was still in so much pain. There was so much grief in that church, it clogged the air."

"It becomes thick with all the emotion. Maybe that's what makes it hard to breathe."

"Maybe. I wished we could've honored the boy he was instead of focusing so much on the brutality of his loss. Jase gave so much to the people in his life. I wanted to hear more of that."

Boden twisted noodles around his fork. "Can you find that now?"

"I'm trying to find more of it. I think everyone who loved him needs it. I was talking to his mom, Kay, about that today. She needs to keep him alive. And talking about him helps."

Boden studied the plate in front of him. "I don't talk about Carissa. Not really."

"You can talk about her to me if you want. I'd love to know her through you." I'd lost the flare of jealousy somewhere along the way. Began to realize that Boden viewed Carissa the same way I did Jase. We'd loved them, but it was more of an immature kind of love. Maybe that would've grown and changed. Maybe it wouldn't have. But it had never gotten the chance.

"She had a real soft spot for animals of all kinds. She was involved in so many rescues, I lost count. Was always fostering a cat or dog. One year, she signed us up to foster kittens whose mother had died. Those kittens had to be bottle-fed every two hours. By the time they were old enough to be adopted, we were so sleep-deprived, I didn't trust myself to drive my damn truck."

A smile curved my lips. "It sounds like she had a good heart."

"The best." Something I couldn't identify passed over his face. "It got twisted somewhere along the way. That sensitive spirit meant she felt it all. Every bit of pain around her."

I reached out, slipping my hand into Boden's. "You can't protect someone from all the pain in the world. At some point, they have to learn to deal with it."

He stared at our joined hands, not letting go. "Sometimes, people deal with it in the worst ways."

"And that's their decision. Not yours."

"Sometimes, outside forces push someone in the wrong direction, though."

I ducked my head, trying to make contact with those hazel eyes. "Was it something you pushed her towards?"

Boden's hand tightened around mine. "No. Drugs were never my scene."

Relief swept through me at that. "Then it's not yours to carry."

"It's more complicated than that."

I waited for Boden to say more, but he didn't. I didn't want to push, not tonight. Instead, I reveled in the simple feel of my hand in his. The comfort it brought. It was that sense of comfort that had another question slipping out. "Will you go with me to the memorial tomorrow?"

Boden's hand spasmed in mine. "I don't know if that's a good idea."

I tugged my hand free, bringing it back to my glass.

"Laiken—"

"You don't have to explain. It was a dumb idea. You're trying to keep a low profile. I get it." But it didn't stop the sting.

Chapter Nineteen

Boden

THE BLADES OF THE ROCKER MADE A MEDITATIVE SOUND as I tipped back and forth in the chair. The sound soothed, but not enough. I tried to focus on watching Ramsey working with the mare, but I wasn't having much luck there either. I tried to force it, picking up my phone and sending a text to the film's screenwriter.

Me: *I think we need to leave room for more silent spaces in the film. Really show the connection between man and horse. I bet Jack can work up something amazing with the score.*

A few seconds later, my phone vibrated in my hand.

Angela: *I like that idea. I've been tweaking the love story thread. I want you to have a look at that too. Sending you the pages tonight.*

Me: *Send them whenever you're ready.*

The last thing I wanted to look at was anything to do with feelings of the heart in any way. Amber eyes full of hurt filled my mind. Laiken and I had continued our dinner last night, but she'd put a wall back up. I didn't blame her for it, either. I'd pushed for more, and then the first time she'd asked for something, for *help*, I'd cut her down. All because of cowardice.

I wasn't sure I could face a coffin at the front of a church or rows of mourners curving around a gravesite. So, instead, I'd left her to face it alone.

My phone rang, and I hurried to pull it from my pocket, hoping to see Laiken's name flash across the screen. I bit back my disappointment and slid my thumb across the glass. "Hey, Dad."

"How are things?"

Amazing. Horrible. Messy. "Good."

"Never did like single-word answers."

That had me fighting a grin—the first one since Laiken had pulled away last night. "One-word answers were always worse than cursing up a storm."

"Damn straight. So, give your old man a little more detail."

"I'm sitting on my front porch, watching a man work miracles with a horse."

"Now, that's better."

I heard a bark in the background and knew Dad must be throwing the ball for his lab, Lex, while we talked. Something about that soothed. I could picture him on the lawn that overlooked the ocean, the dog running back and forth.

"I met someone." So eased by the familiar image of my father and his dog in my mind, the words simply slipped out.

"This someone of the female variety?"

"She is."

My dad was quiet for a moment, the wind humming in the background. "That's a good thing. You deserve to be happy, Bo."

My throat burned. There had been so many days over the past six months where I hadn't been sure that was true.

Dad must've sensed my thoughts because he pushed on. "It wasn't your fault."

"I know. Most of the time. There are a lot of feelings, and they're all a tangled knot."

"That's understandable. I'd give anything to take away what happened. I don't know why Eli seems so hell-bent on taking away what makes you happy. It breaks something in me to see my boys so at odds. But everything I do just seems to make it worse."

My fingers tightened around the phone. "You're not responsible for Eli." The words were so similar to the ones Laiken had given me last night, yet I knew these were the truth.

"Aren't I? I raised him. Somewhere, I missed the mark. Maybe missed a sign I should've seen. Went too easy on him or didn't make him feel like he'd always be loved and accepted."

"Dad—"

"I'm so damn sorry. I feel like I've let you both down."

"You haven't." It stoked that simmering anger in me to think about my father, the best man I'd ever known, feeling the weight of this so heavily. "There's a cruelty in him. I don't know where it came from. A twist of a gene or something he learned along the way. But it's there. And I know he didn't get it from you or Mom."

Dad blew out a breath, the sound creating static through the speaker. "Maybe you're right." He was quiet for a moment. "Have you heard from him?"

I wouldn't lie. My dad deserved the truth, even if it hurt. "A few nasty text messages. One asking for money."

"Hell."

"I blocked the numbers he's texted from. Haven't heard from him in a few days."

"Maybe I'll go check on him—"

"Don't. He needs to find his own way, Dad. You've done enough. He knows he has an open bed at that rehab facility whenever he's ready to make the jump."

Lex barked in the background, and my dad let out a grunt as he bent to pick up her ball. "Maybe you're right. Here I am, unloading on you when I was supposed to be calling for a check-in."

"It's allowed to work both ways."

"You're right. But I want to hear about this girl of yours."

A smile curved my mouth. "She's gorgeous. Has eyes that punch right through you. She's not afraid to put me in my place."

"I love her already. She have a name?"

"Laiken." My tongue curved around the syllables, holding them for a little longer than necessary.

"Laiken. Pretty name. When do we get to meet her?"

I winced. "I don't know about that. I'm pretty sure I screwed things up last night."

"I've done that a time or two. Want to talk it through?"

That was always my dad's offer. Not that he had all the answers, but he could be a sounding board to help me find my path. I'd never been given a greater gift. "She lost a couple friends recently. There's a memorial for one today. She asked if I'd go with her. I said no."

"Why'd you do a boneheaded thing like that?"

His words startled a laugh out of me. "So much for kindness and understanding."

"Well, I didn't raise my son to be an idiot."

A little of the smile slipped off my face. "I'm not sure I can handle it. She needs someone to lean on. I'd probably be a mess just trying to keep my own demons at bay."

"Bo. She doesn't need you to be an unfeeling rock. She just needs to know she's not alone."

I stilled my rocking, replaying my dad's words in my head.

"You don't have to take care of everyone. Or fix things for everyone. Sometimes, it's enough to simply be. To hold their hand and walk alongside."

I swallowed the emotion clogging my throat. "I don't like being weak."

"It's not weakness to feel and to do it deeply. It's weak if you turn away from someone you care about when they need you. It's weak if you turn away because you're scared they'll see that depth of feeling."

Carissa had never handled my *need* well. She liked for me to be a stone fortress that she could collapse into. She rarely helped prop me up in return. But Laiken? She'd done it more times than I could count in just the few weeks I'd known her. She'd asked questions that went deeper, wanting to truly *know* me—and not just the surface-level stuff.

I pushed to my feet, sending my rocker thumping against the porch and startling Peaches awake. "I gotta go. I need to find something I can wear to a funeral."

"That's my boy. Love you, Bo."

"Love you, too, Dad. Thanks for the talk."

"Always."

I just hoped his words of wisdom hadn't come too late.

Chapter Twenty

Laiken

THE PARKING LOT OF THE CHURCH JUST OUTSIDE OF TOWN was packed. I moved between cars and trucks, gripping the strap of my purse a little tighter as my chest mirrored the action. I forced myself to inhale slowly through my nose. I focused on the barest hint of pine in the air. It was almost dormant now.

Groups of varying sizes moved towards the church door. In front of me, a woman I recognized took her husband's hand, leaning her head on his shoulder. The longing for someone to lean on hit me swift and strong. But it wasn't just *someone* I wanted. It was Boden.

I wanted to feel his callused palm pressed against mine. I wanted to feel that fire of his warming me from the outside in. A million chastisements ran through my head, my subconscious calling me every form of stupid. Boden wanted to help but only on his terms.

I rolled my shoulders back as I climbed the steps, my shoes clicking on the cement. I took one last breath of fresh air before stepping inside, hoping it would tide me over for the next hour or so. While the sun shone brightly outside, the entryway of the church immediately dimmed it. As if the building itself knew that we were in mourning.

My gaze swept the space, picking up familiar faces and strangers alike. But it stopped on someone I hadn't seen in far too long. I moved before I had a chance to second-guess myself, navigating around people until I stopped in front of the woman who used to be one of my best friends. "Hi, Marisa."

She blinked a few times as if trying to register my approach. A muscle in her jaw fluttered. "Laiken."

I guessed all wasn't forgiven. I didn't blame her. The last words we'd shared hadn't been pleasant ones. "How are you doing?"

The woman next to her stepped forward, glaring at me. "Like you care."

My pulse thrummed in my neck, but I struggled to keep my breathing even. "Hey, Kerry. Good to see you, too."

She scoffed. "You can run along now. Marisa doesn't need you around."

"I think Marisa can speak for herself."

"This isn't the time or place," Marisa bit out. "You want to talk? We can do it later. But you didn't seem all that interested in what I had to say the last time."

Her words stung. "I'm sorry I wasn't there like you needed me to be. You know where I am whenever you're ready to talk." I started to turn around and then paused. "I hope you're okay."

"Is she for real right now?" Kerry shrieked in a hushed tone.

"Leave it," Marisa said quietly.

I turned and walked away before she could say anything else. But I'd meant those words. I wanted nothing but the best for her. For all of us. Healing. Peace. Only I wasn't sure if that was possible.

Sidestepping one group and then another, I followed the flow of people into the sanctuary. I moved into the back row, and my breath caught. The coffin at the base of the altar was gleaming dark brown with a spray of pink roses covering it. Lisbeth's favorite color. Her favorite flower. Yet it all seemed so wrong.

My ribs tightened in a vise grip around my lungs. Breath

clawed at my throat, trying to get out. Everything about this was wrong. She should be here, walking the streets of Wolf Gap and studiously ignoring me. I'd take a million more of those moments where she looked at me as if I were a stranger, just to have her here.

"Laiken?" A hand closed around my elbow.

My vision swung in the direction of the voice. My eyes met deep brown ones. "Isaac."

Worry lined his face. "Are you okay?"

"I don't think so."

"Come on." He guided me out of the pew, past the stream of people, to a quiet corner of the lobby. "Just breathe."

I nodded, trying to get my lungs to cooperate. It took a few tries, but they finally obeyed. Jerky spasms of muscles, but it at least moved the air in and out.

"Sorry," I croaked.

"You don't have to apologize."

I searched the face I used to know so well. "I wasn't sure if you'd be here."

His brows pulled together. "Where else would I be?"

"I don't know. Hayes said you were out of town."

Isaac nodded, glancing away towards the people still coming in from the cold. "Work trip. He got ahold of me once I was back."

"He told you about what he thinks is happening?"

Isaac's gaze swung back to me. "This is fucked, Laik."

I winced at the nickname no one used anymore. The one that had been retired all those years ago because it had belonged to someone else. "He doesn't know for sure. They could be accidents."

Anger flashed in the dark eyes staring back at me. "Three of us within a year? Either God hates us, or someone is taking us out one by one."

A shiver skated down my spine, and I couldn't help but scan the room for any eyes focused on us. Nothing seemed out of place. "Hayes is doing everything he can to figure out what's going on. We just have to be careful in the meantime."

Isaac scoffed. "Hayes is a good man, but this town doesn't have the resources for this kind of thing. I'm thinking about getting out of dodge for a while. You should do the same."

"I can't. My life is here. My business. My friends."

"None of that matters if you get dead."

My stomach roiled. "I need to find a restroom. I'll see you back inside."

I hurried for the stairs before he could say another word. I remembered from my Sunday school days that there was a bathroom upstairs. It was a single room instead of a row of stalls. I jerked open the door and then slammed it behind me, barely throwing the lock and making it to the toilet before my stomach emptied itself. I heaved and heaved, even after nothing remained.

The cool tile seeped in through my tights, and I fought the urge to let myself sink down onto it. Instead, I pushed to my feet and flushed away the evidence of my sickness. I ran the water as cold as it would go, washing my hands and rinsing out my mouth. I breathed a sigh of relief at the mouthwash and tiny cups on the counter. Swirling the minty liquid around in my mouth, I breathed through my nose.

I spat out the mouthwash and straightened. My reflection might as well have been that of a ghost. I was so pale it was a miracle there was any blood in my head at all. I tried pinching my cheeks, but it only had a minimal effect.

"Get it together," I whispered to the woman in the mirror. "This is not about you."

I squeezed my eyes closed, thinking about Lisbeth's parents. How much they must be hurting. How they needed to know that she was loved and would be missed.

It was enough to have me unlocking the door and stepping out into the hall. The voices were quieter now, and I knew people were likely finding their seats for the start of the service. I hurried down the stairs and rounded the corner, colliding with a wall of muscle.

I immediately stepped back. "I'm so sorry. I didn't see—"

My words cut off as a different set of dark eyes glared back at me. "Never have any consideration for the ramifications of your actions, do you?"

"Jax, I can't do this today. Can you hold on to hatred and vitriol for just twenty-four hours? I'll let you spew it all tomorrow. I just don't have it in me to deal with it today."

He was stunned silent, but only for a moment. His jaw hardened, and I swore I heard his teeth grinding together. "It's always all about you."

"No, it's about Lisbeth. I'm trying to be here for her family. To show up, even though it's tearing me up inside. All I'm asking is that you have a little compassion."

He should know better than anyone. We'd sat at the front of that sanctuary, doing our best to say goodbye to Jase. Jax should know how hard it was to walk in there. I'd never understand why we couldn't support each other instead of battling the way we did.

His hands fisted at his sides. "I heard you're fucking the movie star."

My spine jerked straight, sending sparks of pain through my back. "Excuse me?"

"You heard me. How long did it take for you to spread your legs? Half a second?"

"Who I have a relationship with is none of your damn business."

Jax's knuckles cracked, the sound echoing in the mostly empty lobby. "I guess I just thought you were pickier than that. Took you forever to give it up to Jase. But I guess he wasn't rich and famous. He was just the chump who loved you. And all it did was get him killed."

Chapter Twenty-One

Boden

I PULLED MY TRUCK INTO A SPOT AT THE BACK OF THE church's lot. The space was jam-packed with vehicles. The crowdedness had me loosening my tie a fraction.

Shutting off my engine, I slid out and hit the locks. A few stragglers like me hurried inside. I picked up my pace, moving across the lawn towards the sanctuary.

A tiny form stepped into my path. The little boy's eyes went wide, and his mouth fell open. "You're—you're—"

I held a single finger to my lips. "On an undercover mission."

He bobbed his head up and down. "Rescuing someone? I saw all the movies. The one when you saved the president from the evil guys from Zoltran is my *favorite*."

I smiled down at him but couldn't help glancing around to see if anyone else noticed. A woman who looked to be in her thirties hurried over. "Tim, what did I tell you about talking to strangers? I'm so sorry if he was bothering you. He's overly friendly. We're trying to work on it."

"*Moooooom*, he's not a stranger. He's Boden Cavanaugh. He's the Iron Fist."

The woman's eyes widened. "Holy—" She snapped her mouth closed before the curse slipped free.

"It's so nice to meet you, Tim. I need to get inside, but if your mom here gives me her email, I'll make sure to send you some fun stuff."

"No way! That would be so cool. Give him your email, Mom!"

The woman fished in her purse, pulling out a business card. "Here you go. That's incredibly kind of you. You're making his year."

"No problem. I'd just appreciate you keeping this between us. I'm trying to keep a low profile here."

"Of course," she assured me.

Tim grinned. "Undercover mission. This is so freaking cool!"

I held out a hand for a high-five. "You're officially my sidekick."

The little boy squealed and turned back to his mom as I jogged up the front steps. The person ahead of me held the door open, their eyes flaring a fraction as they took me in. I grabbed hold of the edge of the wood. "Thank you."

"Uh, sure." The guy shook his head and headed for the sanctuary.

I started to follow when I heard a familiar voice. Laiken telling someone that who she had a relationship with was none of their damn business. I turned, moving towards the sound, and then stopped dead in my tracks.

A guy with broad shoulders and a large frame had her backed against a wall, towering over her. I saw red. The words he spewed only turned that anger to fury.

I strode forward and grabbed hold of the man's shoulder, jerking him back. "Stay the hell away from her."

The man's eyes flared, and then he shoved at my chest. "Get your hands off me, you piece of shit."

"I'm not going to stand here while you threaten someone I care about. You think it makes you a man to use your size to intimidate? It makes you scum."

Hands wrapped around my arm, gently tugging me back. "I'm

fine. Really. But I won't be if you punch him—even though it would be fun to watch."

I would've laughed if the rage still hadn't had a hold on me—still licking through my veins, demanding payment from the asshole in front of me.

"Jax, walk away. He'll hit you, and I won't be able to stop him."

Jax scoffed, glaring at me. "You think I'm scared of that piece-of-shit actor? He probably doesn't even know how to throw a punch."

"Come outside, and I'll be happy to demonstrate."

"Now, boys." Gilly sauntered up and stepped between us, placing a palm on both of our chests. "I think violence is the last thing we need right now." She turned, linking her arm through Jax's. "Darling, you're going to escort your most beloved aunt inside now."

"Gilly—"

"No buts. Be the gentleman I know you can be."

He sent one last glare in my and Laiken's direction and then strode towards the sanctuary. I felt Laiken sigh with relief. I turned around, hands framing her face, eyes scanning her body. "Did he hurt you?"

Her eyes widened. "No. Nothing like that."

"Who was that?"

Laiken swallowed, glancing to the spot where Gilly and Jax had disappeared. "Jase's brother."

My muscles locked. I'd only seen that kind of rage on one other person. The type of deep hatred that ate a person alive until you no longer recognized them. *My* brother. "Why is he talking to you that way?" I struggled to get each word out. To keep from grabbing Laiken and taking her far away from here.

"He's angry. Has been since the accident. He can't seem to let that anger go."

Because if he let it go, he'd have to feel the grief. Some people would do anything to avoid that.

I brushed the hair away from Laiken's face, relishing the feel of her skin against my fingertips. Letting the knowledge that she was here and safe soothe the worst of my raw edges. "Why isn't he turning that anger on the person responsible?"

"He did. Jax spent so much time, energy, and money trying to keep Robert Aaron in prison. He wrote letters every month to the parole board. Testified at every hearing. He's the main reason Robert didn't get released before his time was up. When his sentence was coming to a close, Jax hired lawyer after lawyer to try to come up with other things they could charge Robert with. Jax won a civil suit. But it was for monetary damages, and Robert had already filed for bankruptcy from his own lawyer fees."

Laiken's shoulders slumped with a bone-deep fatigue that was written over every part of her. "It was never enough for Jax. He was mad at everyone who could've had a role in things turning out differently."

"What is he mad at you for?"

Tears welled in Laiken's eyes. "We heard Jax was throwing a party that night. Kay and Chip were out of town at one of Serena's cheer competitions. He'd been getting into more and more trouble. The Grangers were all fighting more because of it. Jase didn't want to deal with it. But I pushed. Said we could go and make sure things stayed under control."

I pulled her into my arms, and Laiken didn't fight it. Instead, she burrowed against my chest, grabbing hold of my jacket. "If I hadn't have done that, we'd have been driving in the opposite direction. We never would've come across Robert Aaron."

My lips ghosted over Laiken's hair, the scent of something that was a mix of vanilla and spice filling my senses. "The only thing you're guilty of is caring. You loved the Grangers. You cared about Jax. About Jase. About all of them. What happened isn't your fault."

"I know that. In my head, I do. But my heart doesn't always believe me. We were all shattered by that one moment. And I can't help but think about all the ways it might not have happened."

"That's natural. Human. But Jax doesn't get to dump his shit on you on top of it."

Laiken pressed her cheek against my chest. "I'm tired of it."

"It stops. Now."

One side of her mouth lifted. "I hate to break it to you, but you aren't controller of the Universe. Jax spews garbage. It's what he does."

"He won't if I'm around." I wouldn't let Laiken be exposed to someone who had the same capacity to harbor twisted hate as my brother did.

"You won't be here forever, Boden. Just like you can't be with me every second of every day. I have to find my own way with Jax. I'm just not sure what that'll look like."

A muscle in my cheek ticked. "We'll see about that."

Laiken shook her head and then looked up into my eyes. "You came. You didn't want to. But you came."

"I'm sorry I wasn't here earlier."

"You're here now. That's what counts."

I bent, pressing my lips to her temple. "I'm with you, Laiken. I might not do it perfectly, I might be a mess, but I'm here."

"That's all I want."

Music started, and I pulled back. "We should go inside."

Laiken nodded and slipped her hand into mine. It fit perfectly. Those delicate fingers weaved through mine, balancing something deep within me. A few more of those ragged edges around my heart soothed at the touch.

She led me to one of the back pews, and we slid in next to a man I didn't recognize. His eyes flashed in recognition, and he muttered something under his breath that I didn't quite catch, then turned to face the front of the church. Laiken kept a hold of my hand.

She didn't let go when the music ended, or when the pastor began speaking. She didn't let go when Lisbeth's cousin gave a moving eulogy. She didn't waver once. We leaned on each other, getting through the best we could. And in that moment, I knew this was how it could always be. A give and take. A sort of messy perfection that was the most incredible thing I'd ever experienced. And I'd do anything to protect it.

Chapter Twenty-Two

Laiken

BODEN AND I MOVED QUICKLY OUT OF THE CHURCH. I'D heard the telltale sign of whispers; his name lifted on the stale air filling the sanctuary. As we hit the stone steps, I looked up at him, worry furrowing my brow. "I didn't think so many people would recognize you so quickly. I wasn't thinking."

"It's okay."

"It's not. I want you to have your peace here." He'd lived with eyes on him for so long. I wanted him to have a break from that for once.

Boden slowed his pace as we hit the parking lot. "Word was bound to get around. It's not like I'm hiding out. I'm going to restaurants, The Gallery, the grocery store. Hopefully, now, gossip will spread, and then things will die down."

God, I hoped he was right.

Boden cupped my face in his hands. "You hanging in there?"

"Yeah. It helped to have you there. A lot. Thank you."

He kissed my temple again. The feel of those lips skating across my skin only made me want to lean closer. That flame, pulling me in.

"Will you do me a favor?" he whispered.

"What?"

"Stay with me tonight."

"Boden."

"What?"

The question danced over my skin. "I don't know if I can go *there* with you. I…" My words trailed off because I wasn't sure how to explain that I was terrified—for so many different reasons, I couldn't explain them all.

"You can sleep anywhere you want. Couch. Guest room. My bed. Wherever. I'm not in a hurry. We have all the time in the world."

Only I wasn't sure we did. At some point, Boden would have to go film his movie. He'd have to return to his life in LA. And I would be left behind. I'd already been shattered once. I didn't think I'd survive it a second time.

This time when I woke pressed against Boden on the couch, I fought back the rising panic. I didn't let myself get pulled under the way I had last time. Instead, I simply breathed. I let myself feel Boden's heat, the kiss of the flames that were at the core of his very being.

His hand trailed up and down my back, tracing a lazy, nonsensical design. "You freaking out on me?"

I shook my head against his chest. "You're warm. Like my own personal space heater."

Boden chuckled. "Not sure I've ever been called that before. I guess it comes in handy when the fire died out overnight."

I burrowed deeper into his hold, giving myself a few more moments to revel in the feeling. More than warmth, it was safety, comfort, a sense of being *known* in a way I hadn't felt in forever. "I don't want to move."

"Don't."

"I have to open the gallery in a little bit."

Boden shifted so we were face-to-face and swept my hair out of my eyes. "Have breakfast with me first. I promise that even I can't screw up cereal."

My mouth curved as I searched those hazel eyes. I wasn't even sure what I was looking for. Reassurance maybe? A certainty that was completely unfair to hope for? "What are my options?"

He beamed and shifted to stand, holding out a hand to me. "I've got some healthy thing that tastes like cardboard, and I've got Lucky Charms. What'll it be?"

I arched a brow. "Do I look like an idiot to you?"

Boden chuckled and led me into the kitchen, not letting go until he reached for the box of Lucky Charms. I felt the loss instantly. That sensation sent a jolt through me. But I kept breathing. I focused on making coffee for myself and Boden.

"Cream? Sugar?" I asked as I poured the liquid into two mugs.

"Splash of half and half."

I tipped the carton to Boden's coffee, turning the dark substance a creamy brown. "It feels weird that I didn't know how you like your coffee. I feel like we know each other better than that." He'd held me all night. Been there when I needed him. I should know the daily minutia, too.

Boden took the mug from my hand. "I'd rather know the real stuff."

"And that is?"

"What pulls you to make the art you do? You letting me into your world when you're hurting. Giving me the grace to stumble like you did yesterday and finding our way afterwards."

Warmth bloomed in my belly. Not a sexual heat but something even better. "It's an authentic knowing."

Boden dipped his spoon into his cereal. "Exactly."

We covered the other side of the coin over breakfast. Favorite takeout. His was Thai. Mine was Italian. And dozens of other favorites. Movie growing up. Place he'd traveled to. Way to spend a rainy Sunday. The tiny little intimacies made me paint a fuller picture of the man across from me.

I glanced at the clock on the wall. "I really should go."

"I've got these," Boden said, taking our bowls as he stood. He paused for a moment, the sudden absence of that charming surety in his expression. "Can I pick you up after work? Dinner and a movie?"

I tamped down the panic that rose in me at that question. Because the truth was, I was powerless to say no. I wanted more time with Boden, even knowing he'd leave. "I get done at four." Those flames reached out and licked my skin. But I couldn't turn away. I needed more of these moments with Boden. Something that was only ours.

Before I could consider how unwise making plans with him was, I hurried into the bathroom to change into my clothes from the day before. I didn't worry about pulling on the tights, simply went for the dress. I hated shrouding myself in black even a moment longer than necessary, but I didn't want to get to the gallery in Boden's sweatpants and t-shirt either.

When I walked out, Boden was giving the dogs treats.

"No wonder Gizmo's always so happy to see you."

Boden gave me a sheepish shrug. "I'm not above bribery."

"Good to know." I lifted Gizmo into my arms, ignoring the blooming pain in my back. "I'll see you tonight." My words came out awkwardly as if I weren't sure how to say goodbye.

Boden had no such reservations. He pulled me into his arms and pressed a kiss to the top of my head. "Call me if you need me. Or if Jax shows up."

That thought had my stomach tightening. I didn't have it in me to go another round with Jax this soon. "I will."

"You said that too quickly." Boden brushed the hair away from my face. "Please, call. Even if you don't need me. If you'd just like me to be there. I could be your assistant for the day."

"I bet we'd be the most popular shop in town."

He grimaced. "Having a recognizable face does have its downside sometimes."

I pressed my palm against his chest. "I promise not to sell you out to the residents of Wolf Gap. And I promise I'll call if I run into trouble or get bored."

"Good."

I pulled out of Boden's embrace before I had a chance to reconsider. Those arms could hold me hostage without even trying. I focused on only the next step: getting Gizmo in his car seat and then pulling down the drive. I fought the urge to look in the rearview mirror but ultimately couldn't hold out.

Boden stood there, framed by the door, looking intently at my SUV. Our eyes met in the mirror, and I swore he saw into my very soul. I tore my gaze away and focused on the road.

It had been so long since I'd felt truly seen. There were so many pieces of myself that I held back. Pieces that I could protect if I didn't expose them. But it was as if Boden had a radar for them all.

I pulled into my parking spot behind The Gallery and turned off the engine. Gizmo let out a little whine.

"I know. I didn't want to leave either." I climbed out of the SUV and retrieved him from the backseat, setting him down on the ground. He hurried to the back door. I fumbled with my keys, searching for the right one.

A shadow fell over the door. I jolted, whirling around, keys clutched in my hand as Gizmo let out a series of barks. My hand flew to my chest as I let out a whoosh of air. "Marisa."

"Sorry. I thought you heard me." Her gaze darted around the alley as if she were expecting someone else to pop out at any moment.

A shiver skated down my spine, and I hurried to unlock the door. "I think we're all a little jumpy these days. Come on in."

Gizmo led the way but cast a few leery looks back at Marisa. I made quick work of getting him some breakfast. "Can I get you some coffee, hot chocolate, or tea?"

She shook her head. "No, I'm good."

I set to work making myself some tea. The busy work for my hands helped as I waited for Marisa to speak.

"You're dating Boden Cavanaugh?"

It wasn't the question I'd thought she would lead with, but I didn't blame her for being curious.

"I don't know that I'd go that far. We're…friends." That wasn't right, either. There wasn't a term that felt like it fit Boden and me.

"I'd say it was more than that. I heard he nearly knocked Jax out."

Great. Just what Boden didn't need, the town gossiping about him getting into an altercation.

I poured hot water over my tea bag. "It's Jax. Everyone's a breath away from knocking him out."

Marisa choked on a laugh. "I guess that's true."

How long had it been since I'd heard my friend laugh? I honestly couldn't remember. Was it before the accident? "I'm sorry, Marisa. I hate that I let things get to the point they're at now."

She stiffened, her eyes hardening. "I told you Scott didn't kill himself."

"I never said that he did. Accidental overdoses happen all the time."

"It wasn't an accident, either. We know that now."

I wrapped my hands around my mug, trying to fight back the worst of the chill. "Have you talked to Hayes? Does he know that for sure?"

Marisa's mouth pressed into a firm line. "He says he's still looking into it. But I know Scott. He wouldn't have. He knew how much losing Jase hurt us. He wouldn't have been so reckless with his life."

Except he was. Every time he chased the high instead of getting help like Marisa begged him to do. But none of that mattered now. "I'm so sorry you lost him."

We were both members of a club neither of us applied to join. And it was the last thing I wanted for her.

Marisa's eyes flashed. "Stop placating me."

"I'm not—"

"You don't know the first thing about Scott."

Maybe I didn't. Maybe none of us knew each other as well as we thought we did. "Okay."

"Okay?"

"I'm not going to sit here and argue with you. I don't know what happened. All I know is that we've lost four friends. *Four.* I don't want to lose another. I want us to watch our backs. And if we can, be there for one another."

Marisa turned to stare at my photograph propped up against the wall. The one of the older man with grief etched onto his face. "I think it's too late. We're different people than we were then. I don't even know you."

"You could." I stretched out a hand. "I'm Laiken."

Marisa stared down at my hand for a few long beats before stepping away. Tears filled her eyes. "I'm sorry. I can't. It's too hard."

And with that, she vanished out the back door—just like all the people I'd lost before her.

Chapter Twenty-Three

Boden

I PULLED INTO A PARKING SPOT IN FRONT OF THE GALLERY. Turning off the engine, I sat there for a moment, just watching. Laiken was talking to a couple I didn't recognize. A smile curved her lips, but there was something false about it. Even a dozen yards away, I could read the lines of strain bracketing her mouth. I couldn't tell if they were there from physical pain or emotional.

The couple shook Laiken's hand and exited the gallery as I climbed out of my truck. I double-checked to make sure the window was cracked, but Peaches didn't stir when I shut my door, just kept snoring away. My gaze tracked Laiken as I moved towards the door.

She turned as the bell sounded, a forced smile on her face. It melted away the second she saw me. That small action eased something in me. Laiken wasn't pretending around me anymore.

I crossed the space, my boots echoing on the polished cement floor. I pulled her into my arms. "What's wrong?"

"Long day. A friend who was in the accident with me showed up. It wasn't the easiest conversation. A lot of things to get sorted before the next opening. Patrons coming in. I'm just so tired." Laiken tipped forward, letting her head fall against my chest.

She was leaning. Reaching out. Seeking comfort. It felt so damn good. And I hoped I didn't ruin it by what I was about to say next. "Can you pack a bag?"

Laiken straightened, blinking a few times. "To spend the night?"

"I got a line on a cabin we can use for a few days. It's high up in the mountains. I think it'll be a great place to unplug, take some photos, relax."

"I have to work—"

"I talked to Gilly and Addie. They can cover for you."

Her mouth fell open. "You talked to Gilly and Addie?"

The corner of my mouth kicked up. "I do know how to use a phone."

Laiken scowled at me. "That's not what I meant. You know, you're very pushy."

I nuzzled the side of her neck, breathing in the scent that was only Laiken's. "Not pushy. I go after what I want."

"Spoiled."

I grinned against her neck. "Maybe a little."

"This is the last thing I should be agreeing to."

"Why's that?"

Laiken pulled back a fraction, her amber eyes glowing. "A million different reasons."

There was such pain in those words. A fear I could feel skating across my skin. "But you're saying yes anyway."

"I am."

The feel of victory surged through me, and I laced my fingers with Laiken's. "We'll go as slowly as you want. But I'm damn happy you're taking the first step."

She rolled her lips together. "We're going now?"

"Not giving you a chance to change your mind."

Her eyes flashed. "That's why you didn't say anything last night or whenever you cooked up this scheme, isn't it?"

"I'm not stupid."

She grumbled something about pushy men under her breath as she headed towards the back of the gallery. Gizmo's tags jingled as he got up from his bed. He let out a bark when he saw me, charging over.

I bent and picked him up, wheels and all. "Don't worry. Your girlfriend's in the truck." He licked my face. "You'll get a few uninterrupted days with her."

Laiken started up the stairs, motioning for me to follow. "I'm not sure how we'll tear them apart after that."

I wasn't sure how I'd tear myself away from Laiken, either. The more time I spent with her, the more I wanted. She opened the door to her apartment and stepped inside. "Make yourself comfortable. It'll just take me a few minutes to pack."

"There's snow up there, so bring some gear."

She shot me a wan smile. "I *have* lived here all my life. I know there's snow in the mountains. It's there in the height of summer."

"Just don't want you cranky because you're freezing your cute butt off."

Laiken shook her head, turning back towards her bedroom area. But I didn't miss the hint of pink on her cheeks. As she packed, I studied her space, petting Gizmo as I did. The walls were jam-packed with art. It should've felt crowded. Oppressive. But it didn't. Instead, it made you want to lean closer.

The arrangement of the pieces was art in itself. You could step back and look at the whole or let yourself be pulled into one piece after another. I knew she had taken some of the photos. There were also watercolors. Oils. Pastels. Some had names I didn't recognize. Others were missing signatures altogether.

I completely lost track of time until I felt a presence next to me as I studied a pastel. It was of the mountains here in Wolf Gap. Ominous clouds gathered over it, swirling with pent-up rage. "You did this, didn't you?"

"How did you know?"

"It has that same visceral feeling I got from looking at the photo I bought. That same feeling that grabbed me by the throat and forced me to pay attention."

"Some people don't like that feeling."

I turned to face Laiken. "I do. It reminds me that I'm alive. Challenges me to not look away from whatever it is I'm feeling."

She let out a shaky breath. "When you talk about my art…it's like you say the exact thing I most want to hear."

"I'm not trying to win you over. I'm just speaking the truth."

"Thank you."

All I wanted in that moment was to kiss her. To take her mouth. To lose myself in the swirl of color that I knew the two of us would make. Instead, I forced myself to break the stare. I glanced down at her bag. "You ready?"

A hint of disappointment flashed across Laiken's expression. "If you can grab Gizmo's food and my camera bag, I am."

"I think I can handle that."

Laiken lifted the bag onto her shoulder, and I didn't miss the slight hitch in her movement.

"I can get this, too. Plenty of arm space."

She eyed Gizmo, happily snoozing in my hold. "He might disagree."

"I don't want you to hurt yourself."

"Boden. I hurt every day. It's life. I know how to manage it. I know what my limits are. Sometimes, it's worth it to go past those limits. Other times, it isn't. But you have to let me navigate that."

I bit the inside of my cheek. "I'm just saying I can help."

"And I'm letting you. You're getting the dog, the dog food, my camera. It's enough."

"Okay."

She arched a brow in question.

"You know what you can handle."

"Thank you." Laiken stretched up on her toes to kiss my cheek.

I swore the spot where she kissed me burned. The heat didn't wane as we gathered her gear or when we headed downstairs and outside. Even the bite of cold in the air didn't dull it.

Peaches barked happily the moment she caught Gizmo's scent. Laiken unhooked his wheels and put him in the backseat.

"Will he be okay without his car seat thing?" I asked.

"I've got this." She hooked a short strap to his harness and then clicked it into the seat belt. Peaches nosed her, trying to get to Gizmo. Laiken laughed, and the sound shot straight through my chest. "All right, he's all yours now."

The dogs licked each other and then cuddled up into a ball. I grinned. "I think they'll be happy."

"No kidding." She shut the door but paused before climbing in. "You're sure you want to be holed up with me for a few days?"

I leaned over, tucking a strand of hair behind her ear, and letting my hand linger on her neck. "Never been more sure of anything in my life."

I watched her breath hitch and couldn't help but smile. That curve of my mouth made Laiken scowl. "You don't have to be so cocky."

I grinned wider. "I like knowing that I affect you."

She grumbled something under her breath about me being too handsome for my own good and then climbed into my truck.

I rounded the vehicle and got behind the wheel. "Don't worry. I only use my powers for good."

Laiken rolled her eyes. "Cocky."

"Sure of myself."

"Same difference."

I pulled out of the parking space and headed towards the mountains. We listened to the radio for as long as the signal lasted, flipping back and forth between country and rock stations. When the last signal finally went to static, Laiken clicked off the stereo. "I love it up here."

I glanced over to see her staring up at the snow-covered peaks. "It's pretty incredible. Makes you realize just how small you are in the grand scheme of things."

"I love that, too."

The alert for my four-wheel-drive sounded as the snow

deepened. I focused back on the road, guiding my truck around curves and bends. The road narrowed, the forest closing in around us for a stretch before the trees fell away to reveal a cabin. It was modest in size but expertly designed. It could've been on a Christmas card with its log walls and red front door, all nestled in the snow.

"It's perfect," Laiken whispered. She pushed her face up to the window. "And there are a million backdrops I can't wait to use for photos."

"I can't wait to play assistant."

"You might regret saying that when your toes are freezing."

I parked in front of the cabin and turned off the engine. "I'm tough."

Her lips twitched. "You've already admitted you're a spoiled actor."

"Can't I be both?"

"I guess there's no reason why not."

"Good." I pushed open my door. "Let's check this place out."

We gave the dogs a command to stay and started towards the cabin. Snow covered any sort of path and the front steps, but the porch was dry. I pulled out the keys Hayes had given me and unlocked the front door, tugging it open.

As we stepped inside, a low-level heat greeted us. I was sure the temperature was whatever was required to keep the pipes from freezing. The living area was one big room that held a large stone fireplace bracketed by windows. There was a comfortable-looking couch, a couple of overstuffed armchairs, and bookcases ladened with worn paperbacks.

Laiken was already moving towards those shelves. "It's been so long since I've read a whole book in a few days."

"Now's the time." I could see us here, curled up on the couch. Laiken reading and me simply staring at her.

She plucked a Stephen King novel from the bookcase. "I never read horror when I'm home alone, but since I know you'll be in the next room, it's the perfect time."

I didn't want to sleep in separate rooms. I wanted the feel of Laiken's body against mine. I'd never slept better than the two nights we'd fallen asleep on my couch. But I also didn't want to push. Instead, I shot her a grin. "You can wake me up anytime. I'll chase the bogeymen away."

Chapter Twenty-Four

Laiken

I ROLLED TO MY BACK IN BED, JUST A HINT OF LIGHT SEEPING through the curtained window. The bed felt cold. Not because the heat was too low, but because I knew I could've had Boden's fire next to me. I could've had that heat kissing my skin all night long. Instead, I'd gone to bed alone with nothing but Stephen King to keep me company. Even Gizmo had abandoned me, choosing to curl up on the dog bed with Peaches.

I swung my legs over the side of the bed and stood, crossing to the window. I pulled back the curtain, and my jaw dropped open. I could no longer see any glimpse of my beautiful mountains. Thick, gray clouds covered the peaks, and snow swirled in thick rivulets. The ground, which already had a dusting, was now completely covered in the white stuff.

I hurried out of the bedroom. "Boden?"

He stumbled out of his bedroom, rubbing at his eyes. "You okay?"

"Did you check the weather before we left yesterday?"

He nodded. "It called for snow flurries today. Sun tomorrow."

I grabbed his hand and tugged him towards the front door.

Opening it, a blast of freezing air hit us. "I don't think this is flurries."

There had to be at least two feet already, and it was accumulating fast. Boden's eyes bugged. "Shit. There's no way we'll be able to drive in this."

"You said it was Hayes who hooked you up with the cabin?"

"Yeah, it belongs to one of his friends."

"He knows we're here. He'll get a plow up here once the snow stops." It wasn't as if we could call anyone. There was zero phone service up here. I stepped back inside, closing the door. "I hope you brought enough food in case we get stuck up here."

Boden grinned. "Who do you think you're talking to?"

"What was I thinking? There's probably enough in the kitchen to get us through a nuclear attack."

He shrugged. "Better safe than sorry."

I moved to the dog bed and hooked Gizmo up to his wheels. "Did you see a snow shovel anywhere? Gizmo will drown in that much snow if I don't clear a path."

"There's one in the mudroom. I got it." He was already moving to the small storage space near the front door. I followed behind, grabbing my jacket as I slipped my sock-covered feet into snow boots. Boden did the same and headed outside.

I followed behind, lifting Gizmo into my arms. The wind blew a harsh gust into us, and Boden let out a stream of curses.

"They don't get weather like this much in LA, do they?"

He quickly carved out a small area for Gizmo. "They definitely don't."

I set my little monster down, and he hurried to do his business. Gizmo knew that snow meant you moved quickly. Peaches followed behind, doing the same.

"I don't think Peaches has ever moved that fast before. She's usually sniffing everything under the sun."

"She's not dumb, and it's freaking freezing out here." I hurried to pick Gizmo up, and we headed back towards the cabin.

Boden left the snow shovel leaning against the house, knowing we'd need it again. As soon as we were inside, we ditched the snow gear, and Boden moved towards the fireplace. "At least we've got plenty of firewood."

There were rows of the stuff stacked on the back porch that could keep us warm for weeks. As soon as the fire was going, Boden pushed to his feet again. "So, what do you do in the middle of a blizzard?"

I grinned. "We need hot chocolate and board games."

Boden threw down his cards. "You're a dirty cheater. I don't know how you do it, but you do. Is this a rigged deck?"

I couldn't hold in my laughter. "You found the deck. How could I have rigged it?"

He eyed me suspiciously. "Maybe you planted it here."

"I didn't even know where *here* was. You sprung this trip on me, remember?"

Boden growled something under his breath.

"You really are a sore loser. You know that, right?"

He glared at me. "You would be, too, if you lost all but two hands of gin rummy all day long."

Something about how utterly flabbergasted he was at that truth had me laughing even harder. "I guess gin rummy isn't your game."

"I guess not," he muttered.

I looked around the room. We'd spent all day in front of the fire, eating, playing cards, and talking. It felt so normal. A break I hadn't realized how badly I needed. "How about something a little different?"

"Strip poker?" Boden asked hopefully.

I snorted. "Not exactly. Let me take your portrait."

He stiffened, and I wanted to swallow those words back instantly. "Never mind. That was a dumb idea—"

"No. I just—I haven't had a ton of good experiences with picture taking."

"I get that." I could only imagine how oppressive it would be to feel as though you couldn't leave your house without being hounded by photographers. It didn't matter that what I was doing wasn't the same, it was still a camera in your face.

"Let's do it."

"Boden—"

"No, I want to see how it is you do what you do."

I stared at him for a moment, trying to read beneath his words. I could only see truth there, even if it *was* a little hesitant. "If you want to stop at any point, just say the word."

Boden nodded.

I pushed to my feet and grabbed my camera bag from my bedroom. In under a minute, I had the lens I wanted. One that was perfect for the low light of the cabin. The gray skies had continued all day, and even now that night had fallen, the snow wasn't showing any signs of letting up.

"Scoot back a few feet, closer to the fire."

Boden did as I instructed.

"Turn a little this way." I made a motion with my hand.

The light from the fire hit his face just right, the glow an orangey gold that mirrored what I always felt coming from Boden. I snapped a quick shot to test my settings.

"Wait, I wasn't ready."

A smile teased my lips. "It was just a test shot to see the light and settings."

"Oh." He paused for a moment, studying me. "What do you typically tell your models?"

"We usually just talk."

"About?"

"I've usually approached them because I can sense a sort of pain in them." I toyed with the strap on my camera. "That sounds awful."

"No, it doesn't." Boden shifted his weight so that he was leaning to one side, closer to me. "You felt a kindredness. You wanted to bring that pain to light."

"You don't think it's taking advantage?"

"Do you push people who don't want to talk to you or have their photo taken?"

"No."

Boden brushed his hair out of his face. "I knew that without even asking. You've given people a chance to get their pain out. A safe space to do that in whatever way they're comfortable with."

My chest tightened at his words, at the knowledge that Boden understood me. And not just what I was trying to achieve with my art but also my heart. "You want to go there with me?"

A hint of apprehension passed through those hazel eyes. "Yes."

That word alone was a gift. I raised my camera, balancing my arms on my knees where I sat on the floor. "You get to choose what you let out. Hold an image of something in your mind. Something you want to release."

Boden's eyes moved back and forth as if he were going through a catalogue of images in his mind. His Adam's apple bobbed as he swallowed. "Okay."

"Just hold it there. Lightly in your mind. Focus on the details. One thing at a time."

I pressed my finger down on the shutter. Boden jolted slightly with the first click but soon grew accustomed to the sound. I shifted positions, trying different angles. I could see hints of the emotion swirling beneath the surface, but it wasn't enough. He still had a stranglehold on it.

"Talk me through what you see," I said softly.

"Carissa." Boden's voice was raw. "How she was when we were growing up. When we fell into that puppy love. Where we always should've stayed."

My heart ached for that loss. The innocence that had been stolen in so many ways.

"Paint the picture for me."

"We're at my parents' place in Big Sur. She came with us sometimes in the summers. She's standing at the cliffs. Her hair's blowing behind her, those blond strands wild on the wind. Then she glances over her shoulder. It's the happiest I've ever seen her."

Boden struggled to get the next words out. "I don't know why she couldn't stay that way. If it was something I did. Some way that I failed her."

The first hint of true pain slipped free. I pressed down on the shutter. "You didn't fail her."

A different sort of flame licked through Boden's irises. Ones that spoke of deep-seated anger. "You don't know that."

I clicked again. "Call it an educated guess."

A muscle in his jaw ticked. "She cheated on me."

I stilled, my finger freezing, but I didn't leave the shield of my camera. "I'm so sorry—"

"You don't have to be sorry," he bit out. "I'm just saying that I obviously failed her somehow. Wasn't enough. She went to someone else. To drugs. She didn't come to me. I would've tried to help."

"I know you would've. But people seek out drugs to numb themselves, Boden."

"I know that." He looked towards the flames dancing in the hearth. The grief and anger mixed then, and I took another photo.

"I'm so mad at her. And I fucking miss her. Not our relationship, but my friend. And then I feel guilty for all of it. It's this ugly stew, swirling inside me."

Boden's hand clenched into a fist as he spoke, his knuckles bleaching white. This was it. What I wanted the world to know. That you could feel it all. Every single emotion, all at the same time. To normalize that black stew Boden spoke of.

"Just because she's gone doesn't mean you can't be angry. Just because you realize you were better as friends doesn't mean you aren't allowed to miss her."

A single tear slid down Boden's stubble-covered cheek. It was too much. I couldn't hide behind my lens and not be with him in this. I set my camera down and scooted over to him. I cupped his face in my hands, feeling the stubble and that single track of wetness. "You loved her the best you could."

"I should've let her go a long time ago."

"Maybe so. But you holding on isn't what did this to her. That was Carissa's choice."

Something dark swirled in Boden's eyes. "Maybe."

My thumbs swept back and forth across his face. "You'll see that one day. You will."

He leaned forward, his forehead resting against mine. "It's the first time I've said it out loud. That I'm angry."

"How did it feel?"

"Like some of that weight lifted off my shoulders."

"Sometimes, simply saying the words helps. It doesn't change anything, but you're sharing that burden with another human. It lessens the load some."

Boden's hand slid up the column of my neck, slipping under the fall of my hair. "I'm not just sharing it with anyone. I'm sharing it with *you*. A person who understands me better than anyone ever has before."

My heart thudded against my ribs in a ragged beat.

Boden leaned in closer until his lips were just a breath away. He stilled there. His fire had me closing the distance. My mouth met his in a hungry kiss, one that spoke of bearing witness to pain, of empathy and understanding. One that quickly changed to heat and want. The desire for more. For all that was Boden. For all that was this thing between us.

The sensations that sparked through me had my breath seizing in my lungs. Panic set in and had me jerking back. "I-I'm sorry. I shouldn't have—I can't."

I scrambled to my feet and hurried to my room. All because Boden Cavanaugh made me feel far too much.

Chapter Twenty-Five

Boden

I ROLLED TO MY BACK IN BED. THE SURFACE WAS TOO DAMN cold. The opposite of the heat that had almost burned me alive last night. That one tiny taste of Laiken, and I knew I'd never be the same.

It was so much more than chemistry. That touch of mouth to mouth had been hunger but also understanding. Laying everything that swirled around in my mind out for inspection and receiving nothing but compassion in return.

I understood her impulse to run. It scared the hell out of me, too. I'd given her last night to herself, but that all changed today. There was too much at stake. I'd lived enough years to know that this kind of connection didn't come along often. It was a gift, and I wasn't going to lose it.

Rolling out of bed, I headed for the bathroom. I made quick work of getting ready, pulling on sweats and a tee. I walked out into the living space and listened. I heard Laiken in her bathroom, the water of the shower running.

An image flashed in my mind. Laiken. All that golden skin on display.

"Hell," I muttered. "Not going to help things."

The last thing Laiken needed was me pouncing on her like a horny teenager the second she came out of her room. The dogs looked up from their cozy bed. I scowled at Peaches. "Just rub it in. You got your damn cuddles last night."

Her tongue lolled out of her mouth in a happy pant. I crossed over to them and hooked on Gizmo's wheels. "Come on. I'll clear you a path to pee."

I grabbed my jacket and boots from the mudroom and headed outside, the dogs on my heels. Sun greeted me instead of gray clouds. And more snow than I had ever seen in my life. I wondered how a plow would ever even get up here. As I waded down the steps, I found that it was up to my thighs.

I dug a path that was more like a tunnel and lifted Gizmo down the steps. "There you go."

He and Peaches made quick work of doing their business and then charged back for the stairs.

"Blue balls in more ways than one," I grumbled, lifting Gizmo and setting him on the front porch.

I left the shovel leaning against the house and did my best to brush most of the snow off my boots and pants. Pulling open the door, I stepped inside.

Laiken turned around at the sound. She held an empty mug, and her gaze landed on everything but me. "I was just making some coffee. Do you want some?"

I slipped off my boots, dropping them and my jacket in the mudroom. "Sure."

"Okay." She grabbed another mug from the cabinet. "I think there are plenty of Lucky Charms left if you want them. Or I could scramble some eggs. I don't think even I could ruin that. Or there's bread for toast. Or—"

I took Laiken's shoulders and turned her around to face me. "Hey, what's going on?"

Tears filled her eyes. "I'm so sorry."

"About last night?"

She nodded, a few tears slipping free. "I'm such a mess. But I shouldn't have left. Not like that. You shared something so important with me, and I just…" Her words trailed off as if she couldn't find what she wanted to say.

My thumbs swept across her cheeks, wiping away the wetness. "You got scared. You're human."

"You're not mad?"

"No. Was I frustrated in the moment? Sure. Did I have the worst case of blue balls since the eighth grade? Probably."

Laiken let out a squeak of laughter and then winced. "Sorry about that."

"I'll live." I stroked her cheeks. "But more than anything, I want you to stay in it with me. Even when things get scary or hard or uncomfortable. Talk it through with me. I promise not to push you for something you're not ready for."

"I might call you pushy but never with that kind of thing." She let out a shaky breath. "I don't know if I'm ready for this."

"There's no way to know unless you try."

Her hands fisted in my t-shirt. "I'm scared."

"I know. We can stay right where we are for as long as you need. Until you're ready for that next step."

Laiken leaned forward, resting her forehead against mine. "Thank you."

I pulled her against me, relishing the simple contact. It was enough. For now.

I formed the pile of snow into a ball, packing it tightly as Laiken drew eyes and a smile on our snowman. She stepped back, surveying our work. "It might be days before we have a way out of here, but I don't think I mind. I could make an army of snowmen in that time. He's cute, don't you think?"

She turned to see my response, and I lobbed the snowball at

her. It crashed into her chest, exploding into a million pieces and spraying her face. Laiken's jaw dropped. "You didn't."

I grinned. "Pretty good for an LA native, don't you think?"

She sank to her knees, scrambling to pick up some snow. I hurried to form another snowball, but it was too late. A half-formed one splattered against my face.

"The face? Really?" I abandoned my snowball and ran towards Laiken—or waded quickly. The snow was deep. And the snow gear we'd borrowed from the stash in the mudroom didn't make moving any easier.

Laiken let out a shriek as I dove for her, rolling so that I took the impact. We landed in a deep drift of snow. "Boden! It's freezing."

I shifted on top of her, sprinkling a little snow onto her face. "Shouldn't have played with fire."

She tugged off my hat and dumped snow on my head.

"You minx."

"Shouldn't have played with the Ice Queen."

I went for her sides, tickling her the best I could through her thick jacket.

It did the trick. Laiken squealed and squirmed. "Don't you dare. Boden…" She maneuvered so that she fully sat atop me, straddling my waist. "Victory is mine!"

I gazed up at her, the sun hitting her face and snowflakes glistening in her dark hair. "I don't know. I feel pretty damn victorious right now." Even with the snow seeping into the back of my coat, I wouldn't move for anything.

A smile stretched across Laiken's face. She bent, brushing her lips across mine in the barest of touches. "Thank you for this. It's been the perfect escape."

I fought against the urge to lean in for more, knowing Laiken needed to be the one to make that choice. Instead, I tucked her hair behind her ear. "I'll run away with you anytime."

"Maybe next time we go for somewhere a little warmer."

"I'm down for margaritas and you in a bikini."

She laughed but then straightened.

"What is it?" I sat up with her. That was when I heard the faint sound of an engine.

Laiken moved to her feet, pulling me up with her. "Might be the plow."

It didn't sound quite loud enough. I squinted in the direction of the noise. "Look. I think it's someone on a snowmobile."

Laiken lifted her hand in a wave to whoever it was. "I bet Hayes had someone come check on us and let us know when the plow will get up this way."

Small-town life was so different than anything I'd ever experienced. This neighborly, care-for-everyone-in-your-orbit and making sure everyone had what they needed. It was a breath of fresh air.

The snowmobile slowed and then stopped altogether.

"That's weird," Laiken said.

Something glinted in the bright sun. Metal. Everything slowed to heartbeats.

"Get down!"

A crack sounded as I threw myself onto Laiken, burying us in the snow. Pain bloomed. Then there was nothing but deafening silence.

Chapter Twenty-Six

Laiken

MY HEART THUDDED AGAINST MY RIBS, A CHAOTIC rhythm as I struggled to breathe. The sound of an engine broke through my consciousness. Panic flared. "Boden!"

"Are you hurt? Are you hit?" His hands skimmed over me, checking for injuries.

The sound of the engine moved farther away.

"I-I'm okay." Pain flared in my back from the tackle, but it wasn't horrible. More than livable. "We need to get inside in case they come back." My voice sounded so calm, almost emotionless.

Shock, some part of me realized. A numbness had overtaken my entire being.

Boden rolled to his side, searching out the disappearing snowmobile. "We stay low. Crawl towards the house just in case they have another hidey-hole."

My stomach pitched at the thought, but I nodded. I didn't miss how Boden positioned himself between me and the disappearing shooter. The action made my eyes sting and my throat burn.

We stayed quiet as we worked our way across the front yard to the porch steps. Boden cast one more look in the direction the snowmobile had vanished in and then grabbed my arm. "Go." He pushed me towards the front door, hurrying behind.

I yanked open the door, rushing inside.

"Close all the curtains," Boden ordered as he locked the doors behind us.

Running to window after window, I shut out any way for light or eyes to get in. The dogs whined, sensing our anxiety. Boden jogged into the bedrooms pulling the curtains there, as well. When he came out, his gaze swept over me. "You're sure you're okay?"

I nodded. "You?"

"I tweaked my shoulder when I fell. But I'm fine."

Moving towards him, I pulled off my gloves. "Let's have a look."

I unzipped his jacket. Boden winced as I tugged it off, and I froze. Blood soaked the sleeve of his sweatshirt. "Boden…"

"Shit."

Blood roared in my ears. I couldn't move, couldn't breathe. Someone had shot Boden. That thought spurred me into action, guiding him towards the couch. "Sit. Don't move."

"I'll be fine. Just a nick."

"Don't move," I ordered, then pulled off my own coat. I hurried into my bathroom. I swore I'd seen a first-aid kit in there. Pulling things out from under the sink, I finally landed on the red nylon kit that read *First Aid*. I grabbed it and hurried back out to the living room.

Boden looked a bit pale. My stomach cramped and twisted. "I'm going to cut your sweatshirt and t-shirt off so we don't move your shoulder."

"Damn. I liked this sweatshirt."

"Pretty sure your blood already ruined it."

"Fair point."

I found a pair of scissors in the kit and began cutting down the middle of the fabric. Boden's tee and sweatshirt opened like a jacket. "Lean forward."

He did as instructed. I was as gentle as possible, tugging the fabric free, but I didn't miss his wince. "Sorry."

"It's okay."

As soon as the clothing was off, I zeroed in on the wound. It was a deep gash, but I told myself over and over: *Not fatal, not fatal.* Unless he got some awful infection, and we couldn't get off this damn mountain.

I pawed through the kit, pulling out gloves, a small bottle of hydrogen peroxide, gauze, and tape. As I studied the wound, I worried it wasn't enough. "Hold on."

Running to the kitchen, I pulled open drawer after drawer until I found the one everyone had in their kitchen. The depository of random stuff. I pawed through item after item, breathing a sigh of relief when my hand closed around a tube of super glue.

I hurried back to Boden, and he eyed me carefully. "You're not planning on taking my entire arm, are you?"

I wanted to laugh, but I couldn't get my throat to make the sound. I held up the small tube. "Nope. I'm going to glue you back together."

"Are you for real right now?"

I nodded. "Doctors use medical-grade glue all the time, but this will have to work for now until we can get you checked out."

"If I end up with some weird blood poisoning, you'd better play nursemaid."

"I promise."

"Worth it then," Boden muttered.

I pulled on a pair of the gloves and grabbed the bottle of peroxide. "This will probably be the worst part, but we have to make sure it doesn't get infected."

Boden grimaced. "Do it."

I poured the hydrogen peroxide over his shoulder, catching the overflow with the gauze.

"Holy crap on a cracker, that does not feel fun."

"Sorry. Almost done." I gave it one more good flush and patted it dry. Meeting Boden's gaze, I sent him a silent apology. "Second worst part. I need to hold the wound closed while I glue it."

A muscle in his cheek ticked. "Glove up my other hand. I'll help."

"Are you sure?" It would help to have another set of fingers to hold the gash closed.

Boden held out his hand. I slid the glove on him and positioned his fingers above the wound. "Push down here. Good. Now, don't move."

I felt the restrained pain coming off Boden in waves. I moved as quickly as possible, applying pressure to close the gash and then coating it in glue. Enough to hold but not enough that it dripped down and sealed my fingers to his arm. I blew against the glue. "We're almost done."

"I'm okay."

The tension in Boden's voice told me that he was anything but.

I kept blowing gently on the glue and, within minutes, it was dry. I tested the seal with a featherlight tap. It held.

Slowly, I released my fingers, and Boden did the same. I held my breath as I studied the wound. No blood, and the glue continued to hold.

My gaze traveled to Boden's face. He was still pale, but he smiled at me. "Should I call you Dr. Laiken now?"

I started to laugh, but the laughter quickly morphed into sobs. Not easy tears sliding down my cheeks but cries that rocked my entire body.

"Shit. Laiken." Boden pulled me into his lap, holding me tight against him. "We're okay. It's just a graze. I'm gonna be fine."

"You could've been killed." The words tore from my throat, and the sobs came harder.

Boden squeezed me tighter. "But I wasn't. I'm okay."

I pressed my face into his neck. "Don't leave me."

"I'm right here, and I'm not going anywhere." One of his hands slipped under my t-shirt and sweater, his palm gliding along my skin. "I'm right here."

Slowly, my sobs subsided as I focused on the beating of Boden's heart. Strong and steady. Unwavering. I relished the sound and feel.

I wiped away the last of my tears, pulling back and taking in every detail of Boden's face. That strong jaw with the dusting of stubble. Those hazel eyes so filled with concern for me. I wanted to memorize everything. "I don't want to waste any more time."

His breath hitched. "Laiken…"

I stood from his lap and pulled my sweater over my head, letting it fall to the floor. My t-shirt followed.

Boden's eyes heated as they tracked over my exposed skin. "We've just been through a scare. I don't want you to do something you'll regret later."

My fingers went to the back of my bra, unclasping it. "I'm not going to regret this." I knew that with every fiber of my being. Boden was right. It had been a scare. More than that, it had been a terrifying wake-up call. None of us were guaranteed more than the moment right in front of us. And I had wasted so many of them trying to protect myself.

I dropped my bra to the floor. "I'm done wasting my life. Wasting the opportunities to truly live that are right in front of me." My fingers went to my snow pants and leggings as I kicked off my boots. "Do you want this, Boden? Do you want me?"

He swallowed hard; his gaze zeroed in on my fingers. "More than my next breath."

It was all I needed. I shucked my layers of pants, kicking them away. My hands went to the sweatpants Boden wore, and I tugged them down frantically.

He sprang free, and my hand wrapped around his shaft. Boden let out a groan. I moved on instinct, taking him into my mouth, wanting to feel every inch of him.

Boden let out a slew of curses as his hands tangled in my hair. "Laiken…"

I ran my tongue from base to tip, exploring as I went, paying attention to how each area elicited a response. The tightening of his fingers in my hair, the hitch of his breath. Every reaction drove me higher.

"You keep doing that, and this will be over before it begins." Boden gently tugged me until I released him.

"I was having fun."

"You're gonna be the death of me. But I'll die a happy man." He tugged me closer. "Come here."

I straddled Boden's lap, his tip bumping against my entrance. I wanted him. To feel what it was to be completely consumed by him.

"Shit, condoms," he muttered.

My eyes locked with his. "I'm on the pill, and I've had a checkup."

The gold in Boden's eyes flared. "I've been checked." His fingers flexed on my hips. "I want to feel everything about you."

It was all I needed. I slowly lowered myself onto him, never once letting my gaze stray from his. The stretch was just shy of painful, but God, it made me feel alive. Every nerve ending in my body sparked to life. There was nothing but Boden and me and *feeling*.

I slowly began to rock. Boden took my mouth in a scorching kiss. Our tongues dueled, saying everything we couldn't say with words. One hand came to my hip, and the other moved to my breast. Together, we found a rhythm that was the dance of flame between us. Hungry and tender at the same time. Painting an image that I knew spoke of love and the deepest understanding.

Boden's hips arched against me, bringing him deeper. My walls shuddered around him, and I gasped into his mouth. "More," I begged on a hoarse whisper.

He arched again. I met him thrust for thrust as every one of my muscles trembled. I was barely holding it together, and then suddenly realized that I didn't need to. Not now, not with Boden. So, I let it all go in a cascade of spiraling colors. Sparks that danced across my skin.

I came apart with the man who saw every fractured piece of me and wanted me anyway.

Chapter Twenty-Seven

Boden

THE FIRE WAS DYING. I KNEW I NEEDED TO GET UP AND add more wood, but it was the last thing I wanted to do. Even though my arm throbbed, and my calf cramped, I didn't want to move an inch. Laiken was draped on top of me, her breaths deep and even—so completely relaxed in sleep.

After the day we'd had, I couldn't imagine anything she needed more. Except for maybe a police escort home. That thought had me shifting, easing Laiken onto the couch, and getting to my feet. I pulled on my discarded sweats and moved to the fire, adding a new stack of logs to the dying flames. It flared back up in seconds.

I checked the dogs, who seemed oblivious to the drama of the day and were snoring happily. Straightening, I studied my wound. It hurt like a bitch, but the glue was holding, and there was no redness like you'd see if an infection were taking hold. I pulled back the curtain, peeking outside.

Darkness greeted me, but I still scanned the surrounding wilderness, looking for any flicker of light or hint of movement. There was nothing. I repeated the action at each window—still nothing.

That didn't put me at ease. Walking to the mudroom, I studied the gun safe. There was a keypad lock on it. My guess was a four-digit code, but I didn't have the faintest idea of where to start with it.

I went into the kitchen, opening drawers and cabinets as quietly as possible. I had to hope that the owner of this cabin had as bad a memory as I did and had put the code somewhere. After a thorough perusal of the kitchen, I began to lose hope. But I pressed on, moving to the bookcase.

I scanned the shelves, looking for anything that might be a journal or notebook, something that would keep notes. My gaze caught on a binder on the bottom shelf. I pulled it out. *House Bible* was scrawled across the front.

Opening it, I flipped through the pages. There were plastic sleeves housing manuals on appliances and the heating and cooling system. I made it all the way to the last page when I saw a scrap of paper folded and tucked into the pocket on the back cover. I tugged it out and read the four numbers. 0268.

I hurried into the mudroom. I punched in the numbers and then the lock key. Little green lights lit up, and the sound of a lock turning echoed in the silent room. I pulled open the door. There was a shotgun and two rifles lined up on a rack inside, along with ammunition stacked at the bottom.

I breathed out my first true sigh of relief as my fingers closed around one of the rifles. I took it and a box of its accompanying ammo out. At least now we had a means of defense.

I loaded the gun and laid it on the coffee table. I wanted it within easy reach, just in case.

"Boden?"

Laiken's sleepy voice had me turning around. "Hey. You okay?" She nodded. "Your arm?"

"Not too bad."

Her eyes narrowed on me, and I couldn't help but chuckle. "I could probably use a painkiller."

"There are some in the first-aid kit." Laiken sat up, holding the blanket to her chest. Her eyes widened as she took in the rifle. "Where did you find that?"

"There's a gun safe in the mudroom. I just had to find the code."

Her eyes flicked to me. "You're a regular Hardy Boy."

"Been called worse things." I found a packet of acetaminophen and swallowed them down with cold coffee.

Laiken shivered. "Will you toss me my t-shirt?"

"Hold on, and I'll grab your PJs." I hurried into her bedroom, snagging the blue flannel pajamas that were folded on Laiken's pillow, then stopped in my room for a fresh t-shirt and sweatshirt.

I dropped the PJs in Laiken's lap, and she quickly pulled them on. I instantly missed seeing the expanse of golden skin. Lowering myself to the couch, I pulled her into my arms, ignoring the pulse of pain in my shoulder. I pressed my lips to her temple. "Feel better after a little sleep?"

She nodded, burrowing deeper into my hold. I breathed a sigh of relief that I wouldn't have to battle against any second thoughts. As if she sensed the direction my mind had gone, Laiken said, "I don't regret it. I could never regret you."

I brushed the hair away from Laiken's face and took her mouth in a slow kiss. "I'm damn glad to hear that."

She smiled against my mouth, but the action quickly faded. "What are we going to do? Whoever that was could be anywhere."

My gut twisted as the memory flashed in my mind again. The glint of metal. The crack of the shot. The feel of Laiken's body under mine. I held her tighter against me. "We have a way to protect ourselves now. We stay inside until the roads are cleared and then get our asses back to town."

Laiken shivered in my arms. "This means someone really is trying to hurt everyone involved in the accident."

They weren't trying just to hurt those in the accident. They were trying to kill them. And they didn't care who stood in their way.

Chapter Twenty-Eight

Laiken

THE FAINT SOUNDS OF AN ENGINE ROUSED ME OUT OF A deep sleep. I couldn't remember the last time I'd slept so heavily or this much. Apparently, the trauma of yesterday was taking its toll.

That thought had me jerking upright. "Boden!"

He turned from his spot at the window. "It's okay. I'm pretty sure it's the snowplow. I caught a glimpse through the trees."

The thudding of my heart slowed a fraction as I scanned Boden's form. He was fully dressed, and even from feet away, I could make out the dark circles under his eyes. "Did you sleep at all?"

He shook his head. "I wanted to keep an ear out, just in case."

I swung my legs over the side of the couch and stood, crossing to Boden. I wrapped my arms around his waist and burrowed into his chest. "You should've woken me. I would've taken over so you could get a few hours of sleep."

"Do you know how to shoot a rifle?"

Pulling back a fraction so I could take in his face, my lips pressed into a firm line. "Do you?"

The corners of his mouth tipped up. "My dad was big on target shooting. He taught me young."

"Oh."

He pressed a kiss to my temple. "Stay here. I'm going to try to flag this guy down."

I followed Boden to the mudroom and slipped on my boots and jacket. "I'm not letting you go out there alone."

"Laiken—"

"I highly doubt that whoever shot at us went back to Wolf Gap, stole a snowplow, and is now coming back for attempt two."

Boden's jaw tightened. "They could be hiding out in the mountains, waiting for us to step outside."

That thought had a wave of nausea sweeping through me. We'd only let the dogs out once last night, quickly and under the cover of full darkness. "I don't think anyone would last overnight in these temperatures. They'd freeze."

"I guess you have a point there."

I wove my fingers through Boden's. "We're in this together."

"Together." He squeezed my hand before releasing it and then moving for the rifle. Checking a few things on the gun, he opened the door and stepped out onto the porch.

My gaze swept over the land around us, looking for anything out of place. But there was nothing. The engine of the snowplow grew louder, and it finally peeked out from behind the incline.

Boden lifted a hand in a wave, trying to flag the guy down. The truck slowed, but the engine stayed on. The driver's side door opened, and a man appeared. "You folks weather the storm okay?"

"We actually ran into some trouble. Someone took a couple of potshots at us yesterday. Think you could radio the sheriff from your truck?" Boden asked.

The man's eyes widened. "Shit. You guys okay?"

"Mostly, but I think it would be good if the sheriff came up."

"Of course. Want me to wait it out with you so you have some backup? I've got a shotgun in the back in case of emergencies."

"Thanks, man. I think we're okay for now."

The man ducked back into the cab of his truck. A minute later, he appeared again. "Sheriff Easton and some deputies are on their way. I'll clear a spot for them to park."

"Thank you so much," I called. "We really appreciate it."

A soft bark sounded behind me, and I picked up Gizmo. "Here you go."

I started down the steps, but Boden was right on my heels, his eyes tracking over the land surrounding us. I set Gizmo down and told myself over and over that the shooter was long gone. I carried Gizmo back up the steps, Peaches following, and we hurried back inside.

Once we were there, I turned to Boden. "Let me see your shoulder."

The corner of his mouth kicked up. "Is Dr. Laiken back?"

I glared at him and snapped my fingers. "I want to make sure you're not dying of gangrene or something."

"Fair enough." Boden shrugged out of his jacket and pulled off his sweatshirt. I didn't miss his wince as he did.

Carefully, I rolled up his t-shirt sleeve. The area was definitely swollen, but it didn't look infected. "Maybe Beckett can give you some antibiotics."

"That's Addie's husband?"

I nodded. "He's the doctor in town. We should've told Hayes to bring him along."

"Laiken." Boden brushed the hair away from my face and pressed his lips to mine in a slow kiss. "I think I can make it to a doctor."

My hands fisted in his shirt. "I just want to make sure that you're okay."

His lips brushed against mine again. "You did a great job of taking care of me. The best. We're going to be fine."

I let out a shuddering breath. It would take a while for me to assure myself of that. "I know."

We didn't say anything else as we waited. It had only taken us an hour to get here from Wolf Gap, but waiting for Hayes and his officers felt like it took a millennium. The sound of sirens grew in the air. Boden wrapped an arm around me, moving back to the front door. "They made that trip quick."

I glanced at my watch, seeing that only forty-five minutes had passed. "I think saying *shooting* puts them in hyperdrive."

We stepped out onto the front porch just as three sheriff's department SUVs came to a stop in front of the cabin. Hayes was out of his in a flash. "What the hell happened? Are you okay?"

"We're fine," Boden said.

"He's not fine. He got shot."

He scowled at me. "Shot is a bit of an overstatement."

"Did a bullet pierce your arm or not?"

"It *grazed* me."

"That was a hell of a lot of blood I cleaned up for a *graze*."

Hayes pulled his radio from his holster. "I've got Beckett on call since the driver said you might be injured. Think you need to get to him now, or can we talk first?"

"I'm fine. Really. It's a gash, but it's not infected, and the pain isn't too bad."

I glared at Boden.

He bent and brushed his lips against mine. "The sooner we get this over with, the sooner I get to the doctor."

"Fine," I grumbled.

Hayes' gaze followed us back and forth as if he were watching a tennis match. "You tell me if you change your mind."

Boden nodded. "I'm good."

Hayes nodded and turned his focus to the snow in front of the cabin. "Where were you when it happened?"

Boden gestured to the area near the snowman. "Over there."

"Both of you?"

"We were standing right next to each other," Boden explained.

Hayes scrubbed a hand over his jaw. "So, the perp could've been aiming at either of you."

My stomach twisted at that. I'd assumed it was me, but what if Boden had been the target?

Hayes gestured for Deputy Young and another couple of officers. "See if you can find the bullet."

"Got it, boss," she called.

Hayes headed up the steps, stomping off the snow on his boots when he reached the porch. His eyes tracked over me. "You weren't hurt?"

That bond tugged between us. The one that had cemented our care for each other all those years ago. I urged my mouth into a smile. "I'm fine and dandy. It's just Mr. Hero over here who needs medical attention. He had to go and tackle me into the snow and take a bullet."

My throat constricted on the words. That familiar panic lighting through me at how close I'd come to losing Boden. He seemed to sense that and moved in close, wrapping his arms around me and pressing his lips to my temple. "You're going to have to try a lot harder if you want to get rid of me."

I pressed my face into Boden's chest, breathing him in. The smell of cedar and something else filled my senses. The scent that was Boden. That alone was a comfort.

"Why don't you walk me through what happened?" Hayes urged.

We sat down on the couch and did just that. Hayes took down all the points he thought important and then looked up. "Could you make anything out about the snowmobile or the rider?"

I shook my head. "Not much. I think the machine might've been black."

Boden trailed a hand up and down my arm. "I think you're right. The shooter was wearing a helmet. I couldn't even begin to tell you height or build."

Hayes nodded, making a few more notes in his phone. "I'll get someone up here to follow the tracks. We haven't had any new snow since the storm, so there's a good chance of that."

I picked at the seam of the couch. "Do you think it's someone trying to hurt people who were in the accident?"

Hayes' mouth thinned. "It's looking more and more likely."

Boden stiffened next to me. "What did you find?"

Hayes' eyes hardened. "Robert Aaron has dropped off the map."

"The guy that caused the accident?"

Hayes nodded. "About seven months ago, he simply stopped showing up for work. He made the maximum withdrawal from an ATM and then vanished. There was one credit card hit in the Midwest at a gas station. Then nothing."

I gripped Boden's hand, squeezing the life out of it. "What do you think that means?"

Hayes looked back and forth between Boden and me. "It could just mean he wants to drop off the grid. Maybe people where he was living back east found out about his record, and he wanted a fresh start."

Boden's eyes narrowed. "Or he's lost it and is trying to pick off the people he thinks ruined his life one by one."

My stomach twisted painfully.

"It's something I'm considering." Hayes looked at me. "I don't want you alone for any reason. And either you stay with Boden, or you stay with Ev and me. Don't make me put an officer parked at The Gallery overnight."

I bristled, but Boden nuzzled my neck. "Stay with me. That's where I'd want you, even if this wasn't going on."

I melted a little at that. "Okay. But is there a recent picture of Robert Aaron? We need to know who to look out for."

"I'm working on that, and I'll text it around. We'll have people on the lookout."

"Thank you, Hayes."

He shook his head. "I wish I weren't always two damn steps behind."

I leaned forward and patted his knee. "You're doing everything you can. We know that."

"But sometimes that isn't enough."

Chapter Twenty-Nine

Boden

I GRITTED MY TEETH AS BECKETT EASTON PRODDED MY wound. He shifted his focus from my arm to my face. "That hurt?"

"It doesn't feel like a gentle cuddle," I gritted out.

Beckett chuckled. "I'll write you a prescription for some anti-inflammatories and a painkiller, but Laiken here did an excellent job with your care." He glanced at her. "You ever think about becoming a doctor?"

Laiken snorted. "Seeing as I almost puked looking at all that blood, I think I'll be passing on the medical jobs."

"I get it. Blood's gross," he muttered.

I arched a brow. "Says the doctor."

Beckett shrugged. "I've learned to deal with it, but it doesn't mean it still doesn't make my stomach turn occasionally." He snapped off his gloves. "I'd say you're good to go. But you need rest. Call my office to make an appointment for two days and a week from now. I want to keep an eye on this for signs of infection. If you start running a fever, the site feels hot to the touch, or the pain increases, come in immediately."

"You got it, doc." I rolled down my sleeve and stood from the exam table where Beckett and Hayes had brought Laiken and me back for a full exam.

Laiken threw her arms around the man, and his eyes flared in surprise as he patted her back. "Hey, he's going to be fine. I meant it when I said you did a good job."

"Thank you." She sniffed.

I gently tugged Laiken back into my hold. "I told you I was fine."

"I know, but I needed to hear it from a doctor." She wiped under her eyes. "I was so scared."

The words were barely audible but still made my chest constrict painfully. If this Robert Aaron asshole ever showed his face, I was getting in at least one good punch.

Hayes knocked on the open exam room door. "Everything okay?"

"He's not taking my arm," I muttered.

Hayes chuckled. "That's a good thing. Beckett tried to convince me I was losing a leg before."

"It was one time. You never could take a joke."

"You scarred me for life."

A small laugh bubbled out of Laiken. "I always forget how much of a hard time you give each other."

Hayes' face heated, but he shrugged. "Brothers."

Not all brothers. Some didn't just give you a hard time. Some were so much worse than that.

He cleared his throat and looked at Laiken. "You might want to stop by the Grangers' on your way home. Kay heard through the gossip mill about what happened. Gilly just texted and said she's pretty upset."

Laiken tugged her phone from her pocket. "My cell must've died last night, and there was no service up at the cabin. I'll head over there now."

"We'll both go," I said.

Beckett made a tsking noise. "You need to rest."

I opened my mouth to argue, but Hayes held up a hand. "I'll have one of my deputies drive Laiken. She won't be alone."

"I need to stop by The Gallery after I see Kay and pick up a few things," Laiken said.

"Not a problem. We'll drop you there, and then you can call when you're ready to head to Boden's."

"I'm not dying," I muttered.

Laiken whirled on me, her eyes blazing. "You were *shot*. You need to take care of yourself and heal. I'm not going to lose you because you were being a pompous idiot and wouldn't follow your doctor's orders."

Beckett let out a low whistle. "I'd listen to her, man."

I moved in close to Laiken, taking her mouth in a slow kiss. Three little words hovered on the tip of my tongue. I wanted to let them free so damn bad, but knew now was far from the right time. "I'll go rest if you promise to come home to me as soon as you're done at the gallery."

She melted into me. "I like the way that sounds."

"What?"

"Coming home to you."

"Me, too," I whispered.

Laiken gave me one more peck and then followed Hayes out of the exam room. Beckett grinned at me. "You've got a good one there."

"I damn well know it, too."

He tore two sheets off a prescription pad and handed them to me. "It's good you do because I'd hate to have to break something I'd then have to fix."

I arched a brow.

"Laiken's been through a lot. She's strong, but that tough exterior guards a sensitive heart. I don't want to see her hurt any more than she already has been."

"I care about her. More than care, but I'm not giving you those words before I give them to Laiken. I'll do whatever I can to make sure she's happy and safe."

Beckett clapped me on my uninjured shoulder. "All I could hope to hear. Now get home and follow my instructions."

I chuckled and headed out of the exam room and down the hall. I waved and thanked the older receptionist, who blushed as I passed. Opening the door, I took in a long breath of freezing air. It helped clear away the worst of the cobwebs, but I knew I needed sleep.

The dogs barked from my truck, and I picked up my pace. Climbing behind the wheel, I headed for home. Okay, it wasn't exactly *home,* but it was starting to feel that way. I plugged my phone into my charger and began playing voicemails.

There was one from my mom, checking in. Another from my dad. And, finally, one from a local realtor who said she had a piece of property for me to look at whenever I was ready.

I would take that win. It was time for some good news. Hopefully, it was the perfect place for a second home. I'd just have to find a way to spend a good amount of time here.

I slowed as I approached the gate to Ramsey's property. An SUV I didn't recognize was parked about twenty feet from it, and as I slowed, a figure stepped out from the driver's side of the vehicle.

I pressed fully down on the brake as I took in the man with the same hazel eyes as mine. His were duller, though. A kind of deadening that came from crushing everyone who cared about you. I put my truck in park and slid out.

My brother went for a casual grin. "How was your little getaway?"

I stiffened. "What are you talking about?"

"I asked around about where you were staying. A few mentions of how I wanted to surprise my beloved brother, and people were so chatty. Some chick said you were up in the mountains."

I worked my jaw back and forth, trying to get it to loosen. "How did you know I was in Wolf Gap?"

Eli's grin deepened, going a bit feral around the edges. "You think I don't know where my brother's hiding out? I always know where you are, Bo."

Nausea swept through me, and it only served to piss me off. "What are you doing here, Eli?"

His lips twitched. "No hug? No '*great to see you, Eli*?'"

"No."

A little of his smile slipped. "That's fair, I guess." He shuffled his feet, kicking at a piece of gravel. "Shit, Bo. I'm sorry. I shouldn't have texted what I did. I was messed up. I didn't mean it."

How many times had I heard words like that before? Too many to count. But the remorse never stuck. Not enough to create real and lasting change anyway. "You're right. You shouldn't have."

"I'm trying to apologize. To make amends."

He threw out the word, knowing it would ignite my hope the way it had so many times before. That maybe Eli was back in the program and truly working the steps this time. But that familiar hope didn't flare in me. Because I was done. I'd given all I could to this relationship, and it had bled me dry. "If you want to truly make amends, leave me alone. That's all I want from you."

Eli's eyes flared, shock lighting across his expression. "You don't mean that."

"I mean it. I can't do this with you anymore. I'm done."

His jaw hardened and flexed. "That's not fair. You have to give me a chance to make it up—"

"You can't. This isn't like when you wrecked my car or ran up a massive bill on my Amex. It's not like when you trashed my house while I was filming or showed up high out of your mind when I got you a job on set. Carissa was a human being. I loved her. Maybe not like I should've, but I loved her. And you took her down that spiral of darkness with you. You just had to try to ruin her, too."

Eli charged, shoving me so hard I stumbled back a few steps. "You didn't fucking love her. You didn't know the first thing about her."

I clenched my jaw so hard I wouldn't have been surprised if I chipped a tooth. "You're right. I didn't know her in the end.

Because the girl I fell in love with, the one who was so full of light and had the biggest heart for others? She never would've fucked around on me. She never would've cheated with my own damn brother. But you? I know exactly who you are. None of this is a surprise, except for how far you've taken it."

He sneered at me. "Fucked her in your bed. Did you know that? Those thousand-thread-count sheets you loved so damn much. She came back to me every time she wasn't getting what she needed from you. How does it feel to know that the perfect little façade you wear is nothing but a lie? That you're just second-fiddle to your junkie of a brother?"

"I don't think I'm better than you. I just know I have a heart. And whatever you do to me, you won't make me lose it." The one thing I could hold on to was my character and the fact that I *cared*. I didn't use booze or drugs to turn off those feelings, even when Eli was determined to throw the worst of my mistakes and pain in my face.

"Get off your high horse. You destroyed Carissa. You've ruined everything for me. But now, you're gonna know what it feels like, too."

Chapter Thirty

Laiken

BRETT PULLED HIS SQUAD CAR TO A STOP IN FRONT OF THE Grangers' ranch house. "Want me to go in with you?"

I shook my head and sent him my best imitation of a reassuring smile. "No, I'll be fine. I'm sorry you have to wait for me. Do you have a book or something? I shouldn't be too long."

"Laiken, I'm on duty. I just want to make sure you're safe."

"Right." Because some crazed person was out there, dead-set on taking out everyone from the accident. Except it hadn't been an accident. It was an attack. Both then and now. "Thank you."

He squeezed my shoulder. "We'll find him. Promise."

I nodded and climbed out of the car. But I knew better than most that lots of promises never got fulfilled—ones of forever, and ones of tomorrow. I started up the steps to the front porch when the front door burst open. Gilly charged across the space, pulling me into her arms. "You're okay? You're not hurt?"

I hugged her back, inhaling her familiar scent that was so comforting. "I'm fine. I'm sorry I gave you guys a scare."

Gilly pulled back but kept a hold of my shoulders. "Kay's beside herself. Needed to see you with her own eyes. I guess I did, too."

I squeezed Gilly's hands. "I'm so sorry I upset her."

"She's upset because she cares." Gilly guided me into the house. "And Boden? How's he?"

My throat burned with the onslaught of memories. The crack of the bullet. All that blood. "He's going to be fine, but a bullet did graze him."

"Holy hell. Some idiot hunter. They need to give people eyesight tests before they give them a gun. Someone who doesn't know the difference between an elk and a human being has no business having a firearm."

I could've corrected Gilly, but I didn't want to make her worry any more. I could already feel the frenetic energy coming off her in waves. "Hayes will find whoever it is, and they won't be able to have a gun for much longer."

Gilly grunted and walked me into the living room. Kay sat in a similar position to the one I'd found her in the last time I was here. On the couch, staring out at the fields.

Gilly cleared her throat. "Look who came to see you, Kay. Laiken's here, and she's just fine."

Kay's head whipped in my direction, her eyes frantically scanning my body. "Not hurt."

I eased down next to her on the couch and took her hand. "I'm good, Kay. Just had a little scare is all."

She blinked a few times. "A scare..."

I glanced at Gilly, worry settling in my gut. Kay was far from well. Gilly gave a small shake of her head as if to say, "*Not now.*" I turned back to Kay. "I'm all right now. I promise."

Her eyes struggled to focus, but she finally zeroed in on me. "Who were you with?"

Her voice trembled as she spoke, and my stomach clenched. "I was with my friend, Boden."

Friend wasn't the right term, but we hadn't exactly discussed what we were. *Boyfriend* seemed like such a ridiculous term as adults.

Kay's fingers tightened, her nails digging into the back of my hand. "Boden."

"He's in town doing some research with Ramsey Bishop."

Those nails dug so deep, I knew they'd leave marks. Kay's eyes blazed. "You're cheating on my boy?"

My jaw slackened as I sucked in a breath. "Kay…"

She gripped me tighter. "Answer me."

"I'm not cheating on anyone."

"I never thought you would do something like this. Never." Her voice trembled as she spoke.

Gilly moved to the couch, sinking down next to her sister and rubbing a hand up and down her back. "Kay, you don't mean that. Laiken—"

"I *do* mean it," Kay snapped. Her eyes bored into me. "I thought you loved him."

"I do love him. With all my heart. But it's been a long time. I have to move on with my life. To try and be happy." But this was the first time I'd ever actually reached for it. It had taken almost losing that chance for more to wake me up. I'd found a career I loved in two different ways. I had friends, people I adored, but I'd never actually opened my heart. Not in the real, scary way I was now.

"You promised him forever," Kay said in a hoarse whisper.

My heart cracked at her words. So much pain flooding each and every crevice. "We didn't have a chance at that forever."

Kay stared at me, her lips going white because she was pressing them together so hard. She released her grip on my hand. "Get out."

"Kay," Gilly croaked.

"Get out!" Kay screamed the words so loudly, it felt as if they rattled my brain.

I scrambled to my feet as Kay burst into tears.

Gilly stood, frozen in shock, her eyes going back and forth between Kay and me. I started for the door, but Gilly grabbed my elbow, speaking in hushed tones. "She doesn't mean it."

"I think she does." And it cracked something deep inside me to know that she did. "I can't keep doing this."

A mixture of anger and hurt flashed in Gilly's eyes. "She's been like a mother to you."

"I know that, but all we're doing now is hurting each other."

"Maybe if you backed off this thing with Boden for a little bit—"

I shook my head. "I can't. I can't keep putting my life on hold. It kills me that I lost Jase, but I didn't die with him. I have to *live*."

Gilly's lips thinned, but she nodded. "I'm sorry. About all of this."

"Me, too." I said the words as I slowly backed away from the two women who had always been there for me. Invisible claws shredded my chest. I couldn't help but wonder if this was the beginning of the end. I'd been clinging to Jase through his family, wanting to keep that connection alive, but maybe I was doing more harm than good.

I opened the front door and stepped out onto the front porch. The cold afternoon air was a balm to my burning lungs. I closed my eyes for a moment and simply focused on breathing. My body trembled as I grabbed hold of the porch railing, trying to steady myself.

"You just had to rub it in her face."

I whirled at the sound of Jax's voice. His expression was a mixture of so many things: pain, worry, rage. I clenched and flexed my hands at my sides, trying to get rid of the tingling sensation in my fingers. "I didn't rub anything in anyone's face. The last thing I want to do is hurt your mom."

He scoffed. "What did you think would happen when you ran off for a romantic getaway with a fucking movie star? The entire town was blabbing about it."

"I wouldn't exactly call it a romantic getaway. People don't get shot on those."

Jax smirked. That same cocky tip of the lips he'd had forever, but one that had gotten meaner over the past years. Crueler. "Serves him right."

My jaw dropped. "What happened to you? Did your humanity die with Jase? Boden hasn't done anything to anyone, and he could've been killed."

A muscle fluttered wildly in Jax's cheek. "He's hurting my family. *You're* hurting them."

"I can't stop living my life to protect Kay from hurt. The fact that she would rather I be alone for the rest of my life so that she can pretend her son is coming back *kills* me. And it's so damn unfair."

Jax moved his gaze to the fields in front of us, his hands curling into fists. "Just stay away from her. From all of us. That's what you can do."

Tears clogged my throat. "If that's what you all want, then that's what I'll do."

But it shattered the last piece of Jase I'd been holding in my heart to walk away.

Chapter Thirty-One

Laiken

"ARE YOU SURE YOU'RE OKAY?" Brett's voice cut through my thoughts as we sat in front of The Gallery. "Sorry. I spaced for a second."

He shifted in his seat to face me. "You're allowed to space. You've been through a lot the past few weeks."

Understatement of the century. I opened the passenger door, ready to make my exit. I didn't have it in me for a heart-to-heart with Brett right now. It didn't matter that he was kind or that we'd known each other forever. If I started talking about things now, I'd break, and I wasn't sure it was something I'd be able to come back from. "Thanks for driving me. I'll be here for an hour or so, and then I'll be ready to go back to Boden's. I can drive myself if—"

"Nope. I'll come back in an hour. And we have foot patrols on the street, so you'll have officers keeping an eye on things."

That should've made me feel safe. Instead, it made it hard to breathe. As if I couldn't get my lungs to inflate fully. "Thanks."

I headed for the front door of The Gallery. A shop I had put my blood, sweat, and tears into but one that wasn't mine.

It belonged to a family I had once been a part of but no longer was. And maybe I'd been forcing my way into their ranks since Jase died.

The antique bell over the door let out its familiar jingle as I stepped inside. Even that sound hurt, grating against my skin and embedding itself there.

Addie looked up from the desk. As soon as she took me in, she leapt to her feet. "Oh, God. Laiken." She pulled me into her arms and held me tight. "Beckett swore you guys were okay, but I can't imagine how scared you must've been. You are okay, right?"

I bit the inside of my cheek in an attempt to keep the tears at bay. "I'm okay."

My voice came out as more of a croak, and Addie pulled back, surveying my face. "Come on. Let's get you in the back, and I'll make you some tea. Where's Boden?"

"He's at his place. Beckett said he needed to rest, and I had to do a few things before heading over there."

Serena looked up from where she was stacking crates. She wasn't in her usual attire, this time opting for jeans and a casual blouse. Her blond hair was piled in a top knot on her head, and she'd clearly been building the crates herself. Her eyes widened as she took me in. "Laiken."

"Hey."

Addie ushered me to a chair and sat me in it. Then she moved to our coffee machine and used it to dispense some hot water. Plunking a tea bag into the mug, she set it in front of me and wrapped my hands around it. She pulled a chair close to me and sat. "What can I do?"

My eyes burned, and my nose stung. "This is good. Thank you, Addie."

Serena moved closer, hovering at the edge of the table. "You're okay?"

I nodded, unable to get any other words out.

"Boden?" she asked.

I nodded again. Then I looked up into Serena's face. "Am I hurting your mom?"

She blanched. "What do you mean?"

"I went to see her, and she got so upset that I was seeing Boden... I—I'm not sure what to do. I always thought that it helped that we had a relationship, but maybe I was wrong. Maybe all I'm doing is making things worse."

Serena lowered herself to the chair on my other side. "It's not you," she said so softly I could barely make out the words.

"It sure seemed like it was."

"It's not. She's not well. I didn't realize how bad it had gotten until I was home." Serena swallowed, her eyes reddening. "She still has Jase's room exactly as it was before. Sometimes, she talks about him like he's still alive. When I tried to talk to Dad about getting her some more intensive help, he freaked. And Jax is no help. He all but supports her delusions, thinking he's helping."

I moved on instinct, taking Serena's hand and squeezing. "I'm so sorry, Ser." I hadn't used the nickname in years, one that used to fall off my tongue with such ease.

A tear slipped free, sliding down her cheek. "I don't know what to do. I don't have a vote. I lost that right when I stayed away for so long. Jax was right that I didn't want to deal, but I also wasn't here for my family when they needed me the most."

"You were grieving. None of us make the best decisions in that state. But you're here now. That's what matters."

More tears came. "I hate who I became, Laik. It's like I thought if I put on this other façade, I wouldn't have to be the girl who lost her brother. I wouldn't have to feel that pain."

I wrapped my arms around Serena, tugging her to me and holding on for dear life. As if this glimmer of the girl I'd loved so dearly might vanish if I didn't. "That makes so much sense. But you can't bury that pain. It comes up in other ways."

"Like being a raving bitch."

A laugh bubbled out of me. "Maybe a little." I released Serena but held on to her hands. "I missed you."

"I missed you, too. I just—I couldn't—"

"You don't have to explain. What if we both give each other some grace and start fresh?"

Serena let out a shuddering breath. "I'd like that. I was so scared when I heard you guys had been shot at." Her eyes glittered again. "I don't want to lose you, too."

I pulled her into another hug. "You're not going to."

She nodded against my shoulder, and I released her with one more squeeze.

Addie furiously wiped tears away. "Sorry," she muttered. "Hormones."

Serena laughed. "We're all just a mess today, aren't we?"

"But at least we're a mess together."

A shadow passed over Serena's eyes. "We have to do something about Mom. I'm really worried."

"Maybe we can talk to Gilly," I suggested. She certainly seemed aware of how perilous things were with Kay at the moment.

Serena worried the side of her lip. "Gilly loves Mom more than anything, but she's also terrified of pushing her too far. Of doing something that will hurt and not help."

I understood that fear, but we couldn't let it stop us. "Okay, first step is calling Kay's psychiatrist. He won't be able to share anything about Kay's treatment, but he should listen and hear our concerns. Maybe if the psychiatrist suggests more intensive treatment, your dad and Gilly will listen."

"That's a good idea. Dad does listen to the doctor. I can get his number from Mom's phone book tonight."

I squeezed Serena's knee. "You're not in this alone. I'll help in whatever way I can."

Her breath hitched as she swallowed down a sob. "Thank you. I know I don't deserve that. But thank you."

The bell over the door sounded, and Addie hurried to stand. "I'll deal with whoever that is."

"Thanks." I lifted my mug, taking a sip of the steaming liquid and letting it soothe some of those ragged edges. The last few days had been hellish, but there had been so much good in them, too. Boden. A fresh start with Serena. Knowing how many people genuinely cared about me and had my back.

"I'm guessing you aren't the one my brother is banging since you're already knocked up."

I stiffened at the harsh voice coming from the gallery's main room. Serena and I both pushed back from the table, rushing towards Addie and the man speaking. His eyes scanned over both me and Serena. "She was here the other day, so it's gotta be you." He grinned. "I gotta give it to Bo. He always had good taste."

I let a million different curses in my mind. "You must be Eli."

"The one and only. Nice to meet you, Laiken."

Eli's fingers twitched in rapid movements at his side. My hands fisted as I took that in and noted his disheveled appearance. "Are you looking for Boden?"

"Nope." He popped the P in the word. "Already had a lovely heart-to-heart with brother dearest. I came to talk to you."

My heart hammered in my chest, but I did my best to keep my expression blank. "About?"

"You deserve a warning."

"A warning?"

Eli tapped his fingers against his thighs in a staccato beat, and his mouth twisted in ways that weren't natural. "My brother isn't who you think he is. He likes to swoop in and play the hero. The fixer. But it's for his own selfish wants. He doesn't actually care about you."

My fingernails dug into my palms, all the times Boden had tried to fix things for me playing in my mind. "Good thing I'm not looking for anyone to solve my problems, then."

Eli grinned, revealing stained teeth. "He'll throw you away as soon as he has his hit of feeling all good about himself. He did it time and again to Carissa. And she came running to me every time."

My stomach cramped, nausea sweeping through me. "What?"

That grin widened. "Hey, when he throws you away, I can be there for you, too. Numb all that pain Bo likes to dish out."

"Get out." The words grated against my throat as I spoke.

Eli gave a casual shrug. "Just offering to be a friend. Trust me. When he's through with you, you'll need all the friends you can get."

Chapter Thirty-Two

Boden

I PULLED MY TRUCK INTO THE SHERIFF'S DEPARTMENT PARKING lot. My shoulder throbbed, but I hadn't had a chance to fill the prescription Beckett had written for me. I did my best to ignore the pain as I climbed out of my vehicle and headed up the front steps.

A buzz sounded as I opened the door. The woman behind the desk looked up, and her jaw dropped. I pretended not to see the reaction and forced a smile. "Hi, is Hayes in?"

"Y-yes. Just a second." She lifted the phone and punched a few buttons. She whispered into the receiver and then set it down. "He'll be right out."

A few seconds later, a door opened, and Hayes appeared. "What are you doing here? You're supposed to be home, you know, recovering from being shot."

I grimaced. "I need to run something by you."

He must've recognized the seriousness in my tone because any hints of humor fled his expression. "Come on back."

Hayes led me through the maze of desks. Most of the officers remained focused on their work, but a few sent us sidelong glances. Hayes ushered me into his office and shut the door behind us. "What's going on?"

I lowered myself into a chair opposite his desk, careful not to bump my arm. "I had a run-in when I got back to Ramsey's."

Hayes was instantly on alert. "Do you think it was Robert Aaron? Why the hell didn't you call 911?"

I shook my head. "Not that kind of run-in. My brother."

Hayes sat, his chair making a squeaking sound. "I take it you weren't expecting a visit."

"My brother and I don't have a relationship." I let out a long breath, trying to think about the easiest way to explain things. Searching for the words, guilt grabbed hold. Hayes shouldn't have been the first person in Wolf Gap I shared this with. It should've been Laiken.

"My brother has been an addict since he was in high school. My parents have tried everything they can think of to get him help."

"But an addict has to want that help," Hayes filled in for me.

I nodded. "Eli has always had anger when it comes to me. The more successful I became, the worse it got. He's tried to tear me down in every way imaginable. Sold stories to tabloids, tried to ruin deals for me, trashed personal belongings. I don't know if you heard about my girlfriend passing away six months ago."

"I did. I'm sorry for your loss."

I swallowed, my throat sticking on the motion. The next words were nearly impossible to get out, but I had no choice. "He was with her. I'll never know exactly what happened. Apparently, they were sleeping together. They got high, and she took too much. While he was passed out, she was choking on her own vomit. Not even the sounds of her dying were enough to wake him up."

Hayes muttered a curse. "I don't have words, Boden."

I stared down at my hands. Sometimes, I felt as though I should see blood staining them. "The cops eventually cleared him of all wrongdoing, even though he was the one who bought the drugs.

But not even that was a wake-up call. I cut him out of my life. I had to."

"I'd need to do the same."

"He hasn't handled that well. I thought once I was out of LA, I wouldn't have to deal with it as much, but he still texts. And today, he was waiting for me outside Ramsey's gate."

Hayes straightened in his chair. "What did he want?"

"He said to make amends, but I could tell he'd been high recently. He was hungover. He likely wanted money. That's what it always comes down to with him. More money and to make me suffer."

Hayes tapped a few keys on his computer. "Let me run a search really quick."

I was quiet as Hayes scanned the screen.

"Shit," he muttered.

"What?"

"Eli Cavanaugh was arrested two weeks ago for possession. There was enough that they could charge him with intent to distribute."

I leaned forward, pinching the bridge of my nose. The fact that I hadn't heard from my mom or dad about this told me that they didn't know. But then who had covered his bail and lawyer fees?

"Give me one second." Hayes picked up his phone and began dialing. "Hello, this is Sheriff Hayes Easton in Wolf Gap, Oregon. Could I speak with the detective in charge of the Eli Cavanaugh case?" He paused. "Sure, I can hold."

Hayes tapped a pen against a pad of paper as we waited. "Yes, this is Sheriff Hayes Easton. I'm sitting here with Boden Cavanaugh, who just had a visit from Eli. I was hoping to get the lay of the land and see if there was anything Boden needed to be worried about."

Hayes was quiet for another moment. "No, Boden isn't hoping to get his brother out of a jam. He's wondering if there are things at play that *he* needs to be concerned about. Eli didn't issue overt threats, but they weren't warm and fuzzy greetings, either."

Hayes began scribbling on his pad of paper, his jaw tensing as he wrote. "I appreciate the transparency. I'll have my officers keep an eye out and report anything back to you that we might find." A pause. "No problem. Talk soon."

My foot tapped in a rapid beat as Hayes hung up the phone, but I forced myself to wait for him to speak.

"Your brother is messed up with some seriously bad people and shouldn't have crossed state lines."

My hands gripped the edge of the chair, knuckles bleaching white. "Who?"

"A cartel that's moving product into Southern California. This detective thinks they have your brother dealing to his wealthy friends."

Dealing. A cartel. Eli had gotten mixed up in some bad stuff before, but nothing on this level. "They're sure?"

"This detective seemed to be. She didn't share the evidence she had, but she stated everything as fact. They're taking him to trial. Boden, cartels don't like to take risks with people turning on them."

My gut twisted. No wonder Eli had shown up in middle-of-nowhere Oregon. He was desperate. I released my hold on the chair. "I came to talk to you because Eli knew I was at a cabin up on the mountain." I swallowed against the burn in my throat. "I thought there might be a chance he hated me enough to take a shot at me."

Just saying the words killed something inside me. That I believed my brother could be capable of something like that.

Hayes met my eyes. "And now?"

"I think he's desperate. For money. A place to hide. None of that is a recipe for good things. Especially if he's using."

My phone buzzed in my pocket, and I pulled it out.

Addie: *Your brother is at The Gallery. He doesn't seem like he's in a good state of mind.*

Everything in me froze for a split second. Then I was pushing out of the chair, my panicked gaze meeting Hayes'. "We have to go. Eli's at The Gallery."

Chapter Thirty-Three

Laiken

"WHO THE HELL ARE YOU TEXTING?" ELI BARKED.

Addie fumbled her phone, almost dropping it to the floor. Her eyes widened in panic, and I stepped between her and Eli. "I asked you to leave."

He sneered at me, and for the first time, I saw the glimmers of true hatred in Eli's eyes. "You think you're too good for me? Just like that fucker of a brother of mine."

He lurched forward, grabbing me by my sweater and lifting me off the floor.

Serena charged. "Let her go, you asshole." She slammed her fists into his back, but Eli just let loose a manic sort of laugh.

I brought my knee up, aiming for his family jewels but missed. Eli swore, and his other hand came to my throat, squeezing. "You think you can hurt me?"

I clawed at his arm with my nails as Serena went for his face.

"The sheriff is on his way," Addie cried.

That did it. Eli released me with a shove, his eyes wild. "I'm not done with you, bitch."

I collapsed to the floor as he charged out the front door.

Addie and Serena sank to their knees next to me as I struggled to suck in air. Addie's hand trembled as she rubbed it up and down my back. "Slow breaths, nice and easy."

She slid out her phone. "Beck? We need you at The Gallery." She was quiet for a moment. "Just hurry."

"Oh, God. Oh, God." Serena said the words over and over. "Are you okay? He could've—"

"He didn't," I croaked.

The front door burst open, and Boden and Hayes charged into the room. Boden froze the second he saw me on the floor. Then, in a flash, he was in front of me. "What happened? Did he hurt you?"

"Your brother's a fucking psycho," Serena bit out. "He tried to choke her."

Rage and fear filled Boden's eyes as his hands went to my neck, his touch featherlight. "Laiken." My name was a guttural plea.

"I'm okay." It sounded as if I'd just smoked a pack of cigarettes.

His fingers gently prodded my neck. "Does it hurt?"

I couldn't hide my wince.

"Beckett is on his way," Addie said softly.

"Which direction did he go in?" Hayes clipped.

Serena pointed, and then Hayes was speaking into his radio. "What was he wearing?"

Serena and Addie described it, and Hayes recounted it for the bulletin going out to the department.

Everything hurt. In too many ways to count. I leaned into Boden. He moved fast, sinking to the floor and pulling me onto his lap. He cradled me as if he could protect me from everything bad in the world. Only he couldn't. "I'm so sorry, Laiken. I'm so damn sorry."

"It's not your fault."

"It is. He wouldn't have come here if it wasn't for me. He wouldn't have sought you out."

Panic lit through me so fiercely it stole my breath. My hands gripped Boden's sweatshirt hard. "Don't. Don't leave me. Please." The tears came then. A dump of adrenaline so intense, I began to shake.

Boden held me tighter against him. "I'm not. I'm right here. You have me, Laiken. All of me."

I cried harder. A release of everything that had transpired over the past few days and all I had been holding on to for years. I let it all free.

Some part of my brain registered the bell over the door ringing. Boots on the floor.

"Let's get her to the couch in the back," Beckett said. "Addie, can you find a blanket?"

"Of course."

I became aware of Boden lifting me, settling me on his lap again on the couch. Someone wrapped a blanket around me.

"Laiken, I need you to try to focus on me."

I only shook harder.

Boden held me tighter, pressing his face to the side of mine. "Come on, Laiken. You can do this. Just breathe and focus. Please."

It was the pleading in his tone that broke through my haze. I blinked a few times. Slowly, Beckett's face came into focus.

"There you go." He pressed his fingers to my wrist. "Can someone get me some juice? If you don't have that, anything sugary."

"I have apple juice here," Addie said, hurrying to the fridge.

A moment later, she pushed a cup into my hand.

"Nice and easy sips," Beckett instructed.

The cold liquid was a balm to my abused throat. After a few, I set it down on the side table. "Thanks. Sorry about the freak-out."

Boden's arms tightened around me. "It's natural," he gritted out.

I shifted in his lap so I could take in his face. There was

only one word to describe it: *ravaged*. I lifted my hands to his cheeks, feeling the scruff prick my palms. "I'm okay."

"We don't know that yet." His gaze went to Beckett.

I sighed and turned around so that Beckett could examine me. He gently prodded my neck. "Tender?"

"A little." I had a feeling I'd have a few bruises to show for my encounter.

"What about when you swallow?"

I made the motion. "Just a little. Not too bad."

"Did you black out for any period of time?"

"No."

Beckett straightened. "I think you'll be fine. Come in with Boden for his checkup, and I'll give you both an exam. And for the love of all that's holy, will you two rest like I told you to?"

Addie slipped her hand into his and squeezed. "He can be bossy when he's worried about people he cares about."

Beckett dropped a kiss to her lips. "Speaking of worrying. Have you eaten enough today?"

She grinned. "Told you."

Hayes moved into the back room, Deputy Young on his heels. "You doing okay, Laiken?"

I nodded as I tried to slide off Boden's lap, but he held firm. "I'm fine. Promise. Just shocked me, is all."

Boden growled something I couldn't make out.

Hayes pulled up a chair and sat. "I've got all my officers looking for Eli. We'll find him."

This time, I forced myself off Boden's lap but took his hand in mine, squeezing hard.

"Can you walk me through what happened?" Hayes asked, looking at me, then Addie and Serena.

Addie cleared her throat. "He came in and, right off, I could tell that something was off with him. His eyes were jumpy. He said some crass things, and then Laiken and Serena came out."

I gripped Boden's hand harder. "At first, he was just trying to start trouble. Saying cruel things about Boden. But when he saw Addie texting, he flipped out. I got between them, and he was livid. I told him to leave, and he grabbed me. It escalated from there."

Hayes looked between me and Boden. "I'll need more details eventually, but it can wait for now."

Serena edged forward. "You have to tell Hayes what he said before he left."

Boden stiffened next to me, his body vibrating with barely restrained rage. "What did he say?"

I swallowed hard. "That he wasn't done with me."

Chapter Thirty-Four

Laiken

BODEN RAN A RAG ACROSS AN INVISIBLE SPOT ON THE counter, over and over again. My eyes tracked the movement, worry burrowing itself deeper with each pass of the cloth. I pushed off the counter and moved in close, wrapping my fingers around his arm. "Boden."

He didn't look up, just kept scrubbing. The invisible wall he'd erected between us clawed at me—jagged cuts in my flesh made by his silence. By how he wouldn't meet my gaze.

I squeezed his arm. "Look at me."

"I just want to get this kitchen cleaned up before we call it a night."

"It's clean. I'm pretty sure you could do surgery on this counter." I tugged at Boden, forcing him to turn towards me. The expression on his face had me sucking in a breath. So much pain. It was carved so deeply into the planes of his face I knew it had to have been there for years. But, somehow, I'd missed the severity of his hurt.

I reached up, ghosting my hands over his cheeks. His jaw. Boden pressed into my touch. "I don't deserve that."

My hands stilled. "Why?"

"He could've killed you." The words tore from his throat. "And I brought him into your life."

I gripped Boden's face with a little more force. "His actions aren't on you."

"But they're tied to me. Action and reaction. I always have to think about how what I do might cause him to respond."

I couldn't imagine the kind of pressure that put on a person—needing to analyze every step you took and preemptively brace for impact. I stroked my thumb back and forth across Boden's cheek and jaw. "Why didn't you tell me that it was Eli that Carissa cheated with?"

The muscle in Boden's jaw tensed beneath my fingertips, fluttering. "I didn't want anyone to know."

"Who does?"

"My parents. The police. That's it. Her parents probably suspect. If it got out in the press…"

I could only imagine. The way they'd harassed Boden after Carissa's death had been horrible as it was. But if they got wind of this kind of scandal? They'd go rabid.

I dropped my hands from his face and wrapped them around his waist. "I'm so sorry. I can't imagine how much it hurt to find out."

He rested his chin on the top of my head. "Some part of me knew there was someone else. We weren't sleeping together. Some days she didn't come home, saying she needed the quiet of her place. But the thought of her being with Eli never even crossed my mind. It should've. He always wanted what I had. And if he couldn't have it, he wanted to destroy it."

My hands twisted in Boden's sweatshirt. "Do you know why he's that way?"

Boden shook his head. "It's been that way since middle school. I think my parents thought he was just wrapped up in a bad group of kids, but it wasn't that. He couldn't stand to see me succeed. To see me happy. I don't know what creates that in a person."

I didn't either. As much as Jase and Jax had fought, there was never any hatred there. Anger and frustration, sure. But they had loved each other. Still, that love had created hate for Jax. Love for Jase that ultimately made him hate me. Hate anyone who was still here when his brother was gone.

I stroked a hand up and down Boden's back, my thumb playing over the ridges in his spine. "I wish I could make it better. Had some magical way to fix it."

Boden pulled back a fraction, his gaze sweeping over my face. "He attacks you, and you're here wishing you could fix it?"

"*He's* the one who hurt me. Not you. When I care about people, I can't simply turn that off because it's inconvenient. I wouldn't want to, so don't try to push me away. Because that *will* hurt." It already had. That and the fact that he'd hidden the truth from me.

Boden pulled me back, flush against him. "I'm sorry. It's instinct."

"I get that, but I need you to fight against it."

"I will."

My heart hammered against my ribs. "Are you trying to fix me?"

He released his tight hold on me but kept a grip on my arms. "What do you mean?"

"Eli said you have a thing for trying to fix people."

That muscle was back to fluttering in Boden's jaw. "Yeah, there's some of that in me. But I didn't pursue you because I thought you needed fixing." He let go of my arms and ran a hand through his hair. "That photo called to me. It was like you saw me before we ever even met. It punched into my chest and grabbed hold of my damn heart. It wouldn't let go." His eyes came back to me. "You wouldn't let go."

I wanted to believe every one of those beautiful words, but I couldn't help but wonder if it was simply a pretty speech. "I'm not fixable, Boden. But I'm okay with that. I've learned to love myself just the way I am. The fractures are a gift in so many ways. They've allowed me to see things that I was blind to before. Made me realize how strong I am. I don't want to be with someone who thinks I should be anything but what I am."

Boden moved in a flash, taking my face in his hands and pulling me close. "I don't want you to be anything but exactly who you are. A woman who is fierce, determined, strong. Kind, empathetic, and giving. Everything you've been through has made you into that person. I'm not trying to erase any of it or fix anything about you. Because nothing needs to be fixed."

Tears burned the backs of my eyes, and my throat felt tight.

Boden bent, brushing his lips across mine. "I'd never want to change a thing about the woman who stole my heart. I love you, Laiken. I probably fell the moment I saw your photo. The rest of my body has just been playing catch-up."

"Boden," I croaked.

"It's okay if you're not ready to go there—"

I shook my head. "I love you. I didn't want to. I fought so hard against it. But you stormed into my heart anyway. And I'm so damn glad you did."

The corner of Boden's mouth kicked up. "Told you I was stubborn."

I let out a laugh tinged with a hint of tears. "I love you."

"I love you, too, Laiken. So damn much." He took my mouth in a slow kiss, one that had everything we'd just let free in it.

I forced myself to pull back, gripping his arms. "Wait."

"What?" The heat in his eyes spoke of impatience and promises of what was to come.

"It's been a long day. I need a shower."

Boden grinned. "Then let's get clean together."

He bent and lifted me into his arms, striding towards his bathroom.

I let out a surprised shriek. "Boden, your arm."

"My arm feels damn fine right now. Don't rain on my parade."

So, I didn't. And Boden showed me just how fine he felt—and I soaked up every moment.

A distant ringing pulled me out of a deep sleep. I blinked into the darkness a few times before realizing that the sound was coming from my cell phone on the nightstand.

Boden grumbled something unintelligible and pulled me closer to him.

I smiled into the dark and reached for my phone. A number I didn't recognize flashed on the screen. It was local, so I swept my finger along the answer button. "Hello?"

"Laik?"

Marisa's voice cut across the line, and it was hoarse as if she'd been crying. I pushed up in bed, checking the time. It was after one in the morning. "It's me. Are you okay?"

"Are you home?"

"No, I'm staying with Boden right now."

"Oh, I—never mind. It was dumb."

Boden shifted into a sitting position, worry lining his face. He mouthed, "*Who?*"

"*Marisa*," I mouthed back. "Where are you?"

I heard a car door slam. "I came to The Gallery and was knocking but no one answered."

"You shouldn't be out on your own right now. It's not smart. Let's call the sheriff's department to get you an escort home."

"I'm in my car now." The engine started. "My doors are locked. I'm fine. I just wanted to talk to you. I shouldn't have come in the middle of the night."

"That's okay. I can come meet you—"

"No. Go back to sleep."

I could feel the hurt in Marisa's voice, and it tore at me in more ways than one. I hated that she was in pain, and that we'd grown so distant over the years. "Will you meet me for breakfast at The Bean tomorrow?"

Marisa sniffed, doing her best to clear away the tears. "Sure."

"How about nine?"

"Yeah, that's good."

I gripped my phone a little tighter. "You'll go straight home?"

"I promise. No stopping for shots at the bar."

A soft laugh escaped me. "Glad to hear it. Save it for the espresso shots with breakfast."

"Not nearly as much fun, but I can make it work."

"Good. See you tomorrow."

"Tomorrow...Laik?"

"I'm here."

Marisa was quiet for a moment. "I'm sorry. I was hurting, and I took that out on you. I shouldn't have. You never did that to me after you lost Jase."

"It's okay. I get it. We'll talk tomorrow. Find our way back."

"There's so much I regret..."

"We can fix it. One thing at a time."

She let out a long breath. "Sure. One thing at a time. Night, Laik."

The line went dead, and I slowly lowered my phone.

Boden wrapped an arm around me. "She okay?"

"I don't think so. She was at The Gallery, looking for me."

"Shit. She shouldn't be out with everything going on."

"She's going home now." I turned into Boden's hold, letting him wrap his arms around me. "I lost so much when Jase died. Sometimes, I forget just how much."

"Your friendship with Marisa?"

I nodded. "We were both drowning, and I let her float away."

"That doesn't mean you can't swim her way now that you're stronger."

I looked up at Boden, who always had the perfect, encouraging words. "We're going to breakfast tomorrow."

He pressed his lips to my temple. "First steps. You'll find your way."

I hoped he was right because I didn't want to lose anyone else.

Chapter Thirty-Five

Boden

My jaw fell open as Laiken set down the cereal box. "You didn't."

She gave me a devilish smile and shrugged. "Sorry, not sorry."

I tipped the Lucky Charms box over my bowl. Two measly kernels fell from it, and neither was a damn marshmallow. "You're going to make me eat Grape Nuts?"

"You bought it for yourself."

I sank into my chair at the table. "I bought it knowing I'd never actually eat it because I have the deliciousness that is the luck of the Irish. Which is exactly what I'd be doing right now if I hadn't been betrayed."

Laiken pressed her lips together to keep from laughing.

"Aren't you going to get breakfast with your friend anyway?"

She wrapped her arm around her bowl as if protecting it from me. "That's not for two more hours. I need fuel to hold me over until then."

I let out a growl and poured some Grape Nuts into my bowl. "You're cruel."

Laiken dunked her spoon into her cereal and dribbled a few marshmallows on top of mine. "Better?"

I grabbed her hand and tugged her so she was leaning over the table. Taking her mouth in a slow kiss, I relished her taste—sugar and whatever was uniquely Laiken. "I'll be taking payment like that for the rest of the day."

She laughed against my lips. "It'll be such a hardship."

I beat out a rhythm along with the radio against the steering wheel.

Laiken's lips twitched as she watched me. "I take it your arm is feeling good?"

I worked out a drum solo and then glanced in her direction. "It would be feeling better if I'd had some Lucky Charms."

She rolled her eyes. "Such a drama queen."

"Hey, if I didn't love you, there would've been some serious repercussions for that theft."

"Good thing I know I can get away with it."

I shook my head but leaned over to grab a quick kiss. "You're a monster."

"Watch the road, you crazy."

I chuckled and put on my blinker to pull into the alley behind the gallery. "Living dangerously at ten miles per hour."

She pinched my side. "Just for that, I'm going to steal all your Lucky Charms from now on."

I turned into the alley, and the smile slipped from my face. A sheriff's department SUV and squad car blocked off the street, and a few officers milled around. My ribs tightened around my lungs as images of Eli breaking in filled my mind. Ones where he was determined to get his hands on Laiken.

"Oh, God," Laiken whispered.

My gaze shot to her. All the color had drained from her face. "What?"

"That's Marisa's car."

"Shit." I switched off my engine and climbed out of my truck. I rounded the vehicle to get to Laiken, but she'd already climbed out.

Her hand trembled as she reached for mine. I tugged her to my side and then wrapped that arm around her.

Hayes strode towards us. "I was just about to call you."

"Where's Marisa?" Laiken asked.

His jaw hardened. "We don't know. One of the neighboring businesses called in an abandoned car with its door open this morning."

"She called me last night. Said she wanted to talk, but I was at Boden's. I told her to get an escort home, but she didn't want one." Tears filled her eyes and tracked down her cheeks. "She was in her car. I heard the engine start and the locks engage."

Hayes straightened at that information. "You're sure?"

Laiken nodded.

"Points to someone she knew," I surmised.

Hayes jotted down something in his phone. "Could be. Or someone had a gun and she felt she had no choice."

"What about cameras?" I asked.

"None of us are very big on security," Laiken said softly.

Hayes grimaced. "We've asked around, but so far, no video."

Laiken gripped my jacket. "Is there anything?"

Hayes looked back at the vehicle and then returned his gaze to Laiken as if trying to decide whether or not to share something. "There's blood at the scene."

Laiken's hand spasmed, and she made a small noise in the back of her throat. I pulled her tighter against me. I would've given anything to shield her from this.

"It's not enough to end her life or even be a critical wound, but it's enough that we know the person is injured. I've already got a sample headed to the lab," Hayes said.

A sick feeling invaded my gut. "Does Marisa look similar to Laiken?"

Laiken turned in my arms. "We have a similar build. Her hair is a little lighter than mine but it's brown, too."

"Enough that they could be mistaken for each other in the dark," Hayes filled in.

My gut twisted. "Have you located my brother?"

Hayes shook his head. "We had one possible sighting, but once we got there, he was gone."

"You don't think...?" Laiken's words trailed off as I was sure a million dark what-ifs filled her head.

"He would have to realize pretty damn quick that he had the wrong woman." And I had to hope Eli would let her go once he realized that he couldn't use her.

Hayes held up a hand to stop my guessing game. "We don't know what happened. If it was Robert Aaron or Eli or someone else altogether. The only thing we can do now is work the evidence and get searches going for Marisa."

"Tell us what we can do," Laiken said.

A car door slammed, and we turned to see Gilly heading our way. Her face paled as she took us all in. "Did you find her?" she asked Hayes.

"I'm afraid not. We'd like to do a search of The Gallery premises just to make sure we aren't missing anything inside."

"Of course." Gilly slid a key off her ring and handed it to Hayes. "Look anywhere you need to."

"Thank you." He started back towards his officers.

Gilly turned to Laiken and pulled her into a hug. "When he called, I thought it was you. That you'd been taken. Cherub, I was so scared."

"I'm okay." Laiken's voice trembled. "But I don't know that Marisa is."

Gilly pulled away from Laiken but kept a hold of her shoulders, her gaze moving from Laiken to me. "We need to get a search going." She pulled out her phone and hit a contact. It rang and rang. "Jax was probably out late with those friends of his." She paused for a moment, listening. "It's Gilly. Marisa is missing, and we need all the people we can get for a search. Call me when you wake up."

She hung up and began typing out a text. "I'll let Chip and Serena know, too. My book club ladies. They're great at spreading the word." Gilly nibbled on her bottom lip. "I'm not sure if I should tell Kay." She looked up to meet Laiken's gaze. "She's not been herself lately, and I don't think this would help—"

Laiken squeezed Gilly's hand. "We should shield her while we can. I can call Everly, Hadley, and Addie. They'll get the word out in their circles. We'll find her."

Gilly shook her head. "What's happening around here?"

I didn't have an answer for her, but whatever it was, it wasn't good.

Chapter Thirty-Six

Laiken

I SLUMPED AGAINST THE BATHROOM COUNTER AS I SET DOWN my toiletries bag. Everything hurt. My eyes burned, my back ached, and my legs felt as if they might give out on me at any second. But hours of scouring the woods and driving around town hadn't given any of us a clue as to where Marisa might be. It was as if she'd simply vanished into thin air.

A soft knock sounded on the open door, and Boden stepped into the bathroom. "You find all the space you need?"

I did my best to force a smile. "I'm taking up half your shower with my girly-smelling stuff now."

Boden brushed the hair out of my face. "I like having your girly-smelling stuff next to mine."

"Not afraid it'll turn your shampoo pink?"

"I'm not scared of a little pink."

"That's good." I grimaced as I shifted against the counter.

Boden massaged my neck. "Your back hurting?"

Normally, I tried to hide my pain from others, not wanting them to pity me or try to throw me solution after solution. But I found myself wanting to let Boden into my world. To let him see everything. "It's not feeling great."

"How about a bath?"

"That actually sounds perfect."

Boden released me and turned to the large soaking tub. He switched on the water, holding his hand beneath the flow. After a few seconds, he lowered the drain. Pulling open the shower, he surveyed the contents and grabbed my bodywash. He poured a healthy slug into the water, and bubbles immediately started to form. "You soak, and I'll go make you some tea."

I moved into Boden's space, pressing my body against his and seeking his lips. "I don't know what I did to deserve you."

"Obviously, you were an angel in a previous life."

I chuckled and stepped back. "Good to see that ego hasn't suffered any hits lately."

"Never." He sent me a wink and headed out of the bathroom.

I set my bag of toiletries on a stool next to the bathtub. Peeling off my clothes, I left them in a pile on the floor and stepped into the water. The heat was heavenly. I sank into the suds and closed my eyes for a moment. The warmth soothed my tense muscles, and I wished it could fix the rest of my problems along with it.

After a few minutes, I shut off the water and reached for my razor. I soaped up one leg and began methodically moving the blades across my skin. Something about the move was calming. An action I could take with a tangible result.

But it only made the frustration hit harder when I reached that spot behind my knees and at the backs of my thighs. As I tried to move to gain access, pain radiated up my spine. I bit back a curse and slammed my razor down with a little more force than necessary.

Boden's eyes widened as he stepped into the bathroom. "What's all that about?"

"Just my body not doing what I need it to."

He lowered himself to the floor, setting my mug of tea on the stool. "Tell me."

My face flushed; the heat of embarrassment pooling in my cheeks. "It's nothing."

Boden dipped his hand into the water and absentmindedly stroked my leg. "It's not nothing if it has you slamming toiletries down."

I worried my bottom lip, searching for words I didn't especially want to find. "There are some things that are harder for me to do than others."

He picked up the razor, twirling it between his fingers. "Shaving?"

"I can reach most of my legs easily, but there are spots where it's hard. It's painful for me to reach them. Same with painting my toes." I let my polish-free nails peek out of the water. "I miss brightly colored toenails."

I used to have a thing about them. As many wild colors as I could find. Sometimes, I'd paint them in a rainbow. Serena and I had gotten good at drawing little flowers or hearts on our nails, too. Now, I couldn't bend over for the length of time required to get the polish on.

Boden's hand trailed up my leg, his fingers leaving delicious shivers in their wake. "Where is it hard for you to reach?"

I swallowed hard, trying to get a handle on my ragged breathing. "Behind my knees. The backs of my thighs."

His hand left the water, and he set down the razor. Boden's gaze locked with mine. "Trust me?"

I stared into those hazel eyes, watching the gold dance under the lights of the bathroom. "Yes." It was just one word, yet it was everything. Somehow, I'd come to trust this man more than anyone else in my life.

Boden lifted my shaving cream from the stool and dispensed a good amount into his hand.

"Boden—"

His eyes cut to me. "You said you trusted me."

I swallowed my words and nodded. He inclined his head to the leg closest to him. "Lift."

I did as instructed, resting my heel on the edge of the tub. Boden smoothed the foam over my knee and thigh in long, gentle strokes. The motion soothed the edges of my soul that had torn and become ragged over the course of the day.

He rinsed his hands in the water and picked up my razor. His focus was laser-sharp as he dragged the blades over my skin. He attacked the job as if he were an engineer at a nuclear plant and one wrong move could mean disaster. Yet he was completely calm at the same time.

Boden slowed as he reached the spot behind my knee, taking the time to straighten my leg. In mere moments, he was done. "Switch."

I followed his orders, and he got to work on the other leg. My throat and eyes burned as I watched him work. No one had ever shown me this kind of care. Something so simple that meant everything.

As I took Boden in with his intense focus and gentle intensity, I realized that fixing things was Boden's love language. The way he showed those in his life that he cared. It wasn't an unhealthy obsession but an enactment of that love.

He dragged the razor over one last spot. "There. All done."

I let my leg slide back into the water. I rubbed my limbs together, reveling in the silky feel. I never got them this smooth. My gaze lifted to Boden's. "Thank you."

His eyes heated, that gold in them sparking. "It's never a hardship to have my hands on you."

I leaned forward, my breasts rising out of the water. My lips met his in a tender kiss that turned hungry.

Boden let out a sound that resembled a growl as he moved into me. The action forced me back, reclining against the tub. His hand slipped into the water, but this time he didn't stop at my thighs. His fingers delved into the heat at the apex.

He teased me with lazy strokes as our tongues dueled. Each pass of his fingers over and around my clit drove me higher. As two fingers slid inside me, I moaned into Boden's mouth.

His hand curled in a new kind of stroke. This one hit a spot that had me seeing stars behind my closed eyes. Boden pulled back from my lips as he continued his ministrations.

"Open your eyes."

I couldn't seem to get them to obey—too lost in sensation.

"I want to see that amber dance when you come. I want to see you shatter."

The pure need in his voice was enough to have my lids fluttering open.

"That's my girl."

"Boden." His name was a plea on my lips.

"Need more?"

"Yes." I couldn't find it in me to care that I was begging. I simply needed more. More of everything I was feeling.

A third finger slid inside me, and Boden's thumb circled that bundle of nerves. My hips rose to meet him, silently asking for even more. His movements sped up, and my head tipped back on the end of the tub. Boden's other hand found my breast, rolling my nipple between his fingers.

Sensation sparked across my skin. Everything in me tightened. There was a hint of pain cascading along my spine, but I didn't give a damn. Everything else felt so alive—pinpricks of light and feeling everywhere.

"Open your eyes." Boden's gravelly voice cut through my haze.

I forced them open. I wanted to be with him in this moment, to let myself shatter without losing him for even a second.

Boden's thumb pressed down on my clit as his fingers drove deeper. My mouth fell open in a silent gasp. It was as if I were pulling in everything around me. Each spark and sensation, the flame that was Boden, and all the love pouring out of his eyes. I took it all, and when I came apart, it was with Boden cemented on my very soul.

Chapter Thirty-Seven

Boden

"I'D PAINT YOUR TOES RIGHT NOW IF WE DIDN'T HAVE TO leave for dinner." The idea that Laiken hadn't been able to do something so simple that she obviously loved ate at me. I'd paint her toes every damn day if it would put a smile on her face.

Laiken arched a brow. "Really?"

"Hey, my fine motor skills are excellent."

She let out a throaty laugh. One that had me fighting the urge to tug her into the bedroom for more of what we'd started earlier. Instead, I simply pulled her into my arms and brushed my lips against hers. "Love you."

"Love you, too. I wish we hadn't agreed to go to dinner."

I brushed the hair away from her face. "I want to get to know your friends better."

Addie had wanted everyone over for dinner after the search, saying we needed some time together. I didn't disagree with that plan. I knew the day had been rough on Laiken and the time with people she cared about would help.

"Addie is an amazing cook." Laiken's stomach growled with that.

I pressed a kiss to her temple and released her. "Let's get you fed." I picked up two bully sticks from the counter and tossed them to Peaches and Gizmo on their dog bed. "Be good while we're gone. No parties."

Peaches barked and then dove for her bully stick.

Laiken grinned. "I think that means *screw you*."

I chuckled as I grabbed my keys and headed for the door. "She never listens to a word I say."

"How does it feel to know there's a woman you can't win over with your charm?"

I tugged Laiken out the door and locked it. "I won you over. That's what matters."

She scoffed as we headed down the steps. "Maybe I'm still making up my mind."

Opening Laiken's door, I moved in close as she got in. I buckled her seat belt and took her mouth in a slow kiss. "I've got you. No use in denying it."

She huffed. "Bragger."

The corner of my mouth kicked up. "Secure in the knowledge you're mine."

Laiken gripped my sweater, pulling me back to her. "Just remember, you're mine, too."

"You've got all of me. All the time."

A shadow passed over her eyes even as she smiled. "Glad to hear it."

As I rounded the front of the truck and climbed behind the wheel, I had to wonder if Laiken was thinking about the future. How things would work when I had to leave for this movie and all the days after that. I couldn't imagine being away from her for a week, let alone months. But I wasn't sure she was ready for an invitation to come with me, either.

I backed out of the makeshift parking spot in front of the cabin and headed for the gate. As I waited for it to open, I took

Laiken's hand in mine, resting it on my thigh. "We'll figure it out. One day at a time."

Her hand tightened around mine. "One day sounds good."

The drive into town was quick. We hadn't gotten any more snow, and the roads were clear. Laiken pointed to a white farmhouse. "That's Addie and Beckett's."

I pulled behind another SUV and shut off the engine. "Let's do this."

"Prepare for chaos."

"I love a little chaos."

As we walked up the path, the front door burst open. "Laiken!" a little girl shouted, running down the front steps.

Another girl, who had to be her twin, followed behind, shutting the door softly behind herself. "Birdie, you left the door wide open."

"I knew you'd get it." Birdie flung herself into Laiken's arms. "It's been forever."

Laiken ruffled the girl's hair, a big smile on her face. "Way too long. I need to see what new tricks you're working on." Her gaze lifted to me. "Birdie here is an amazing skateboarder. And Sage is an expert botanist."

Sage sent Laiken a shy smile. "I've been working on my photography of the new plants I find in the woods. I want to show you."

"Of course. Girls, this is Boden."

Birdie looked up at me with an assessing expression. "Is he your boyfriend?"

I choked on a laugh.

Laiken squeezed the girl tighter to her. "I guess he is."

Birdie's eyes narrowed. "You better treat our Laiken good. She deserves the best."

A flare of warmth lit in my chest at the fierceness of the little girl's words. "You're right. She does. And I'll be working every day to make sure she gets it."

"Good," she harumphed.

Laiken's eyes twinkled. "They'll be watching you now."

"On my best behavior," I said, making an X over my heart.

We headed up the path, and the door opened again. This time, a blonde and a man with dark features filled the space. The woman grinned. "Are you two causing trouble?"

"Duh, Mom," Birdie said.

Sage giggled. "Birds was threatening Laiken's new boyfriend."

The woman's eyes widened. "Sorry about that. They love their Laiken." She stepped forward, extending her hand. "I'm Hadley, and this is my husband, Calder."

I shook both their hands. "Nice to meet you. And I like that they're looking out for their girl." No, I loved it. Knowing that others had Laiken's back and cared for her.

Calder chuckled. "Just don't step out of line. They can get vicious."

"*Dad*," Birdie moaned.

"It's the truth, kid. Now, let's get inside before we all freeze to death."

We followed the family inside to the sounds of laughter and the faint strains of music.

Hadley motioned us along. "Everyone's in the kitchen."

As we stepped into the space, my gaze swept the room. I recognized Addie and Beckett. There was a blonde woman I didn't recognize, and another who I registered with a flash of shock. The same one I'd seen on the hill at Ramsey's ranch. The one who'd had the playful tussle with the dog.

Her eyes widened a fraction, and then she quickly averted her gaze. I noticed that she was on the outskirts of the group, rubbing the head of a German Shepherd while sitting at a breakfast nook while everyone else gathered around the kitchen island.

Laiken tugged me forward. "You know Addie and Beckett. This is Hayes' fiancée, Everly."

I shook the woman's hand, who was sitting on a stool at the island. "Nice to meet you. I'm a fan of your fiancé's."

She grinned. "I am, too. Even though he didn't believe there was a movie star in our midst. He made me think I was losing my mind."

I chuckled. "Now you can hold this over his head for years to come."

"I like the way you think."

Laiken led me towards the familiar stranger. "This is Shiloh, the last of the Easton clan. Shy, this is Boden."

The woman didn't stand or offer a hand. She simply dipped her head in a sort of greeting. "Nice to meet you."

"You, too." I crouched to greet the gorgeous dog. "Is he yours?"

Shiloh shook her head. "Koda belongs to Hayes."

"Nice to meet you, Koda." I gave him a scratch behind the ears. "Can I get you a beer?" Beckett called.

I straightened, heading back to the island with the rest of the group. "I wouldn't turn one down."

"You?" he asked Laiken.

She shook her head. "I'll take a soda if you've got one."

"Get her a Cherry Coke," Addie ordered.

Beckett's lips twitched. "That's her drug of choice."

"Except I can only have one a day right now." She rubbed her belly. "As soon as I pop this one out, I'm having at least three."

Everly laughed and rubbed her back. "I'll bring a six-pack on ice to the hospital."

She grinned. "You are the best cousin ever."

We lost ourselves in conversation about nothing serious. No one mentioned the fact that Hayes wasn't here because he was still searching for a missing woman. We didn't speak about shootings or possible murders. We laughed and ate, and I fell in love with Laiken's friends. There was no pretense. They didn't pretend that I wasn't an actor, but they didn't make a big deal out of it either.

Calder and Beckett did their fair share of good-natured ribbing, and Hadley asked me all sorts of random questions about other actors I'd worked with. But they mostly wanted to know about *me*. What I was interested in. How I'd ended up in Wolf Gap. We talked about the town.

When I mentioned having talked to a realtor, Laiken's eyes flared. I guessed it was as good a time as any to let her in on that small detail. The whole table chimed in on areas I should consider looking. The only one who didn't say a word all through dinner was Shiloh.

I couldn't help but be curious about the mysterious woman and wanted to ask Laiken about her the first moment I got.

My phone buzzed in my pocket as we cleared the table. A voicemail from my dad. Apparently, I'd been too caught up in conversation and had missed his call.

I pressed a kiss to Laiken's temple. "This is from my dad. I need to check it real quick."

"Of course. Take as long as you need."

I nodded and headed for the back deck. The air bit into my skin, but the feeling was pleasant after the big Italian feast. I lifted the phone to my ear and listened to the message.

"Hey, Bo. I talked to the private investigator. He has nothing. It's like Eli dropped off the face of the Earth. I'm so sorry he's putting you through this." My father's voice cracked, and my heart right along with it. I could kill my brother for what he was putting them through, not to mention what he'd done to Laiken. "I'm calling it an early night, but let's connect tomorrow. Love you."

The line went dead. My dad had sounded so tired. A bone-deep fatigue that didn't come from lack of sleep but from years of pain.

The sound of the back door closing had me turning around. Shiloh appeared with Koda at her side.

"Hey," I greeted, trying to clear the lingering thoughts about my father and Eli.

"Please don't tell anyone you saw me at Ramsey's."

Interesting. Why watching someone work with horses had to be a secret, I had no idea. "I don't keep secrets from Laiken."

Her eyes hardened a fraction. "Fine," she gritted out. "Just don't tell anyone else. I don't need my business spread around."

It was more words than I'd heard her say all night. "I haven't yet, and I have no plans to start."

Shiloh jerked her head in a sort of nod and took off for the house. She almost collided with Laiken but dodged her at the last second. Laiken's gaze went from me to Shiloh and back again. "What was that all about?"

I watched Shiloh disappear around a corner. "I have no idea."

Chapter Thirty-Eight

Laiken

BODEN'S HAND TRAILED UP AND DOWN MY SPINE AS I LAY sprawled across his chest. "I like your friends."

"I'm glad. They're good people."

"Good people can be hard to come by."

"Probably harder in LA, where you're wondering if they're pursuing a friendship out of genuine interest or whether they want something."

His fingers stilled for a moment and then started their movement again. "You're right there. I can count the number of genuine friends I've had in my life on one hand."

That made me so incredibly sad for Boden. I'd had my share of hardship over the years but always had the knowledge that people in my life cared about me. "What you got from the people at dinner was pure authenticity."

Boden tipped up my face so I was looking at him. "I know that. I felt it every moment of tonight."

I kissed the inside of his arm. "I'm glad."

He stared at me for a moment, but it was as if he didn't see me.

His eyes were unfocused as he puzzled over something. "Can I ask you something?"

"Of course."

"Can it stay just between us?"

I studied the man beneath me. The planes of his face, the stubble along his jaw, those soulful eyes. "As long as you aren't about to tell me you're a serial killer or plotting to overthrow the government, I can keep a lid on it."

His mouth curved. "I might want to be king one day..."

I snorted and then kissed the underside of his jaw. "Of course, you do. All right, ask away."

"What's Shiloh's story?"

I stiffened a fraction. Somewhere along the line, I'd become protective of Shiloh, wanting to shield her from prying eyes and nosy questions. But I knew Boden wasn't just asking out of morbid curiosity. There had to be a reason.

"She was kidnapped when we were in the fifth grade."

All the muscles beneath me tensed. "But they found her."

"Ev saved her. Everly's father suffered from some serious delusions and took Shiloh, saying he rescued her from her evil family. After days passed and he wouldn't let her go, Ev rode her horse miles into town in the dark and told the sheriff."

Boden let out a long breath, one I hadn't realized he'd been holding the entire time I spoke. "I can't imagine what they've been through. Their family seemed so..."

"Perfect?" I finished for him.

He nodded. "But I guess no family is."

I traced circles on his pec. "No, I think that's impossible. But the Eastons love one another, and they love Ev and Addie as if they've always been a part of the brood."

"And they love you, too."

"I guess so." Even though I was a newer addition to their group, they had all welcomed me with open arms.

I looked up at Boden. "Why did you ask?"

He worked his jaw back and forth. "She comes here sometimes."

I sat up, the sheet falling to my waist. "Shy comes here? To Ramsey's?"

Boden nodded. "I've seen her a few times now. She sits on the hill and watches Ramsey with the horses. I've never seen her talk to him or anyone else. She just sits with that wolf-dog of his and watches."

I worried the corner of my bottom lip. Shiloh had always had a thing for animals—horses in particular—but I couldn't imagine her family being thrilled at her being on this ranch. Ramsey had been cleared of the crime he'd been accused of, but *rough around the edges* was an understatement when it came to describing the man. He'd gotten into more than one fight at local bars, and now he mostly stayed to himself.

"Does she seem okay when she comes here?"

Boden toyed with a strand of my hair. "I get the sense she's never completely okay. And with what she went through, I think that's understandable."

My chest squeezed as an image of Shiloh filled my mind. The day she finally returned to school. Everyone had stared as she walked down the hallway, and I hadn't missed how her hands trembled. She knew what it was like to have your life upended by a single event. One moment, and you were never the same again. Maybe Ramsey understood that, too.

"He's a good man," Boden said.

"I never said he wasn't."

"I can feel the tension running through you. The worry. Ramsey might not be warm and fuzzy, but I've seen him with an abused and broken horse. There isn't a cruel bone in his body."

I bent, taking his mouth in a kiss, pouring everything I felt for him into it. "You're a good man, too."

"I'm trying."

"You're succeeding."

And maybe Ramsey's brand of goodness was exactly what Shiloh needed. Because I knew better than anyone that a kind, fixer heart could change everything.

"Crud. Where did I put my boots?" I rushed around the living room until Boden caught me around the waist.

He pulled me flush against him. "How about you call in sick and we stay here all day? No boots needed."

I rolled my eyes. "Some of us work for a living."

"Hey, I work."

"I haven't seen a lot of evidence of that recently."

Boden chuckled and released me, tapping me on the butt. "Your boots are in the closet."

I made a beeline for the main bedroom. We'd kept the gallery closed all of yesterday for the search, but we were going to open it for a few hours this morning before things resumed this afternoon. Hayes and the sheriff's department were putting together new search grids, but so far, there was no sign of Marisa.

The thought had my stomach cramping. The temperatures had reached below freezing last night. All I could hope for was that she was at least somewhere warm.

I shook off the onslaught of images in my mind and pulled on my boots. "I'm ready."

"Do you want to take the dogs or leave them here?"

I glanced at Peaches and Gizmo, all curled up on their dog bed. "Let's leave them all cozy. We'll be back by lunch."

Boden bent to whisper in my ear as we headed for the door. "And what currency will you be paying me in for my assistant duties today?"

A pleasant shiver skated down my spine. "Sexual favors, of course. Maybe some Lucky Charms if you're really good."

"Combine the two, and I'll combust on the spot."

A laugh burst out of me as I hurried to Boden's truck and climbed in before he could open my door. "I never knew you had such strange fetishes."

He turned on the vehicle and immediately reached for the seat heater controls. "What can I say? I'm a weirdo at heart."

"Weirdos are my favorite people."

"Works out well for me then."

"That it does."

Boden pulled out and headed down the gravel road. He braked, reaching up for his gate fob, and then froze.

"What is it?" My gaze followed his to the gate. Something had been tossed over the metal. It took several moments for the image to register. Dark hair, masses of it. A too-still body. So much blood.

Only one word escaped my mouth. "Marisa."

Chapter Thirty-nine

Boden

I MUTTERED A CURSE AND PULLED LAIKEN INTO MY CHEST. She didn't need to see this. No one did, but this was her friend. Someone she'd spent such a formative portion of her life with.

With my free hand, I picked up my phone and hit Hayes' contact. He answered on the second ring. "Everything okay?"

"We found Marisa."

There was nothing but muted background voices for a moment. "It's bad?"

"Bad as it gets."

"No chance she's still breathing?"

My gaze traveled to the pool of blood, the lack of color in the woman's face, the blank eyes. "There's no chance."

"Where are you?"

"The gate at Ramsey's property."

Hayes muttered a curse. "You should call him, too. We'll have to question all of you."

I could only imagine his response and knew I should brace for it.

"Stay in your car. This could be a lure to get you out in the open."

Hayes' words had me scanning the forests around us, looking for any sign of movement. There was none. But that didn't mean someone wasn't out there.

⌐

Laiken shivered, and I pulled the blanket tighter around her shoulders, scooting in closer. The heat was on and the fire blazing, but I couldn't seem to get her warm.

Hayes took a seat on the coffee table in front of us and handed Laiken a mug of tea. "Ev always says tea helps when nothing else does."

Laiken's lips fluttered as if she were trying to smile and couldn't quite get her mouth to obey. "Ev speaks the truth."

She wrapped her hands around the mug and held it close to her chest. Her eyes had a slightly glassy look, and her gaze was a bit unfocused. Shock. There was nothing I could do. I simply had to give her time and be there for her.

Ramsey stared out the window, watching the sheriff's department officers crawl all over his property. "You need anything else from me, Easton? Or can I tend to my horses? Your people are making them edgy."

Hayes glanced back at Ramsey, a muscle in his jaw tensing. "Sure. I'll be in touch if we have any other questions."

"I'm sure you will," Ramsey muttered and stalked out the door.

Hayes shook his head. "That guy is a piece of work."

"Did his security cameras show anything?" I asked.

Hayes slid his phone out of his pocket and read a message. "We got nothing. Whoever did this spray-painted them from a distance."

I rubbed a hand up and down Laiken's arm. "That has to be someone who knows the property, right?"

"Or someone who's been watching," Hayes said.

Laiken shivered again, and I tightened my hold on her. "So, we're back to square one."

Hayes' eyes shifted a fraction. "Not exactly."

Laiken straightened. "What did you find out?"

Hayes navigated to the notes app on his phone, seeming to scroll through whatever he had typed there. "A few things." His thumb stopped moving. "Both Mitch and Lisbeth had high levels of narcotics in their systems when they died."

Laiken set her tea down on the side table and took my hand, squeezing it. "The same kind?"

"Yes. Both had high levels of opiates."

She swallowed, her eyes traveling to the officers working outside. "And you'll test Marisa?"

"We will."

"What about the search for Robert Aaron?" I pushed. "Someone has to have seen something."

"They did." Hayes ran a hand through his hair. "Got a call from police back east this morning. After my call, they did a more thorough search of Aaron's rental house. They brought dogs to search for drugs and blood evidence."

"Oh, God," Laiken whispered, her body going tense next to me.

"They found him buried in the backyard. Their medical examiner says she won't have a cause of death for some time, but that it was some kind of a brutal attack."

Laiken lifted her eyes to Hayes. "What's happening?"

"I don't know. It's unlikely Aaron's death is related to this. It's a very different signature. Different location. And he's a man with a record, it's possible he had less than savory connections in his life."

All of that was true, but none of it put me at ease. Nothing changed the fact that someone was killing people involved in Jase's accident.

Hayes ran a hand through his hair. "Aaron has a brother who's local. He defended Robert at every turn—"

"I remember him from the trial." Laiken gripped my hand

harder. "He testified. Suggested that we must've been doing something to egg his brother on."

"That's the one. He's harassed the Granger family on more than one occasion. Blames them for his brother going down."

"They never told me," Laiken said softly.

"I think Chip hid it from Kay to shield her. It usually happens when Ray has been drinking. I sent officers up to Ray's cabin to bring him in for questioning, but we can't find him anywhere. And his boss said he's missed the last few weeks of work."

My muscles were wound so tight, it felt as if one could snap at any moment. "You have a picture of him?"

Hayes tapped on his screen a few times and then flipped his phone around. "He look familiar to you?"

I shook my head, but Laiken let out a small gasp. "I've seen him around The Gallery before. He never comes in, but I remember noticing him staring at me a couple of times."

Fear punched me right in the solar plexus. How close had Laiken come to being one of this man's victims? "Where does he live?"

"In the mountains," Hayes replied.

"Somewhere he might be able to ride a snowmobile from to shoot at us up there?"

Hayes lowered his phone. "It's very possible, and there was a snowmobile on his property covered by a tarp."

I let some very creative curses fly.

"His face is everywhere now. We've got bulletins out to all surrounding counties and states, and we put Ray's face on the twelve o'clock news. We will find him."

I just hoped it was in time.

Chapter Forty

Laiken

I GOT UP FROM MY DESK, AND BODEN IMMEDIATELY APPEARED from the back room. "Hey, where are you going?"

I fought the urge to growl. "To pee. Is that okay?"

Serena hid her giggle with a cough, and I glared at her. Over a week had passed since Marisa's death, and Boden had been my ever-present shadow. He accompanied me to work, driving me each way. And if I stepped out for coffee or lunch, he was right there. I appreciated that he was worried, but I was about to scream.

My phone dinged.

Kay: *Will you come to dinner tonight?*

I stared down at my device, nibbling on my bottom lip. I flipped the screen around to Serena.

Her brows lifted as she scanned the screen. "You up for that?"

"I guess it depends on if she still thinks I'm being unfaithful to Jase."

"Who is it?" Boden asked, moving in close.

"Kay inviting me to dinner."

Pain lanced through Serena's eyes. "She's wrong, Laik. Jase

would want you to be happy. He never would've wanted you to put your life on hold because he wasn't here anymore."

My throat burned. "I don't think he would either." I glanced up at Boden. "And I think he'd like Boden. Even if he is a hovering stalker these days."

Boden's mouth pulled down in a frown. "I thought you liked being around me."

Serena stifled another laugh.

I patted his chest. "I do. I just don't need an armed escort to take me to pee."

Boden had gotten an expedited concealed-carry permit and had taken to carrying a gun with him each day. Every time I caught a glimpse of it, my stomach twisted, a reminder that someone was out there watching. Waiting.

Boden brushed the hair away from my face and pressed a kiss to my temple. "You can never be too safe. I should probably follow you into the shower tonight, too. Safety in numbers."

Serena let out a little squeal. "I can't take it. You two are gonna make me combust."

I rolled my eyes. "Please don't encourage him."

Boden nibbled the column of my neck. "I've got all the encouragement I need right here."

"Well, then, good thing I'll be at dinner without you."

Serena raised her hand. "I volunteer to switch places with you."

A laugh burst from me, the first in over a week. And it felt so damn good.

Boden pulled up to the Grangers' house and put his truck in park. I leaned over and pressed a kiss to his cheek. "I shouldn't be too late."

"Just call whenever you're ready, and I'll be here in five." His phone dinged in the cupholder, and he swiped it up. His jaw tightened as he read. "It's from Hayes. He said they picked up

Ray at a hunting cabin. He had a rifle and a scope with him. But he's not talking."

I let out a breath that felt as if it had been trapped in my lungs for months. "I hope this means it's over."

Boden leaned his head into mine. "I hope so, too. They just need to get him talking."

"Hayes will get him to open up." He had an unassuming way about him when he wanted it. Ray would be spilling his secrets before he knew what had happened. I linked my fingers with Boden's, squeezing. "I feel like I can breathe again."

"I'm glad, but until we know for sure, I want you to be cautious. No going anywhere by yourself."

"You take overprotectiveness to a new level."

Boden chuckled and gave me a quick kiss. "You love my overprotective ass."

I pinched the side of his butt. "You do have a great ass."

"I'll let you get your hands on it later tonight."

"Don't turn me on before I have to go to dinner with people who are basically my second parents."

Boden grinned. "Serves you right for giving me a hard time."

I shook my head and opened the door. "See you in a few hours."

"Love you."

I'd never get tired of hearing those words from his lips. "Love you, too."

I shut the door and jogged up the steps. As I reached the top one, the door opened, and Gilly waved me inside. "Get in here before you freeze to death."

I hurried inside and wrapped Gilly in a hug. "How are you?"

She gave me a quick squeeze and released me. "You know me—made of the tough stuff."

"I hate that it seems like a requirement lately."

Gilly wrapped an arm around me. "Me, too. But I think tonight is the first step in some healing."

I glanced over at her. "How does Kay seem?"

"A little better, I think. But things are still rocky."

Serena and I had both placed calls to Kay's psychiatrist, who promised that he was aware of Kay's declining state and was doing all he could to help. But he couldn't speak about specifics due to patient-client confidentiality.

"I'm just glad she invited me to dinner."

Gilly squeezed my shoulders one more time and released me. "Me, too."

"Hey, Laik," Serena called from her spot in the kitchen. "Hope you're good with tacos."

"Have you ever known me to turn down tacos?"

She chuckled. "Not once in the history of time."

Jax scoffed as he grabbed a beer from the fridge and then muttered something under his breath. Serena sent him a glare. At least, I couldn't hear his words. When it came to Jax, I was happiest being blissfully unaware.

Chip crossed the room and gave me a quick hug. "Glad you could make it."

"Thanks for inviting me." My gaze shifted to Kay. "Hi."

She gave me a wobbly smile. "Hi, honey."

That simple greeting made my heart ache. I wanted Kay's *hi, honeys*, warm hugs, and cookies hot out of the oven. I didn't want to lose the woman who had taken me shopping for every homecoming and prom dress. The one who had listened when things were bad with my mother and never judged. The one who cheered until she lost her voice at every gymnastics meet.

I stepped into her open arms. Her hands trembled, and she engulfed me. "All's right now that you're here."

But I couldn't help but wonder if she would still feel that way, knowing Boden had dropped me off. I wanted Kay in my life, but not if I had to pretend to be someone I wasn't. Boden was becoming an important part of my life, more and more, and I needed her to be happy for me—even if it wasn't what she'd always dreamed of.

The sound of a scuffle in the kitchen had Kay releasing me. I turned to see Serena giving Jax a little shove.

"Get the drinks, would you?" she asked with a pointed stare.

"I'll help," Gilly said, hurrying into the space—I was sure hoping to defuse the situation.

"Sit," Chip invited. "Serena made one of those fancy charcuterie boards."

"Ser, you're officially in charge of food at the opening," I called.

"I got you covered. Just don't forget to give me a budget."

Chip coughed as he leaned forward. "Really, don't forget to give her a budget. I've regretted not doing it since her Sweet Sixteen."

"I heard that, Dad," she yelled.

I couldn't hold in my laughter. "Trust me, I'll confirm the budget at least ten times."

Serena sent us both exaggerated glares. "I'm gonna put those crazy-hot ghost peppers in both your tacos."

Gilly appeared, handing Chip and Kay a glass of something fruity. "Serena made sangria."

Jax shoved a glass into my hand. "Here."

"Thanks." I repeated *don't punch him* over and over in my head. I took a sip and turned to Serena. "This is amazing."

She took a sip from her glass. "I think this is my best batch yet."

"Let's put this on the menu at the opening, too."

"You got it."

Gilly grinned at the two of us. "This is just what we needed. Some good family time."

"She's not family," Jax muttered.

"That's enough," Chip said.

I held up a hand. "It's all right. Jax is free to make it as clear as possible that he isn't my biggest fan." I stared in his direction. "That doesn't mean he's going to scare me off."

Jax smiled back at me, but it had a feral edge. He said something, but the words sounded garbled, and his silhouette began to blur. I blinked a few times, trying to clear my vision, but it didn't seem to help. I tried again. The blurring got worse.

I thought I heard my name, but I didn't take my eyes off Jax. "What did you do to me?"

Chapter Forty-One

Laiken

MY HEAD THRUMMED TO AN ANGRY BEAT. MY MOUTH tasted like dry cotton. I struggled to get my eyes to open, but they didn't seem to want to obey.

My neck ached, and I realized it was because my head was bent at an awkward angle. I strained to straighten it. When I finally succeeded, my eyes fluttered open.

I blinked against the overhead light. It wasn't overly bright, but it felt blinding. My vision revealed things in snapshots. Bursts of images. Chip slumped over in his recliner. Serena with wide eyes. Kay with tears streaming down her face.

I moved to sit up on the couch, but as I did, I felt bindings on my wrists and ankles. My hands were trapped behind my back. Panic flared, and my breathing grew more shallow. Short, quick bursts of air rushed in and out of my lungs.

Struggling to piece things together, I tried to think of the last thing I remembered. Coming to dinner. Serena's sangria. The wooziness after I'd taken a few sips from the glass that Jax had handed me.

"Laiken, are you okay?" Serena's voice trembled as she spoke.

"What happened? Where is he?"

Before she could answer, the back door slammed against the wall. Isaac filled the doorway, blood dripping from his temple, his eyes glassy. His gaze swung around the room, panic filling his expression.

Someone shoved him forward. "Keep walking."

That voice. One I knew almost as well as my own, yet harder than I'd ever heard it.

Isaac stumbled forward, crashing into the couch and struggling to right himself on the cushions next to me. Gilly stepped forward, her face twisted in rage. She tossed a section of rope at Isaac. "Tie your feet."

"Gilly, what are you doing?" I asked softly.

Her head snapped in my direction. "Shut up. I don't want to hear a word out of your mouth."

My heart hammered against my ribs. The woman I'd loved for so many years was completely unrecognizable. Everything about her had twisted and knotted into something so much darker.

Gilly raised a gun in Isaac's direction. "Bind your legs."

Isaac's eyes flashed, a hint of that stubbornness coming through. "Why? You'll kill me either way."

She strode forward and smacked him across the face with her gun hand. I heard the crunch of metal against bone. Kay let out a strangled sound. Gilly just sneered at Isaac as he cradled his jaw. "I can make your end painless or full of agony. I'd let you ask Robert Aaron about how the painful version goes, but I don't think he's coming to the phone anytime soon."

Bile surged up my throat, and I struggled to swallow it down.

"What have you done?" Kay stared up at her sister, her eyes full of tears.

Gilly turned so her gun was still pointed at Isaac but she

could face Kay. "I had to fix it. You know that. You were suffering so much. I had to end the people who caused your pain. I kept hoping it would be enough, but you kept getting worse."

"This—this isn't right. It's not the way—"

"They didn't care that they stole Jase from you," Gilly clipped. "They didn't give one damn. I have to fix it. Have to protect you."

"Gilly—"

"No! That's why you're tied, too. I knew you might not see it my way. Knew your heart would be too kind. But this is the way it has to be. We have to root out the evil. The reason he's gone. Then, you'll be free. They don't love him like we do. They forgot. Moved on. But we never will."

Kay began crying in earnest, and Serena had gone pale. Chip still wasn't rousing, but his hands and legs were tied, too. No one scattered around the living room had the freedom to move.

Gilly tossed the final piece of rope hanging over her shoulder to Isaac. "Your hands. Tie them tight. If you don't, I'll know."

Isaac let out a low moan but did as she instructed. I watched him loop it around his wrists the best he could. Then he lifted his gaze to Gilly. "I can't tie it."

She scowled but strode over. "The safety is off on this gun. I'd hate to have an accident if you move too quickly."

Isaac's jaw tensed. "I'm not fucking moving."

She slapped his face with her open palm. "Mind your language."

I watched closely and saw Isaac rotate his wrists as Gilly knotted the cord around him. As she stepped back, railing about what a good-for-nothing man he was, Isaac's wrists relaxed, and the ropes loosened a fraction. I met his gaze, and he gave the smallest incline of his head towards Gilly.

He needed someone to keep her occupied. Distracted. Then

he could set to work on his ropes. I swallowed and turned my gaze to Gilly. She paced back and forth.

"Where's Jax?" It was the first thing I could think to ask. But now I was dying to know the answer. My stomach twisted at the possibilities. Was he helping? Had she hurt him?

Gilly chuckled. "I might've given the boys too much of my special brew." She crossed to Chip, patting him on the cheek. His eyes didn't even flutter. Then she moved in my direction. I sucked in a sharp breath, waiting for what, I didn't know. Instead of coming to me, she ducked behind the couch.

With a groan, she tugged on something. "Here's your best pal, Laiken. Did you miss him?"

She dragged him by one arm in front of us all and then let go of his hand. It fell lifelessly to the floor. Serena began to cry. I trained my eyes on Jax's chest. I didn't move or breathe until I saw it rise and fall. Not dead. Just unconscious.

I forced myself to focus on Gilly. To get her talking. "Why?"

A muscle in her cheek fluttered wildly as her grip on the gun tightened. "Everything's a chain reaction. If just one of you would've made a different choice, none of this would've happened. So, you all have to pay the price."

I swallowed against the burn in my throat. "You made a choice that night, too. If you hadn't left Jax alone to have his party, we wouldn't have had to come back to the farmhouse—"

Gilly charged, her hand lashing out, slapping me across the face. "Shut up, you whore! You're a traitor and a cheat. You spread your legs for the first man with money and power to come your way. You never loved Jase. Or you never would've betrayed us all this way."

My head rested on the arm of the couch as stars danced across my vision, and I tasted blood in my mouth. I tried to focus on getting air into my lungs, waiting for the pain to pass as Gilly raged about my treasonous ways.

My gaze caught a flicker of movement. Jax's fingers against the area rug in front of me. His eyelids fluttered, but never fully lifted. I sent up a silent prayer for him to wake up, to find a way to get us all help.

Gilly's hand fisted in my hair, yanking me upright. "Are you listening to me?"

She gave me a shake for emphasis, and fiery-hot pain shot up my spine. "I'm listening," I croaked.

"I didn't realize it at first. I thought you should be saved before you showed your true colors. But it was always you. You were the one who made everyone come back here to check on Jax. Always the high and mighty fixer. If it weren't for you, none of this would have happened. You have to die to set us all free."

Chapter Forty-Two

Boden

I PULLED INTO A PARKING SPOT A COUPLE OF SHOPS DOWN from the pizza parlor. The idea that Kay Granger might hurt Laiken more than she already had made me grumpy as hell. I was going to soothe my foul mood with pizza.

Shutting off the engine, I climbed out of my truck. Now that the sun had gone down, the air had an extra bite to it, and I tugged my jacket closer. As I walked, I debated between a Hawaiian pizza and a meat lover's. Who was I kidding? Hawaiian would always win.

Something pressed into my lower back. "Keep walking unless you want to lose a kidney. Maybe a piece of your liver, too."

My muscles snapped tight, but I forced myself to keep walking. "What the hell is wrong with you, Eli?" We were on a public street. Did he seriously think he could shoot me here and get away with it?

"I'd rather not shoot you, but I'll do what I have to. It's so damn hard to get you or that girlfriend of yours alone. You might want to look into a little therapy on codependency. You guys are a textbook case."

Rage lit through me at the thought of Eli getting Laiken alone. "Did you kill Marisa?"

His steps faltered. "Who the hell is Marisa? I didn't kill anyone. You're always blaming me for things that aren't my fault."

"I can't imagine why," I clipped.

Eli dug the gun into my back. "I'd watch my tone if I were you. My finger could slip."

"What's the plan, Eli? You obviously haven't thought this out."

"That's where you're wrong, brother dearest. We're gonna take a nice walk around the block and head back to my car. How much do you think our parents will pay to get their favorite son back unscathed? I'm sure it's more than enough to buy me a nice life in Mexico. Might have to send them a finger or two just to make sure they know I mean business."

He'd completely lost it. But maybe he'd always hated me this much. Been this callous towards our parents. Because the only person Eli had ever cared about was himself.

I'd have to make a move before we turned the corner onto a less populated street. I didn't want anyone caught in the crossfire, but I wouldn't mind help afterwards. I mentally ran through my attack. Stomping his foot, elbow to the gut, and an uppercut to the jaw. I sent up silent thanks to my trainer, who'd made boxing a part of our routine.

A bell over the pizza parlor door jingled as a laughing group stepped outside.

"Boden," Hadley called. "What are you doing in town?"

Calder helped Sage into her coat as Birdie tugged on her mittens. All I could think about were those two innocent faces and the gun just feet away. I cleared my throat. "Just showing my brother around town. Eli, this is Hadley, Calder, and their two daughters."

Calder's gaze hardened at Eli's name. He knew what my brother had done to Laiken. I widened my eyes, hoping he would get the message to get gone. He lifted his chin in greeting. "Nice to meet you. Welcome to Wolf Gap."

"You, too." Eli gripped my shoulder as the gun dug deeper into my back. "We should get going so we can find some dinner."

"Of course," Hadley said, ushering the girls around us. "See you later."

"Later," I gritted out.

"Don't say a fucking word. You do, and they're toast," Eli growled.

I moved on instinct, slamming my heel down on the toe of Eli's boot. At the same time, my elbow came back into his gut. He cursed, but I was already turning around, my fist connecting with Eli's jaw.

He crumpled to the ground like a sack of potatoes. I dove for the gun, clamping a hand on Eli's wrist so he was forced to release. Footsteps sounded on the pavement as I got a hold of the metal.

"Shit, you got him?" Calder asked.

"Wouldn't mind some help or the cops."

Calder and I rolled my brother to his stomach, holding his hands behind his back. Eli cursed and writhed. "Get the hell off me."

I dug a knee into his back. "Don't move."

"Hayes is on his way," Hadley called.

"That was so freaking cool!" Birdie yelled. "I want to do that."

Calder shook his head. "Maybe next time, you take down the bad guy away from my hellraiser of a daughter?"

"Deal."

I pinched the bridge of my nose as I leaned against Hayes' SUV. The headache that had formed sometime over the past hour didn't show any signs of abating. The call I'd had to place to my parents hadn't made things better. My mom had broken down in tears, and my dad had said curse words I'd never before heard him utter.

Even though I told them not to come, Dad had already contacted his pilot. They'd be on their way first thing tomorrow. I just hoped Eli wouldn't con his way out of this one with them, too.

Hayes strode towards me. "Hadley had to get to the fire station for her shift, and Calder needed to get the girls home, but I got enough of their statements for corroboration. Eli's on his way to lockup."

I nodded numbly, unable to get out any words.

"I talked to the detective in LA. Possession of a firearm and traveling across state lines gets his bail revoked. They'll hold him until his trial. But now he'll have an added charge of attempted kidnapping in the state of Oregon."

This wasn't something the news media and paparazzi would miss. The press would descend on Wolf Gap and follow me wherever I went. "This town is going to turn into a circus. I'm so damn sorry about that."

"We'll deal. None of us are pansies around here. We protect our own, and you've become one of them."

His words meant more than I could express. I wanted to become part of the fabric of this place. To have this be my haven when the rest of the world got crazy. And I wanted to build that haven with Laiken.

I glanced down at my phone for the thirtieth time tonight. She still hadn't called or texted me back, and it was after nine now.

"What's wrong?" Hayes asked.

"Laiken isn't answering my calls or texts. That's not like her."

"Where is she?"

"I dropped her at the Grangers' for dinner. But that was over four hours ago." She might've simply left her phone in her purse, but something didn't feel right. I pushed off Hayes' SUV. "I'm gonna drive out there and make sure everything's okay."

Hayes clapped me on the back. "We'll drive out together. How about that?"

"Sure." But the fact that he was offering made dread slide through me. Laiken was fine. Just caught up with reconnecting with Jase's family. I told myself the same thing over and over as we drove. But with each passing moment, I believed it a little less.

Chapter Forty-Three

Laiken

THE ECHO OF MY HEARTBEAT RATTLED MY RIBS WITH ITS force. "Gilly, don't do this."

Something that almost resembled sadness passed over her features. "I'll miss you. I'll shed tears at your funeral. But this is the way it has to be."

Did Gilly honestly believe that she would get away with this? There were too many witnesses. Unless she killed everyone. But that didn't fit with her plan to set them all free.

"It won't work." My gaze shifted to the side to see that the ropes around Isaac's wrists were completely loose. He held them in a way that made it look as if they were still in place, but he needed the ones on his ankles off, too.

Gilly scoffed. "It's worked perfectly at every turn. I left you in charge of The Gallery, but I'm not an idiot. We need a scapegoat." She pointed her gun at Isaac. "He really has been depressed since Jase's accident. Some might say unstable."

Isaac stiffened on the other side of the couch.

"It's such a shame how mental illness can take hold. It's quite brutal. He's picked off everyone, one by one. Showed up here tonight and terrorized us all, holding us hostage. Only I kept a small firearm on my person since these attacks started. Just in case. I'll save us all."

She turned to me, laughing. "Well, *almost* all of us. He'll kill you first, Laiken. I'm sorry about that. I'll make it clean, though. Headshot, nice and simple."

"You fucking crazy bitch," Isaac growled.

Gilly reeled, pulling her hand back and punching him in the nose. He keeled over as blood poured into his hands. "You broke my nose!"

"I'll do a lot worse if you don't watch your tongue."

Isaac stayed bent over, moaning lowly.

"Such a baby." Gilly ran a hand through her hair.

"It's enough," I said quietly. "Everyone in this room has suffered. We've all felt the worst pain. Isaac and I will never forget. But if you kill us, our suffering will be over."

Did Gilly think Serena and Kay would let her get away with this? Was her mind so warped that she thought they would simply go along with it afterwards?

Gilly paused in her pacing, seeming to think about my words. My gaze darted to Isaac as he worked on the ropes around his ankles. He needed to move faster.

"She's right," Serena said, trying to sit up in her chair. "They won't suffer if they die. They have to be alive to feel it. Don't you think, Mom?"

Kay nodded, tears still streaming down her face. "I don't want them dead, Gilly. I want them to remember. To never forget my boy."

"Stop it! All of you stop! You're trying to trick me. The only way for us to be free is for them to be gone. It's the only way for us to *heal*."

What a messed-up version of healing Gilly had in her head. I couldn't help but wonder how she'd hidden this sickness and obsession for so long. How she'd seemed to care for me so deeply. Or had she just kept me close to make sure that I was grieving appropriately? The truth was, I hadn't shown any signs of moving on until Boden.

My heart clenched at the thought of him. He'd already lost one woman he'd loved; I couldn't put him through that again. I wasn't sure he'd survive.

Isaac peeked up at me. His hands and feet were free.

Blood roared in my ears. "*I'll help.*" I mouthed the words to him.

Isaac nodded back, mouthing a countdown. "*One, two, three.*"

On three, we both burst forward. All I could do was hop and throw myself at Gilly. But Isaac, he could run. Thanks to his head wounds, his gait was clumsy, and I knew he likely had a concussion. Still, I hoped he had enough adrenaline to spur him to freedom. We were miles from help, but I had to hope.

I caught Gilly's legs as I fell, holding on for dear life, trying to give Isaac as much of a head start as possible. She cursed and kicked at me. One of the blows connected with my chin, and I saw stars.

My grip on her loosened, and she clamored to her feet, running out the door after Isaac. Serena dropped out of her chair, crawling over to me. But it was another flash of movement that had me jerking back. Jax sat up, patting his pockets. "She took my fucking phone."

"House line?" I asked.

He shook his head. "We got rid of it last year. We never used it."

He scooted closer to me, working at my ropes. "Get to the barn and get the keys to the work truck. Then drive like hell."

"We'll all go." As soon as my wrists were free, I started on my ankles.

Jax moved to Serena's bindings, shaking his head. "You and Serena go. She won't hurt Mom and Dad."

I hoped he was right. I pulled the rope around my legs free and stood. Wavering a bit, I reached out to steady myself on the couch.

Serena was right there, gripping my arm. "You can do this. Lean on me."

"Nobody move," Gilly gritted out as she shoved Isaac through the door a second time. Now, blood dripped down his shoulder, staining his shirt.

Nausea swept through me. This wasn't happening. We were so close to freedom.

Isaac slammed his head back into Gilly's face with one word on his lips. "Run!"

Chapter Forty-Four

Boden

HAYES PULLED TO A STOP IN FRONT OF THE GRANGERS' house, and we climbed out of his SUV. It was eerily quiet. Hayes and I shared a look and headed for the front steps.

He lifted his hand to knock on the front door, but with the first strike, the door swung inward. One hand moved to his gun, removing it from his holster, and the other went to his radio, calling for backup and asking them to come in quietly.

Hayes handed me his keys. "Go wait in the SUV. Backup will be here soon."

Instead of obeying, I slid my gun from my holster. "I'm not letting you go in there alone." And I sure as hell wasn't leaving Laiken alone either.

Hayes muttered a curse but turned his focus towards the house. "Stay behind me."

I did as ordered but my gaze swept over every space I could get my eyes on, hoping to see dark hair and golden skin. Amber eyes that saw to the very core of me.

"Carson County Sheriff's Department," Hayes called.

"In here," a woman's voice called. "We're in here."

We moved into a living room that looked as if a tornado had hit it. Tables and chairs were upended, and a woman hovered over Isaac, her hands pressed to his shoulder. I knew she had to be Kay. Tears streamed down her face. "She shot him. She just shot him."

"I'll be okay," Isaac croaked. "You gotta get the bitch."

"Who?" Hayes barked.

"Gilly," he answered. "She's chasing Laiken and Serena. She's batshit crazy. Killed all those people."

Kay only cried harder. "I'm so sorry. I didn't know."

"Is he—?" I asked, inclining my head towards the man slumped over in the chair.

"He's alive," Kay said. "Just drugged."

Hayes pulled his radio again. "Holy hell." He started relaying the situation to his dispatcher, but I was already moving.

"Which direction?" I pressed Isaac and Kay.

"The front door," he gritted out.

"Jax got a shotgun from the gun safe and went after them," Kay called as I ran for the front door.

My ribs shook with the force of my heartbeat, and blood roared in my ears. I had to find Laiken. A million horrible scenarios raced through my mind. I never should've left her here alone.

Hayes was on my heels in an instant. "I told you to stay behind me."

"I don't care what you told me. I have to find Laiken."

"Don't be stupid and get yourself killed."

I opened my mouth to argue when a shot cracked the air. Everything in me locked, then I took off running in the direction of the sound. It seemed to come from the barn and outbuildings.

My lungs burned as I pushed my muscles harder. Hayes matched me, stride for stride. Another shot sounded. Closer. On the side of the barn.

We ran towards the noise. Just as we were about to round the corner, a body slammed into mine. Petite. Dark hair. Golden skin.

Laiken let out a strangled sound.

I yanked her into my arms. "You're okay. I've got you."

"Gilly. She has a gun. She's shooting."

"Get to the barn," Hayes barked. "Lock yourselves in the office and wait for backup. I'll give them your location."

This time, I listened, tugging Laiken towards the structure. All I could think about was getting her safe. Secure. Behind locked doors and thick wood.

The horses whinnied as we ran inside. A few pawed at their stall doors.

"Back there," Laiken said.

I jogged towards where she inclined her head, pushing her inside. I shut the door behind us and flipped the lock. It wasn't a deadbolt, just one of those flimsy doorknob deals, but it was something.

My gaze swept over Laiken as I moved towards her. The side of her face was swollen, and she had a nasty gash near her eye. "You're hurt."

My hands went to her face, gently probing. Laiken's entire body shook. "Gilly. She blames us all. Said we had to die."

What in the holy hell had happened over the past few hours? There was plenty of time to find out. Right now, I just needed to hold Laiken.

I holstered my gun and pulled her into my arms. "I've got you."

"Laiken," Gilly singsonged. "I know you're in here."

The voice was almost childlike as if she were playing a game. The tone made my skin crawl, and I held a single finger to my lips.

"Let's see just how noble you are. You said you loved Jase. Would you give your life for his sister?"

Laiken went rigid against me.

"Don't come out, Laik. She'll kill us both," Serena yelled.

"Shut up! You never mourned him the way you should've. You're probably part of the reason your mother is such a mess."

Their voices were close. Too close.

Tears streamed down Laiken's face. "I have to help her."

"Hayes will hear her. Backup is coming."

I saw the emotions flit across her features: pain, grief, resolve.

Laiken moved for the door, but I tugged her back. "Serena's right. You step out there, and you're both goners. Give both of you a fighting chance."

Laiken's tears came faster, but she nodded. I slid my gun out of my holster again, bracing for anything.

Sounds of footfalls on the cement. Then quiet. A silence so painful, I wanted to rip out my ears.

Wood cracked as the door flew open. Gilly gave Serena a hard shove towards me and raised her gun.

Everything came in staccato beats. The half seconds between inhales and exhales. It was as though I was moving through molasses. The glint of the gun taunted me as I pushed Serena to the side. I couldn't get my weapon raised.

Laiken's eyes went wide, panic and fear blooming there. I couldn't lose her. In such a short time, she'd come to mean everything to me.

I did the only thing I could. I dove.

The bullet cracked the air. A shock of pain lit in my chest. Then I was falling.

Chapter Forty-Five

Laiken

WE HIT THE FLOOR WITH AN ANGRY THUD. I INSTANTLY clawed at the floor and tried to get out from under Boden. He wasn't moving or making a sound. *No. No. No.* This wasn't happening. I wouldn't lose him.

Another shot sounded, and this time it was Gilly who crumpled to the floor. But I barely noticed as she screamed and writhed in pain.

I rolled Boden to his back. Dark red blood covered his chest, spreading across his sweater. My hands hovered above him for a moment, not knowing what to do. Stop the bleeding. That was all that mattered.

I pressed hard against his chest, and Boden let out a pained moan.

"Boden. Open your eyes." Tears slid down my cheeks, splashing onto my hands. I leaned all my weight onto him.

Gilly screamed as Hayes cuffed her, the sound grating on my eardrums.

"Boden, please."

His eyes fluttered, then nothing.

I wanted to give him my blood. To tear open a vein and pour it into him.

A shadow swung over us, and my head jerked up as Jax lowered himself to the floor. He reached out to do something, and I batted him away. "No! Don't touch him. Don't you touch him."

His eyes flared. "I'm going to check his pulse."

"No. You'll kill him just so I hurt more. You don't get to touch him."

I was sobbing now, my whole body shaking as sirens sounded in the background, and Gilly screamed louder.

All color leached from Jax's face. "I won't. I just want to help. I'm taking EMT training classes."

"No!" I screamed. "Get away from us!"

The sobs came faster and harder. Hands gripped my shoulders, and I kicked out. Hayes cursed, but I didn't stop. He gripped me tighter. "The EMTs are here. Let them help."

But I couldn't. Some part of me was so sure that I was the only one who could keep Boden alive. The only one who could fix him.

"A little help here?" Hayes yelled.

"Shit," Deputy Young said as she aided Hayes in pulling me away from Boden.

I screamed and kicked. And then I simply broke. I collapsed into Hayes' hold and let everything go.

I rocked back and forth in the waiting room chair. The hard plastic bit into my spine, but I welcomed each flare of pain. I wanted my body to hurt. If I was in enough pain, then maybe my heart wouldn't feel as if it were being shredded to pieces in my chest.

A shiver wracked my body. A moment later, a sweatshirt landed in my lap. Worry lined Beckett's face. "Put that on. You getting pneumonia isn't going to help anyone."

I pulled the warm fabric over my head. I couldn't do anything about my wet hair. The hospital had to offer me a shower because

I'd been covered in blood. Boden's blood. So much of it, I didn't know how he was still breathing.

He'd coded in the ambulance on the way here, but they'd gotten his heart beating again. Boden was strong. The strongest man I'd ever known. He was a fighter—for himself and for me.

A sob crept up my throat, but I swallowed it down. Addie tried to reach out for my hand, but I tugged it away. I couldn't. Didn't want anyone to touch me.

All I wanted was Boden's warm hand in mine. To feel that flame of his, heating every inch of my skin. To see the gold in his hazel eyes blazing brightly.

Tears burned the backs of my eyes, a few slipping free. I felt the others' stares on me. Everly's stoic concern. Hadley's frenetic worry. She had been one of the EMTs to work on Boden. She knew how bad it was.

Calder rubbed a hand down her back. But he didn't offer us any reassurances. He knew from being a firefighter that no outcome was guaranteed.

I picked up my rocking again.

Hayes appeared in the doorway, and my movements stilled. "Anything?"

He shook his head. "Nothing from the doctors. I got ahold of Boden's parents. They're on their way."

Oh, God. His parents. They'd already been through so much.

"Gilly?" Beckett asked.

"Shoulder wound, through and through. They stitched her up and will keep her overnight for observation. Then it's a psychiatric facility. The courts will decide if she's competent enough to stand trial."

It wasn't enough. How many lives had she destroyed? All while playing the concerned aunt.

Nausea swept through me, and I knew I'd lose whatever food I had in my stomach. I launched myself from the chair and ran for the single bathroom around the corner. The door banged open, and I sank to the floor, emptying my stomach in heave after heave.

Cool hands pulled my hair away from my face. "That's enough. There's nothing left," Hayes said softly.

I ordered my body to stop, to put an end to the motions. But it was as if some part of me thought this was a way to fix everything. Finally, the heaving slowed, then halted altogether.

I rested back on my heels, and Hayes flushed the toilet. He helped me to my feet, guiding me over to the sink. As I rinsed my mouth, he poked his head out the door. "See if you can find some mouthwash."

I kept rinsing, trying to cleanse the foul taste. Finally, someone brought a travel-sized mouthwash. I swirled it around in my mouth until all the horribleness was gone. If only it could clear everything else, too.

Hayes gripped my shoulders gently and turned me around. He ducked down to meet my gaze. "You hold on. There is so much left to fight for. Don't quit on me. We've been in tough spots before, you and me. We'll make it through this, too."

My eyes filled, and I let my head fall to Hayes' chest. He wrapped me in a hug. "Boden is fighting for you. You fight for him right back."

"I will," I croaked.

My body trembled, and Hayes pulled open the door to the bathroom. "Let's get you sitting down."

As we stepped out into the hallway, we caught sight of two women in scrubs striding towards us. "Boden Cavanaugh's family?"

I gripped Hayes' hand so tightly, I was sure I'd leave bruises. "I'm his girlfriend."

The older woman nodded. "I'm Dr. Padman. Mr. Cavanaugh's surgeon. He's still in serious condition, but I was able to repair the vein tear and remove the bullet. The next twenty-four hours will give us more information."

"He made it. He's alive."

The woman's mouth curved, and she patted my arm. "He's alive, and Nurse Smith can take you to him."

"Go," Hayes said. "I'll fill everyone in."

I nodded, already moving to follow the nurse down the hall. I didn't say a word as she led me to the elevators and took us up several floors. I kept up with her, step for step, as she led me to the ICU and buzzed someone to let us in.

She stopped in front of an open door. "He has a machine breathing for him, along with a few other things helping him function in all the ways he needs to without putting stress on his body. I know they're scary, but they're helping."

"Thank you." The words didn't sound like they had even come from my mouth—nearly unrecognizable to my ears.

Nurse Smith moved to the side, and I walked in.

The sight in front of me stole all the air from my lungs. So many tubes and wires. A bandage covered his entire chest. His face was swollen. And I couldn't see those eyes.

Boden was almost unrecognizable. Yet some part of his soul called out to mine. That flame was still there, and it pulled me closer.

I moved as though I had no control over my limbs. Striding across the linoleum floor and sinking into another of those awkward chairs. I landed with a jolt of my spine but barely noticed.

The hand closest to me had nothing but a hospital bracelet on it. I took it in mine. The warmth of his skin had tears slipping free and cascading down my cheeks. I swore I felt the beat of his heart in that hand.

"Fight," I whispered. "Please, fight. I can't lose you."

Chapter Forty-Six

Boden

THE BURNING IN MY CHEST STARTED DRAGGING ME OUT of the swirling darkness. The pain was a hot branding iron. Intense and unceasing. I tried to back away from the feeling, but a hand squeezed mine. Hard.

"Boden. Come back to me."

I knew that voice. It took me precious moments to place it. Laiken.

Dark hair. Amber eyes. Skin like gold. Strength. Vulnerability. The largest of hearts.

I fought against the darkness, trying to move towards her light. She'd become a beacon, almost from the moment I met her. From the first time I saw into her soul in that photo.

My eyes fluttered, the bright lights making them sting. Laiken squeezed my hand harder. "Boden?"

"Hey," I croaked.

A second later, she placed a straw between my lips. "Tiny sips. You've had a tube down your throat. That's why it's sore."

The cool liquid tasted like heaven, but after a few swallows, she tugged it away. "The nurse said not to give you too much, or you could get sick."

My mind whirled as I tried to put the pieces together. Images flashed in my mind. Running with Laiken. Hiding in the office. Gilly. The gun.

"You're okay? You aren't hurt?" I tried to sit up, but white-hot pain had me letting out a curse instead.

"Don't try to move." Laiken's hands were on my shoulders as tears pooled in her eyes. "You were shot. You shielded me." Her voice cracked as she spoke, the tears sliding down her cheeks. "You almost died. Your heart stopped."

Shit. Things had been closer than I could've imagined, but none of it mattered. I lifted a hand to her cheek. "Tell me you're okay."

"Thanks to you." She leaned her forehead against mine and simply stayed there for a moment. When she straightened, I didn't miss the strain of pain tightening her features or the bruise and healing gash on her face.

"You're hurting."

She shook her head. "I've just been sleeping in a cot in here the past few nights. That's all."

"Why didn't you go home?"

Laiken looked at me as if I had a head injury instead of a shot to the chest. "I wasn't leaving you."

"Get in this bed," I ordered.

She let out an exasperated sigh. "You have staples in your chest. I'm not getting in your bed."

"Only on one side." The pain was localized; on my left side. I could tell that now. "Come here."

Slowly, Laiken pushed to her feet and rounded the bed. Her movements were stiff, and I knew she was in more pain than she was letting on. First thing, I would call Addie and get her to take Laiken home—just as soon as I assured myself that she was okay.

Laiken carefully perched on the edge of the bed.

"Lay down."

"Spoiled movie star," she muttered.

I chuckled but immediately regretted it.

"Don't do that," Laiken said. "Do you need a nurse? Pain meds?"

"I just need you."

She melted at that, slowly lowering herself to my side and curling around me. Her fingers linked with mine. "I was so scared."

My chest burned, but this time it had nothing to do with my injury. "I'm so sorry."

"You have nothing to apologize for. I'm the one who's sorry. I didn't see it. There wasn't a moment where I thought Gilly could hate us all that much."

I swept my thumb back and forth across the back of her hand. "I don't think anyone saw it."

"Not until it was too late."

"Hayes got her?" After that first blast of the shot, everything went fuzzy.

Laiken nodded. "He shot her in the shoulder, but the injury wasn't serious. She's in a prison medical bay now."

"Is everyone else okay?"

She scooted in a little closer to me. "Isaac's a couple of floors down. He'll make a full recovery, but he'll need some physical therapy."

"What about the Grangers?" I hadn't missed the fact that Laiken hadn't said a word about them.

"They stopped by to check on you, but I just couldn't—I'm not ready."

I tilted my head to press my lips to her temple. "Laiken."

"It's too much. Jax's rage at me. Kay's disappointment in me for moving on. It all fueled Gilly more. I'll talk to them soon. I just can't do it right now. And I couldn't do it while you were lying here unconscious."

"Okay. You go at your own speed. Just don't let too much

time pass. Anger like that can fester, and they've been a second family to you."

Laiken stiffened. "Your parents are here."

"Shit." I'd forgotten all about Eli and them coming up here. "Where are they?"

"Your dad just took your mom back to their hotel to rest." She toyed with a thread on the blanket. "They love you so much. And they've been so worried. I should text your dad."

I squeezed her hand. "Let them get some rest. They'll have good news to come back to."

"They'll be so happy."

"Have they been to see Eli?" I asked.

"Your dad met with Hayes and saw Eli once. But he's not providing him a lawyer. Eli's already on his way back to the LA county prison."

My throat burned. I didn't want this for Eli or my parents. But it was time for Eli to face the ramifications of his actions, and it sounded like my parents were finally going to let that happen.

I brushed my lips against Laiken's temple again, reveling in the silky feel of her skin. "That's good."

"I can't believe he tried to kidnap you."

"He's lost all sense of logic and reason. I can only hope that this is his rock-bottom and that it'll be enough to scare him straight."

Laiken burrowed in even closer to me. "I hope so, too. For all of you."

I let myself soak in her warmth. That would heal me faster than anything, knowing that Laiken was by my side. "I love you."

Her eyes lifted to mine. "I love you, too."

I watched the golden amber of her eyes spark and dance. "This is a forever kind of love, Laiken."

She stiffened. "Don't. Please don't promise me forever. I've already had forever ripped away from me once. I almost had *you* ripped away from me."

My heart ached for everything she'd been through. And I was furious at Gilly for putting her through more. I swallowed all that down and brushed my lips against Laiken's. "How about I promise you today? And I'll do it again tomorrow. And every day until we're old and gray."

Laiken's eyes shone with unshed tears. "I love that plan."

Chapter Forty-Seven

Laiken

ONE WEEK LATER

"DO YOU WANT A FRESH BATCH OF MAGAZINES OR ANY other snacks?" I asked as I straightened Boden's hospital blankets.

"Stop stalling."

I made a face at him. "I'm not stalling. I want to make sure you have everything you need before I leave."

Boden grabbed my hand and tugged me so I bent over him. He brushed his lips across mine. "I'm fine. My mom and dad will be back with lunch any minute."

"But I should wait until they get here in case you need something."

He lifted a remote attached to his bed. "I have this handy-dandy call button. A nurse can help me with whatever I need."

"I'm sure they can," I muttered. More than a few nurses had been extra *helpful* these past few days.

Boden chuckled, and this time there was no wince in his features. "Don't be jealous."

I scowled at him. "Don't be smug."

"I won't be smug if you stop stalling."

I swallowed the growl that wanted to surface. "Fine. I'm going. Want me to bring you anything back?"

"Wouldn't say no to a milkshake."

"Strawberry or chocolate?"

He'd been alternating between the two, and I was happy to be his sugar dealer.

"Strawberry."

I bent to kiss him one more time. "Love you."

"Love you, too."

As I walked out the door and down the hall, my heart tugged. It hadn't gotten easier to walk away from Boden. There had been so many touch-and-go moments in the forty-eight hours he'd been unconscious. I knew letting him out of my sight anytime soon would be a challenge. Yet I forced myself to keep walking.

I opted for the stairs instead of the elevator, trying to burn off some of my nervous energy. As I headed for the exit, I pulled on my sunglasses. I braced as the doors slid open.

Voices screamed my name, asking invasive questions as flashes went off. A security guard hurried over. "I'll escort you to your car, Ms. Montgomery."

"Thank you."

We hurried through the throng of people and towards the parking lot. The press had descended less than twenty-four hours after Boden had been shot, and they showed no signs of leaving even though both his and his father's publicists had released a joint statement that Boden would make a full recovery. They were vultures. Some of the headlines I'd seen had turned my stomach. And I'd found one photographer trying to sneak onto the ICU floor. James Cavanaugh had called in private security then and there.

Boden had tried to give me my own guard, but I didn't want it. I couldn't take having someone with me all the time when I was barely holding it together. I needed those quiet moments in my SUV to let the tears flow. I'd come so close to losing Boden, and it would take some time for me to reassure myself that everything was okay.

I gave the security guard a smile as I beeped my locks. "Thank you. Again."

"Anytime. Just call the number if you want an escort back inside."

"I will."

I climbed behind the wheel and started the engine. No one followed me as I pulled out of the parking lot. A few had tried the first couple of days after Boden had woken up, but they'd finally given up when all I ever did was go to restaurants or back to the cabin on Ramsey's property.

I couldn't bring myself to return to the gallery. Not yet. But I'd be facing the worst of it today. I guided my SUV out of town, taking the roads I knew by heart. Houses gave way to ranches and farmlands, and before long, I was pulling up to the Grangers' house.

I stared up at the façade that I could've drawn by memory. The place that had always felt like home. Only this time, I shuddered. I knew there had to be a way to reclaim the space, but I wasn't sure that I was strong enough to do it.

A knock sounded on my window, and I jumped.

"It's just me," Serena said. "Sorry."

I pushed open my door. "I was lost in my own world."

"I should've made more noise."

She looked so unsure, worry creasing her face. It was all I needed to pull her into my arms. "I'm so glad you're okay, Ser."

Her body shook as she cried. "You, too. How's Boden?"

"Driving me up the wall, so he must be healing."

She laughed through her tears. "I love you, Laik. I'm sorry I lost so much time with you by being a bitch. I missed you."

"I missed you, too. We've got all the time in the world now."

Serena released me but took my hand. "We do. Mom's getting some hot chocolate and bringing it out to the front porch."

It was cold, but the sun was shining brightly, and I was glad that I wouldn't have to venture inside the house quite yet. "Sounds good."

Serena led me up the front steps just as the door opened. Chip held a ceramic pitcher while Kay followed him with a tray of mugs. As soon as Kay laid eyes on me, hers began to fill with tears. "Laiken."

"Hi," I croaked.

She set down the tray on a table and moved towards me. I thought she'd hug me, but she stopped herself. "I'm so sorry. For so many things."

"We all are." It was the most truth I could give her.

Chip wrapped an arm around his wife's shoulders. "How's Boden doing?"

"He's good. They should release him from the hospital in the next couple of days."

He'd need physical therapy, and his movie had been delayed, but he was alive. And that was what mattered.

"Want to sit?" Kay offered.

"Sure." I lowered myself to one of the rockers, Serena taking the one next to me.

Kay clasped her hands tightly in her lap. "I didn't know. Had no idea she'd fixated like that."

"It's not your fault, Mom," Serena said. She turned to me. "Gilly was feeding Mom medications she shouldn't have been on. It took us a few days to figure it out. We're guessing she thought she was helping numb her pain but—"

"It was making me lose my mind." Kay let out a shaky breath. "I can't believe some of the things I said, Laiken. You'll never know how sorry I am. I want more than anything for you to be happy. It's what Jase would want, too. If this Boden does that, then he's an answer to our prayers."

My throat and eyes burned. "I don't want to hurt you—"

"Oh, honey." Kay leapt from her chair and came to me, sinking to her knees and enveloping me in a hug. "Seeing you happy and thriving would never do that. Never."

"Thank you. I'm so sorry about Gilly."

"Me, too." She held tightly to me for one more moment and then let me go, pushing to her feet and settling back in her rocker. "I never told any of you kids because it was so painful, but Gilly was in a car accident when she was younger. She hadn't had her license long and skidded on some black ice. It was a bad accident, and our little brother was in the car."

Kay wiped a stray tear from her cheek. "He didn't make it."

"Kay, I'm so sorry."

"Me, too. It wrecked our parents. He was so young at the time. Only nine. A surprise baby when they'd thought they were done. I named our Jase after him. Maybe that was a mistake—"

Chip squeezed her hand. "You were honoring his memory."

"I was trying to. But I think when our Jase died, it created one more crack in Gilly. This year being the tenth anniversary, Robert Aaron getting out, me struggling…it was all too much. She'd had some issues in the past, but nothing like this."

I held tightly to the arms of my chair. "Grief changes us. We just have to make sure it doesn't twist us into something ugly. And, sometimes, if we're lucky, it can make us more beautiful because we recognize pain and can help ease it in others."

Kay reached out and squeezed my hand. "You're so right, my beautiful girl."

We talked and sipped hot chocolate for another hour. We reminisced about Jase and shared stories of growing up here on this land. Then I hugged them all goodbye and headed for my SUV.

As I reached the bottom step, Jax rounded the house. I stopped, holding up a hand. "My emotions are all wrung out. If you're gonna yell at me, please save it for another day."

He grunted, his hands fisting at his sides. "I blame myself. I was a selfish asshole in my teens and early twenties. All I wanted was a good time and didn't care who I hurt. I knew I shouldn't have thrown a party that night. That I'd gotten Jase in trouble before for the same thing. But I didn't care."

He swallowed, his gaze shifting to the fields around us. "All that rage…it was eating me alive. I knew if I turned it inward where it belonged, I'd never survive. So, I cast it out. To anyone who was associated with Jase and the accident. When I didn't have access to Aaron anymore, I turned to you and the rest. But it was me that I really should've been screaming those ugly things at."

"No." I strode forward and gave Jax a little shove. "You are not to blame for this. The only one who is responsible is Robert Aaron. And he's dead. You have to let this go. Or it'll kill you. I don't want that for your parents or sister. I don't even want that for you. I wouldn't mind a little swift kick in the ass, though."

His lips twitched. "Fair enough. I'm sorry, Laiken. You loved my brother so damn well. He'd want you to have everything you dreamed of."

"If you make me cry right now, I really will be mad."

Jax held up both hands. "I'll stop. If you need anything, help around the gallery, anything fixed, just let me know."

It was an olive branch. I could hold on to all my anger and hurt, or I could take it. But I couldn't do both. We might never be close the way we used to be, but we didn't have to be enemies, either. "I'll call if I need something."

"Good." Jax bobbed his head. "You'd better get back to that movie star of yours. I heard celebrities can be pretty demanding."

My mouth curved. "Spoiled, too." But I wouldn't change a damn thing about him.

Chapter Forty-Eight

Boden

"THIS COUCH IS HEAVEN." I stretched out an arm for Laiken to join me on the massive sectional in my parents' rental house as Peaches and Gizmo burrowed into my other side. They'd been stuck to me like glue since I got home, and it was damn adorable.

Her mouth pulled down into a frown as she sat. "I still think you should've stayed a few more nights."

"I agree," my mother said, setting down a tray of snacks.

"I slept a million times better in a real bed last night without nurses bugging me every ten minutes."

"They were bugging you to make sure you were still alive," Laiken said with an exasperated sigh.

I leaned over and pressed a kiss to the top of her head. "That's what I have you for."

"I'm not a medical professional!"

My dad chuckled as he joined my mom on the couch. "He'll have you pulling your hair out before you know it."

"Or turning it gray," Mom muttered. "This one did that to me."

"Hey." My dad gave her a quick kiss. "I'm worth it."

"Some days."

I couldn't hold in my laughter. This time, my chest barely twinged. "I missed you guys."

My mom smiled over at me. "We missed you, too."

I toyed with a strand of Laiken's hair. "Any word from Eli?"

I wanted to kick myself as soon as the words were out of my mouth. The smile slipped from my mother's face, and that muscle in my dad's cheek began to flutter. He wrapped an arm around Mom's shoulders. "I've talked to him twice. I told him I'm here for him, to listen and support him, but I'm not paying his legal fees. I guess the cartel he was working for isn't either because he has a court-appointed attorney now."

It was the right thing, but I knew it was harder than anything my parents had ever had to do. "I'm sorry."

"It was time." My mom looked up at my dad, patting his knee. "We should've taken a stronger stance years ago, but it's hard when it's your baby. The one you changed diapers for and nursed at three in the morning."

"This is your way of loving him," Laiken said softly.

Mom turned to her, eyes glistening. "That's a good way to look at it. I'm loving him by letting the consequences of his actions take hold. All I can hope for is that it wakes him up."

I hoped the same thing, but I knew it was a long shot. Sometimes, people were too far gone, with too much anger in their hearts.

Laiken bent her head and pressed her lips to my arm on her shoulder. She always seemed to sense when I needed that point of contact—that little extra soothing touch.

As I lifted my gaze, I met my dad's eyes. There was so much in them. Pride and joy for me at what I'd found. We'd gone for a drive yesterday, much to my mom's and Laiken's chagrin, and had one of our epic talks. I'd told him what Laiken had come to mean to me, and he only said one thing. *"This is what I've always wanted for you. Someone who cares for you as much as you do them. It's time for you to be happy, Bo."*

It was time. What the shooting had taught me was that there

was no time to waste. You had to live every moment fully and couldn't be afraid to chase what you wanted most.

I squeezed Laiken's shoulder. "Come with me?"

She shifted in her seat. "Your mom just made snacks."

Mom waved us off. "They'll be here when you get back, and I can get some cuddles with those pups while you're gone."

Laiken's lips pressed together. "I don't know if you should be in a car again—"

"Ten minutes," I pressed. "I have something I want to show you."

"You've been locked up in a hospital for almost two weeks. What could you have to show me?"

The corner of my mouth kicked up. "Come with me and you'll find out."

"You're nothing but trouble. You know that, right?"

"That's what makes me so fun."

Laiken shook her head but stood. She hovered as I climbed to my feet. By the time we reached Laiken's SUV, I was breathing heavily. It was crazy how two weeks of no activity could have me huffing and puffing. But I'd get back in shape. The doctors had already cleared me for short walks, and I'd be meeting with a physical therapist tomorrow.

I buckled my seat belt, and Laiken started the engine. "Where to?"

I gave her turn-by-turn directions. We wound through backroads until we reached a gate. "Plug in this code. Two, nine, one, three."

Laiken arched a brow but did as instructed. The large iron gate swung open. We made our way down the gravel road until we reached a house. It looked like the quintessential mountain lodge—a mixture of wood and stone. The colors chosen went perfectly with the surrounding landscape of fields, forests, and those epic mountains.

Laiken slowed to a stop. "Who lives here?"

"No one right now. Come on." I got out of her vehicle before she had a chance to argue.

"This isn't taking it easy."

"Just a few more minutes."

We walked up the front steps, Laiken matching my turtle's pace. I pulled a set of keys out of my pocket and unlocked the door. We stepped inside the empty house.

The entryway was open, leading into a massive living space, which poured into a kitchen and dining area. I knew that a conservatory and library were on the other side of the house, and that a screening room and a game room were below us. Above were six bedrooms and a playroom. There was a garage with a gym above it, as well.

I couldn't imagine a more perfect place to call home. But Laiken had to love it. She slowly strode towards the massive windows at the back of the house. "These views are incredible."

"So, you like it?"

She spun in a circle. "What's not to like? Why—?" She stopped herself before finishing her question. "Are you thinking about buying it?"

I moved in close to Laiken, pulling her into my arms. "I am. But I only want to do that if you'll live here with me."

Her amber eyes glistened. "Boden, we've only known each other for a couple of months."

I brushed the hair away from her face. "I know everything I need to know about you. This has been trial by fire, and there's no one I'd rather have by my side. In battle, rest, and for everything in between."

"Boden…"

"I don't want to waste a minute of this beautiful life. This second chance we've both been given. I want that life with you."

"Okay."

A grin split my face. "Okay?"

She nodded, an answering smile stretching her mouth. "I want a life with you more than I ever thought possible."

"Love you, Laiken." I wove my fingers through hers. "I promise you today."

"Today is my favorite day."

Epilogue

Laiken

THREE MONTHS LATER

"WHERE ARE WE PUTTING THIS PHOTO?" HAYES asked, lifting the image of me in the field that had brought Boden into The Gallery.

Boden pointed to the fireplace. "It's going over the mantel."

I made a face at him. "Don't you think that's a little pompous? Having a picture of myself hanging in such a prominent spot?"

He grinned and looped an arm around my waist, pulling me in close. "I want it where I can see it every single day."

"You see her every single day, isn't that enough?" Beckett asked, coming in with a box.

Addie smacked his shoulder. "He's being romantic."

He bent to brush her lips with his. "I'll show you romantic."

Her cheeks heated, and then her eyes widened. "The baby's kicking."

Beckett instantly set down the box and knelt in front of

Addie. "How ya doing in there, buddy?" He pressed his hand to her belly, wonder filling his gaze. "He's strong."

Addie's smile wobbled a bit. "He'll probably be a soccer star."

My eyes filled with tears. I was so happy for my friends and overly emotional with all the changes taking place. Boden's arms tightened around me. "Hey, what are the tears for?"

I wiped at my eyes. "Just happy. Sometimes, your cup overflows, and you have to let it out somehow."

Boden chuckled, nuzzling my neck. "You're so damn adorable."

Boden's dad, James, and his mom, Bette, strode in carrying boxes. James' gaze swept over my face and then narrowed on his son. "What did you do to make her cry?"

"Seriously? You automatically assume I made her cry?"

"She's standing in your arms, Bo."

I laughed and crossed to James, kissing his cheek. "I'm fine, just emotional about Addie feeling the baby kick."

Bette beamed, setting down her box. "That was my favorite feeling."

"You can feel him if you want. He's pretty strong," Addie offered.

"I'd love to."

Boden's parents and my friends had become close over the last few months. James and Bette had wanted to be with their son as he recovered and had fallen in love with the town of Wolf Gap. They'd ended up buying another property just down the road.

"How many art and photo supplies can one person have?" Jax moaned as he carried in a particularly large box.

"I made that one extra-heavy just for you," I quipped.

He rolled his eyes. "Where does it go?"

"In the photo studio out back."

Jax whirled on Serena, who had followed him inside. "You said the house."

Her lips twitched. "Oops. Payback's a bitch."

"Language," Kay chided as she and Chip came in with yet more boxes.

It was crazy how much stuff I'd managed to pack into that tiny apartment over The Gallery. After Gilly had taken a plea deal that put her in a psychiatric facility, she'd signed over the space to Serena. The two of us were sharing management now and made a great team. She was an ace at promotion and events, and I handled all the art.

Hadley and Everly came in with two more wrapped photos. Hadley shook her head. "I still can't believe you've been taking these photos and didn't tell us. It's amazing."

"It really is," Ev echoed.

Hayes wrapped an arm around her. "You have a gift."

Heat rose to my cheeks. "Thank you. It feels good to finally share them."

Boden pulled me back into his arms. "Told you."

"You don't have to gloat."

"But he always does," Bette muttered.

"Mom, you're supposed to be on my side."

"I'm on Laiken's side," she shot back.

I couldn't hold in my laughter. Between the Cavanaughs and the Grangers, I felt so incredibly loved and supported. It dulled the sting of my mother not bothering to visit after my ordeal. In some ways, it was freeing. I didn't have to feel guilty when she dropped snide comments about me not coming to see her back east. I simply let her go. We'd always have the occasional phone calls, but she wasn't my support system.

"Got the pizza," Calder hollered from the entryway.

"We got loads of ice cream, too," Birdie said.

Sage grinned. "Made sure we got some strawberry for you, Boden."

Boden lifted a hand and high-fived Sage. "You're the best."

Calder raised the stack of boxes. "Should I stick these in the kitchen?"

As soon as the smell of pepperoni hit my nose, my stomach

roiled. I tried to force down the nausea but knew this was one episode I wouldn't be able to fight. I took off for the bathroom at the other end of the house.

As soon as my knees hit the tiled floor, I emptied my stomach into the toilet. A few moments later, a hand pulled my hair back, holding it. Boden rubbed his other hand up and down my back. "Is your stomach still bothering you? I thought you'd gotten over that bug."

As my heaving eased, I flushed the toilet and moved to the sink. I rinsed my mouth out with water, and Boden ducked under the counter. "My mom stocked the bathrooms with toiletries last night." He held out a bottle of mouthwash to me, worry creasing his brow.

"Thanks," I croaked, then swished the minty liquid around in my mouth.

"Maybe we should have Beckett take a look at you."

"I think I know what's wrong." My heart hammered against my ribs as Boden's brows rose in question. "I'm pregnant." The words were barely a whisper.

Boden went stock-still. "What?"

"I know this isn't exactly something we were planning but—"

He moved in a flash, pulling me into his arms. He framed my face with his hands. "Nothing would make me happier than starting a family with you. I'm just a little annoyed that you stole my thunder."

"Stole your thunder?"

Boden slid a box out of his pocket. "Planned on asking you to marry me today. First day in our new home. First day of our new life." He opened the box and pulled out a diamond ring that took my breath away. "Marry me, Laiken."

Tears spilled down my cheeks. "You want to make a family with me?"

"You already are my family. You and this little one in here." He pressed a hand to my stomach. "Marry me."

"Yes." It was the only word I needed.

Boden slid the ring onto my finger. "I promise you today."

"I keep thinking every today is the best, but you keep topping it."

"And I'll never stop trying."

THE END

Bonus Scene

Laiken

"AYEEEEEEEEEEEEE!"

I couldn't hold in my laughter as James swung from the rope on the ridiculously extravagant playhouse. The company had offered to install it for us, but Boden had wanted to put the thing together with his own two hands. He had quickly regretted that decision. It had taken him, Hayes, and Beckett an entire weekend to assemble it, and much cursing had been heard.

James released his hold on the rope, flying through the air. I held my breath as he hit the grass. He tucked into a sort of roll and then threw his hands into the air in victory. I swore my eldest son had rubber where his bones should be.

Colin grabbed the rope from his spot atop the play structure as it swung back. He always had to follow in his big brother's footsteps.

I lifted my camera just as he caught hold. My lens focused on his beautiful face, the perfect mix of Boden and me. My dark hair, Boden's hazel eyes. I pressed the shutter, capturing his adorable determination.

Vulnerable, honest emotion still drew me. I always sought it out in my photography. But now, it was more balanced. I found authentic joy as much as I found real sorrow. And I was no longer scared of showing my view of the human experience to the world.

I'd done a few exhibits in New York, Chicago, LA, and even one in London. But my favorite place to show my work was still The Gallery. Serena had fully taken over now. Her eye for artists had grown with each year, and she was thriving in the role. And I got such joy from watching her soar.

Colin let out a yell as he sailed through the air. He let go of the rope and threw himself into a flip. My lungs constricted. Memories of a night so many years ago played at the edges of my mind. But as Colin landed with a laugh, I released my hold on them. They no longer took me out at the knees.

Instead, I helped Kay and Chip honor Jase by doing work that I knew would make him proud. Kay and I had started a literacy program that Boden had helped hugely with. We went into schools to work on reading with the students and provided one-on-one tutors to anyone struggling. It was a great way for members of the community to give back.

Kyle's face peeked out of the playhouse. He bit his bottom lip as the rope swung back and forth. On the third swing, he caught hold. My stomach twisted. My sweet youngest was more reserved than my other two hellions. He thought everything through, needing to know all the possible outcomes. He looked at the ground, so far down for a four-year-old.

"Come on, Ky. We don't have all day," my eldest griped.

"James," I warned.

He flushed. "Sorry. We all go at our own speed."

"Because we all have our own paths to take," Boden said as he settled behind me on the small hill. His legs wrapped around me as I leaned back against his chest. "They've definitely memorized your mantra," he whispered in my ear.

My mouth curved. "They each have strengths and methods. Those should be celebrated."

I needed to do everything in my power to make sure our boys were close. Maybe because I'd seen what it had done to Boden's family—and to Jase's—when brothers were at odds.

Colin edged forward. "You got this, Ky. If you aim towards that tree, there's nothing to hit but air."

He traced the path with his finger in the air, and my chest warmed. Pressure built behind my eyes as they started to water.

Boden nuzzled my neck. "Are you crying?"

"No," I shot back. "I just get a little emotional seeing our boys working together."

He chuckled against my skin, the action sending delicious vibrations down my spine. "You're so damn cute."

"Little ears," I warned.

"They can't hear me." His lips trailed down my neck. "And if we went inside, they couldn't see us, either."

"The last time we left them alone out here, Colin broke his wrist."

Boden groaned. "Fine, you have a point."

Kyle took a deep breath and stepped off the playhouse platform. He swung back and forth twice before letting go and stumbling to land on his butt. His brothers cheered, descending on him in a sort of dogpile.

A tear slipped free, sliding down my cheek. Boden wiped it away with his thumb. "Love your heart."

"Love yours more." I looked up at him. "How was your meeting?"

"Good. I'm acquiring the script. I love the idea of an all-female cast of superheroes, and she has a unique voice."

I smiled up at him. "I loved the first pages I read."

Boden had moved away from acting and into more of a productional role, focusing on finding projects for his company. Then, every summer, we packed up the kids and went wherever the project took us. Sometimes, Boden directed something. Other times, he acted. We'd taken the kids to Australia, Thailand, France, and all over the United States. It was a chance for them to see different walks of life, and we all stayed together as a family.

Boden pressed a kiss to my shoulder. "I'm excited about finding the right director for this one and seeing it all come together."

I burrowed deeper into his hold. "You don't want to take the helm?"

"I think this one should have a female director. And if I did take it on, I'd have to be gone for six months, at least. I don't want to do that. I'd miss you all too much."

I tipped my head back so I could see Boden's face. I'd memorized his angular jaw and warm eyes within the first moments of meeting him. After years together, I could've drawn them from memory. "We can figure something out if you want to take this on. Get the boys tutors and—"

Boden took my mouth in a long, slow kiss. The kind that warmed me from the inside out. He brushed his nose against mine. "I love our life here. We've found a balance that works in every way. And I think it makes my art better, too. Because I'm living."

I reached up to kiss him one more time. "I was just thinking something similar. I see more colors because of our life together."

He ran a hand along my jaw. "Every damn color under the sun."

"It does make it a lot more convenient that you don't want to take that job."

"Why's that?"

I set my camera in my bag and pulled out a photo. It was mostly black with brushes of white. I held it up so he could see. "Because of this."

Boden went rock-solid beneath me. "Is that—? Are you—?"

"I'm pregnant."

After I'd had Kyle, the doctor had said that another pregnancy would be unlikely. I'd felt a stab of disappointment, but we had three beautiful boys, and they—along with Boden—were my world. So, I hadn't been tracking my period. It had taken me more than three months to realize that my already irregular period hadn't come at all.

"Laiken."

My name on his lips was a hushed prayer. I didn't need to ask if Boden was happy. His voice said it all.

I grinned up at him. "Do you see something different with this one?"

Boden's hand found my belly as he studied the ultrasound. "Is that…?"

"Twins. Girls."

I hadn't been able to resist finding out the sexes when the doctor asked if I wanted to know. I was so sure that I was incapable of creating girls in my womb that I'd nearly fainted when I heard the news.

Boden tipped my head back to meet his gaze. "Every time I think this life can't get better…"

"I love you." And I felt those words with every cell of my being.

His lips brushed mine in the barest touch. "I promise you today."

"Today is my favorite."

Acknowledgments

This book. I might've coined it *The Devil Book* while writing it. It pulled just about every emotion out of me during the writing and editing process. Part of that is because it was so important to me to get the chronic pain piece of the story right. Part of it is because some stories are simply harder than others. In the end, I hope the blood, sweat, and tears were worth it. I hope that Laiken and Boden touched your hearts and gave you an escape for a little while.

I always enjoy seeing who was a part of the author's journey when they create a story. I had an army behind me for this one. Firstly, a massive thank you has to go to Sam, who listened to me whine and moan when I struggled and dropped everything to read my rough draft when I needed some outside perspective. I truly don't know what I would've done without you on this book. To Emma, who talked through plot and character points, read early chapters, and then demanded that she be able to finish the whole thing. You gave me a boost I so desperately needed, and I'm incredibly grateful. Laura and Willow, thank you for being cheerleaders, sprint partners, and a balm to the soul when this career and life are so challenging. You celebrate the wins, soothe the losses, and make me cackle-laugh every single day. #LoveChainForever. My slackers, thank you for the accountability and encouragement, the laughter and sweet support. Grahame, thank you for the friendship, check-ins, and your ever-ready offer of help. You are the best!

To all my family and friends near and far. Thank you for supporting me on this crazy journey, even if you don't read "kissing books." But you get extra special bonus points if you picked up one of mine, even if that makes me turn the shade of a tomato when you tell me. And a special shout-out to my STS soul sisters: Hollis, Jael, and Paige. Thank you for the gift of twenty years of your friendship and never-ending support. I love living life with you in every incarnation.

To my fearless beta readers: Angela, Crystal, and Trisha, thank you for reading this book in its roughest form and helping me to make it the best it could possibly be!

The crew that helps bring my words to life and gets them out into the world is pretty darn epic. Thank you to Susan, Chelle, Julie, Jaime, Kara, Hang, Stacey, Jenn, and the rest of my team at Social Butterfly. Your hard work on this novel is so appreciated!

To all the bloggers who have taken a chance on my words… THANK YOU! Your championing of my stories means more than I can say. And to my launch and ARC teams, thank you for your kindness, support, and sharing my books with the world. An extra special thank you to Crystal, who sails that ship so I can focus on the words.

Ladies of the Catherine Cowles Reader Group, you're my favorite place to hang out on the internet! Thank you for your support, encouragement, and willingness to always dish about your latest book boyfriends. You're the freaking best!

Lastly, thank YOU! Yes, YOU. I'm so grateful you're reading this book and making my author dreams come true. I love you for that. A whole lot!

Also Available from
CATHERINE COWLES

The Tattered & Torn Series
Tattered Stars
Falling Embers
Hidden Waters
Shattered Sea
Fractured Sky

The Wrecked Series
Reckless Memories
Perfect Wreckage
Wrecked Palace
Reckless Refuge
Beneath the Wreckage

The Sutter Lake Series
Beautifully Broken Pieces
Beautifully Broken Life
Beautifully Broken Spirit
Beautifully Broken Control
Beautifully Broken Redemption

Stand-alone Novels
Further To Fall

For a full list of up-to-date Catherine Cowles titles,
please visit www.catherinecowles.com.

About

CATHERINE COWLES

Writer of words. Drinker of Diet Cokes. Lover of all things cute and furry, especially her dog. Catherine has had her nose in a book since the time she could read and finally decided to write down some of her own stories. When she's not writing, she can be found exploring her home state of Oregon, listening to true crime podcasts, or searching for her next book boyfriend.

Stay Connected

You can find Catherine in all the usual bookish places…

Website: catherinecowles.com

Facebook: facebook.com/catherinecowlesauthor

Catherine Cowles Facebook Reader Group: www.facebook.com/groups/CatherineCowlesReaderGroup

Instagram: instagram.com/catherinecowlesauthor

Goodreads: goodreads.com/catherinecowlesauthor

BookBub: bookbub.com/profile/catherine-cowles

Amazon: www.amazon.com/author/catherinecowles

Twitter: twitter.com/catherinecowles

Pinterest: pinterest.com/catherinecowlesauthor